The Last Dragon Home

by

Glenn T Ryan

1st Edition

Arts House Publications

First Published by Arin House Publications

2013

National Library of Australia Cataloguing-in-Publication entry

Author: Ryan, Glenn T., author.

Title: The last dragon home / Glenn T Ryan.

ISBN: 9780987461933 (paperback)

Series: Dragon wars; Book 1.

Dewey Number: A823.4

Visit
www.facebook.com/TheLastDragonHome

For Milly and Mighty

Inveniet viam vestram

Chapter 1

'Come on, Mollie. It's time to go.'

'I really don't feel like it. Can't I stay home?'

Esmae frowned at her daughter. 'No, you're not old enough to stay here by yourself. What if a group of bandits came to rob us? What would you do?'

Mollie looked around the bare cottage. 'What would they take? Two chairs, a table, the mirror that isn't big enough to see your whole face in? I doubt whether they'd be able to lift our beds.'

'That's not the point. I wouldn't care if they did take what we own. I would worry about you the whole time I was at the fair. *Maybe* if you'd let me teach you some more magic?'

'Not that again, Esmae. I already know enough to get by.'

'Well, you don't know one tenth of the amount required to stay home by yourself. Maybe that should be a lesson to you. Now grab your coat and let's go. Bring a scarf as well. And one more thing…'

'Yes?'

'Since when did you start calling me *Esmae*?'

Mollie Adkins smiled at her mother and followed her out the door.

For a long time they scrunched along the dirt path that would take them to the main road, pulling their coats tighter around them as they marched. The stars were clear overhead, and the moon was the thinnest sliver of yellow. The wind found the smallest holes in their clothes and whispered through to their skin.

1

'Why don't we buy a horse, Esmae?' Mollie asked as she huffed along.

'You know why.'

'Yes, but wouldn't it be good for times like this? No walking everywhere. We'd be at Gibbon by now.'

'I thought you didn't want to go to the fair anyway. Now you're telling me you want to get there faster. Look, we're at the crossroads already.'

Mollie didn't answer. She stood in awe as carriage after carriage passed her by, all heading north along the main road.

She had never seen so many horses before; each of them was magnificent in stature. Every single noble, peasant and merchant in the surrounding villages of Danmurk Shire snaked their way to Gibbon, passing close to Mollie. She smelled the musty horses and gawked at the painted carriages they pulled.

'Keep going, Mollie,' said her mother. 'It's impolite to stare.'

The two joined the line and weaved their way along the road. Heads down they marched, until Mollie's calf muscles began to ache with the endless walk. Her mother was about to tell her not to lag when a voice called out to them from a nearby cart.

'Hoy, you ladies.'

Mollie and Esmae stopped and turned. A small carriage drawn by a single steed pulled alongside them.

'You two wanna lift? Save yer legs?'

The driver of the cart was a thin, pink-faced man who had blond stubble poking recklessly from his cheeks.

'Yes!' Mollie said.

'Ah, do you know who we are?' Esmae asked in complete surprise.

The driver rubbed the front of his nose.

'Yeah. S'pose you an yer young'un are the Witches of Danmurk ... right?'

'We have been called such things.'

The driver shrugged his shoulders. 'Not my fault if Danmurk is full of superstitious tookers—' He stopped short, eyeing Mollie. 'Er, people.'

'Very well. Thank you. As long as you keep minding your language.' Esmae ignored the driver's hand and instead turned to help Mollie on the rear of the cart before gracefully climbing on herself.

'Name's Terry, by the way,' the driver announced with a yellow-toothed smile.

No one answered.

They rode in silence. Soon, an expensive looking carriage tried to pass them. It came close enough for Mollie to see inside. She smiled when she saw the family within had two boys her own age.

'Hello,' she called across.

The passengers glanced over to see who was greeting them. They saw Mollie's grinning face, her glinting blue eyes and her waves of hair that were blacker than the night sky. They took in her face and the light dusting of freckles on her high cheeks.

They also saw Esmae, who looked almost identical to Mollie except that her hair was in a bun and her eyes were lined with small wrinkles—no freckles either.

They were unmistakable.

The boys went pale with fright and crouched below the window. The boys' father slid the curtains shut and their mother urged the driver to speed up. They passed quickly—no one dared look back.

'See, Esmae! That's why I should have stayed home.'

'Never mind,' Esmae whispered, rubbing her daughter's cheek. 'Why don't you try talking to the horse?'

Mollie shrugged and closed her eyes.

'Hello,' she spoke into the animal's mind.

Suddenly the cart jerked and swayed, causing Terry to hoy and howl and reach for his stash of sugar cubes to calm his horse.

'Don't be frightened. I won't hurt you,' Mollie said as she gripped the armrest to keep from falling.

The beast blew fiercely through its nose and tried to turn its head to face her. 'How can I hear you with my head and not with my ears?' he demanded.

'It's something I've always been able to do,' Mollie answered in a soothing voice. 'Please don't be scared.'

'I thought only animals knew how to talk to each other like this!'

Mollie could hear his voice inside her head, deep and gruff. 'Some humans can too. Not many though—actually, just mother and me. What is your name?'

The horse was silent for a while.

'Bramble,' he answered. 'If you don't mind, I'd rather not talk while I'm working. My master wouldn't like it.'

'He seems nice though,' Mollie replied. 'Except he smells like old wine.'

'He *is* nice. I guess *I* don't like the idea of talking to you. It's not natural.'

'What harm is there in talking? I know it's not much further to town, but we can pass the time by chatting. Have you ever been to Gibbon before?'

The horse said nothing.

'I said have you ever been to Gibbon before?'

Still no answer.

Mollie flopped back in her seat and shook her head at her mother.

'Never mind,' said Esmae, patting her daughter's shoulder. 'You'll meet lots of other teenagers tonight. They will talk to you.'

'We both know that's a lie.'

Esmae took a deep breath to argue, but then stopped herself and sighed.

'True. But there are a few items I need from the fair and I couldn't leave you at home alone. So I tell you what—how about we *try* to have fun? No matter what other children—or horses—say. We can just pretend they don't exist. We can roam around the fair like we own it. How does that sound?'

In the distance, Mollie could see several massive fires burning on Gibbon's fairground. Around the big fires came the smaller glow of nearly one hundred lanterns dangling from wooden posts. She could faintly hear a mix of laughter, excited squeals, voices selling cheap tickets for sideshow games and hawkers hollering for business.

'You're right. I say we do it,' said Mollie and gave her mother a wink. 'Watch out Gibbon, the Witches of Danmurk are coming!'

Chapter 2

The lights were getting brighter.

The wind blew the smells of exotic meals and cooked meat to Mollie's nose.

Her anticipation mounted with each clop of Bramble's hoofs, until at last, they entered the wooden gates of the Gibbon Fair.

It was more wondrous than Mollie had thought possible, and she was at once glad that Esmae had forced her to come. There were stalls selling fabrics and lace, stores selling delicious rare food, and there were *sideshows*.

'Not so bad after all?' Esmae asked, raising her voice to be heard.

'I guess not. It would be better if there weren't so many people.'

'You'll be fine. Here's a few coins. Have fun, and I'll meet you back here in an hour.'

Mollie slowly walked off and found the part of the fair with the fewest children. She spied a game where the player had to throw a small hoop around a pole. It didn't cost much, and the main prize was a silver bracelet with a delicate heart-shaped charm.

Mollie stared at it and thought about how lovely it would be to own something as precious as jewellery. She imagined it in the empty top drawer of her bedside table, shining against the bare wood.

She paid the attendant and threw her hoop. It went spinning off to the left of the pole, nowhere near the target.

The attendant, a large woman with a mole on her forehead, laughed at Mollie's throw. 'You'll have to do better than that!' she squawked.

Not to be outdone, Mollie paid for another turn.

The lady hastily grabbed the money with a dirty paw and stepped back to watch.

When Mollie held the hoop this time, she noticed it felt much heavier on one side. It had been weighted to cheat the player out of a fair throw.

Two can cheat at this game, Mollie thought as she focused. She let her mind reach out and touch the elements around her. For an instant she heard her mother's voice in her head. *We never use magic for personal gain, Mollie.* Her eyes went back to the bracelet.

She quickly looked around to make sure no one was watching, then swung the hoop through the air. As she did this, she let her mind *feel* for the elements around her. Esmae called this *gathering*. She gathered air together to make small currents of wind to keep the hoop flying straight. At the right instant, she used the earth's power to pull the soaring ring downward.

Shooomp, spin, spin, spin.

The hoop lay flat on the ground, the pole standing proudly in its centre.

The attendant put a chubby hand over her mouth. 'A direct hit! No one's *ever* done that before!'

'Can I play again?' Mollie asked in a sweet voice as she took the bracelet and slipped it over her wrist.

At that moment, a small family approached the stall—Mollie recognised them as having passed her earlier when she and her mother rode in Terry's cart.

The father spoke quietly to the hoop lady, whose eyes widened and fixed on Mollie.

'No more games for you,' she barked when the father had finished speaking to her. 'Once you win you can't play again. Now go away before I box your ears.'

Word spread quickly through the fair that there was a girl with blue eyes and black hair who could cheat at the games.

Every time Mollie tried to win a prize at a stall, she was ignored or told to go away.

Her money sat useless in her hand. The coins felt like cold, heavy stones.

Everywhere she went, people stared at her. She could see them making way for her; parents were pulling children in the opposite direction. Not one would meet her eyes.

Mollie rubbed her eyes with her sleeve and decided to look for Esmae. But everywhere she looked, there were more people, whispering, pointing. She wanted to call for her mother at the top of her lungs so she could go home, but instead, Mollie turned and ran to the back of the fair.

She sat down on a rock and breathed heavily, hiding her face in her hands and wishing her mother had just let her stay home.

She stayed that way for a few minutes then heard someone calling to her. She slowly looked up. At the back of the showground, tucked away in a corner and surrounded by a knot of children, was a large painted van. On it was a picture of a ferocious looking dragon and a dazzling pink unicorn.

A sign above read:

CUDGEL'S WONDERS: WHITESTAFF AND WENDY

'Come and see the mythical beasts,' called a short, bald man. 'Only one gold coin to look.'

Mollie crept hesitantly over to him. 'Are they real?' she asked.

He looked down at her and wiped his thick black moustache. He had a large stomach and eyes the size of peas. 'Of course they are, yer dimwitted child! Give ol' Cudgel a gold coin and see for yourself.'

'Here you are,' she said. 'It's not like I can spend it anywhere else.'

Cudgel took the money with glee and pointed her to a large, barricaded wagon.

'The only way to see 'em is from up there. Walk up that plank and look down into the enclosure. You'll see the marvellous beasts for yerself. Next!'

Mollie walked over to the walkway and followed it up and onto a viewing platform. From this raised level she could see down through the barred roof of the wagon.

The structure was divided into halves by a walkway. One side contained Wendy, the unicorn. Her enclosure was no bigger than Mollie's bedroom. There was straw on the ground and a trough that contained little water. The windows were boarded over so no one could sneak a free peek at the mysterious creatures.

Mollie focused on Wendy. It was instantly obvious to her that she was not looking at a unicorn. All she saw was a painted horse that had a paper cone stuck to its forehead with white, gummy glue.

Mollie felt sorry for the horse. The only view she would have had from inside the barred cage would have been the sky above or the opposite enclosure, which was identical in size and shape.

'Your master must be very cruel to dress you up like that,' Mollie said to the horse.

'What do you mean, child? Dress me up like what?' Wendy's voice answered inside Mollie's head.

'You know, paint you pink and stick that silly thing on your head.'

'Well, I never!' squealed Wendy in reply. 'Are you insinuating I am not a real unicorn?'

'It does look like—'

'Look like what? You have never *seen* anything as beautiful as me. You've never seen anything so— AHHHHHHH.'

The horse screeched and bucked. 'The butterflies!' she yelled. 'They've come for me again.'

Mollie watched aghast as Wendy threw herself into a blind rage. The horse kicked through the bars and barged the walls with her shoulder. She chuffed and whinnied and made a horrible commotion.

'Stop!' Mollie pleaded. 'You'll hurt yourself!'

9

'Don't mind her,' a soft voice whispered in Mollie's brain.

Mollie's eyes searched for the speaker. 'Where are you?'

'Over here. In the other cage.'

Mollie looked down toward the room opposite Wendy, and there, lying on a straw bed, was what Mollie guessed to be a dragon.

'She thinks magic butterflies come to steal her beauty when she's not looking. She also thinks she's the last unicorn on earth.' The dragon's voice was husky and faint.

'Well... She is definitely unique,' Mollie replied.

'Well put. Very tactful.'

Mollie smiled at him.

'My name is Whitestaff. But I guess you know that already from my picture on my master's van.'

'Yes. My name is Mollie.'

'I know I don't look much; most children who come to see me are very disappointed. They expect a larger, more ferocious looking animal, don't they?'

Mollie didn't know where to look.

'I guess so.'

'Don't be embarrassed, human. I know only too well. I'm so weak I can hardly lift my head. I only wish I slightly resembled that proud looking dragon in the painting, not a miserable lump of white scales. Then I'd give them a show.'

At the finish of his sentence, Whitestaff broke into a coughing fit. Mollie waited patiently for him to finish.

'Where do you come from? Why are you so sick?' she asked.

'I don't really know. I have an idea, but it's a long story. While we are asking questions, why can *you* talk to animals?'

'Well,' she said. 'My family is a bit ... different.'

Whitestaff narrowed his gaze on Mollie and sniffed the air.

'Yes, I can see that right enough.'

Chapter 3

'I'm not a witch if that's what you're thinking, though everybody calls me one. I don't have warts and I don't have a cauldron.'

'No, that's not it at all. I smell something about you. Something special…'

'I'm a sorceress,' Mollie continued over the top of him. 'Not a witch. The two are very different.'

In the opposite cage, Wendy had calmed herself and began slurping water from her trough.

'You smell good to me. Like strawberries and sugar.'

'Thank you, Wendy.'

'What for? Who are you? Aren't I the prettiest unicorn in the world?' Wendy asked, looking at her reflection in the trough water, already forgetting the first two questions.

'Are you saying you know magic?' the dragon asked in his rustling whisper.

'I know some,' said Mollie. 'But I wish I didn't.'

'That seems strange to me. If I knew magic, I would be out of here in a flash.'

'Yes, but when you know magic, no one will talk to you. They avoid you and make up stories about you. You can never have any friends. It's terrible.'

'No one talks to me anyway, except Wendy, and she… well…'

The two looked over to Wendy, who was singing to her reflection.

'Yes, well it's different when you're a girl. I've never had one friend in my life. Except my mother, I suppose.'

11

'How many do you think I've had, human?'

Mollie's face fell. 'None.'

'That's right. It looks like you and I are in the same boat. The only difference is you don't have a cage.'

'You poor thing! Can't you get out somehow?'

'No. I'm too weak to walk even a few steps. And believe me, I've tried. But I have managed something, see. I've made a peephole in the wood here so I can look out. If only I were small enough to squeeze through.'

'Is there anything I can do?'

Whitestaff thought for a moment then his face brightened.

'Why, yes there is! The voices! You'll probably be able to hear the voices.'

'What voices?' Mollie looked over to Wendy, then back to the dragon.

'No, no, no. I'm not mad. These voices are real, right enough. I can hear them now. Listen.'

Mollie obeyed and strained her ears. She thought she could hear something through the hubbub of the fair. She listened for a moment more, but the sounds faded.

'I can hear them calling me. Other dragons maybe? Calling through the night.'

'I thought I could hear something,' Mollie offered.

'I'm not surprised,' Whitestaff replied. 'You really are fantastic.'

'You don't think I'm bad, or… weird?'

'Definitely not! I think you are the most wonderful human I have met!'

'What about me?' Wendy demanded, rejoining the conversation.

Whitestaff gave her a smile. 'You are lovely too, Wendy.'

'I think you two are both great,' Mollie blurted. She couldn't wait to tell her mother she had finally made some friends.

'All right, girlie. That's long enough.'

Cudgel's voice made them both jump. He was standing at the bottom of the platform with the lady from the hoops game at his side.

The lady jabbed her round elbow in Cudgel's mid-section and whispered something.

'All right, Audrey, all right,' Cudgel said to the woman. He turned back to Mollie. '*Get down* I said.'

'Just a minute longer, please sir. I only just got up.'

Cudgel looked to the woman beside him and the two began to whisper to each other.

Glad for the distraction, Mollie quickly turned back to the dragon.

'What do you want me to do? Tell me fast.'

'Look inside Cudgel's van for anything strange or unusual. I need to know where those voices are coming from and why. They might hold the key—'

'Hurry up girlie, or Audrey and I will come up and drag you down by the hair.'

Mollie looked down and saw Cudgel beginning to climb up towards her, his face red and sweaty despite the cool night air.

'Fine, I'm coming,' she said, and quickly made her way down.

Mollie rushed past Cudgel's groping hands and back towards the nearest crowd. She mingled in with the people and decided to watch Cudgel and the hoop woman from a safe distance.

Audrey appeared fussed about something. She was waving her arms and pointing.

She's still angry I won at her stupid game, Mollie thought.

Cudgel was shrugging his shoulders and wiping his moustache. Every now and then he would shake his head and chuckle. The woman stomped off after the exchange and Cudgel began crying out for business again.

What do I do now? Mollie asked herself.

Chapter 4

Back in his cage, Whitestaff wondered the same thing: *What do I do now?*

On four shaky legs, he managed to stand briefly, walk a few steps, and then collapse in a huffing heap.

It's useless. There is nothing I can do.

'*Dragon,*' a voice called to him through the dark, '*make your way home. Join us once again.*'

Whitestaff lifted his head to listen.

'I want to,' he said aloud, 'but I don't know how.'

'*Come home… Come home… Be with your own kind.*'

'I'm trying to, but I'm trapped. I'm not strong enough to get out.' Whitestaff's tone was pleading and helpless. 'Why can't you hear me?'

'*Come home, dear dragon. We need you here.*' This time it was a female voice that beckoned.

Whitestaff tried fruitlessly to stand again. He struggled with his legs and beat his tiny wings until he could no longer move.

The voice began to fade.

'Don't go,' he wailed.

But it was too late. The calling had stopped.

'What are you doing, dragon?' Wendy asked from her bed of straw.

'Nothing, Wendy. Go back to sleep.'

'How can I sleep with you making that terrible noise? What's the matter?'

'Just tired, Wendy. It's been a difficult day.'

'Were you calling that girl back? She's great, don't you think?'

Whitestaff nodded. 'Yes, she certainly is special. I bet she could have helped too. Never mind.'

'Helped what? Don't tell me you're trying to escape again. I thought you gave up on that idea.'

'I had. Until I saw Mollie, that is. For a second there I thought I had a chance. I finally found someone who could help. Did you hear those voices before?'

Whitestaff waited for Wendy's answer. He got a soft snoring sound instead.

Who are they, those voices that keep calling me? Why am I here? Am I the only dragon alive? Where did I come from? These questions repeated themselves in his mind as they so often did.

In his earliest memory, Whitestaff was surrounded by trees. He could hear birds whistling and insects zooming past his ears.

He was hungry, but he couldn't move. None of his muscles worked. Then, as the light faded from the day, he heard footsteps.

Crunch, crunch.

Somebody, or something, was coming closer to him. It was a human: a man. Whitestaff felt a sharp stick prod his soft scales. He gave a small gasp of pain. The man then picked him up and carried him to a barn, fed him, and gave him water. The next day the man stuck him in a cage. He had been Cudgel's prisoner ever since. Most of that time had been spent alone, until a few years ago, when Cudgel painted Wendy.

At first Whitestaff was relieved he had been found and fed. His relief didn't last for long though.

One day Cudgel tried to make Whitestaff do tricks. He figured that rather than show an ordinary dragon that just lay there, he'd make more money showing off a dragon that could stand on its head, or balance on one leg.

Of course, Whitestaff couldn't even stand properly, let alone do somersaults, so Cudgel would often get very mad.

'What's the use of yer?' he'd shout. 'Useless bag of bones, yer are. I feed yer and water yer, and yer just lie there!'

Following this speech, Cudgel would poke the dragon with his stick, digging in the sharp end between Whitestaff's scales.

Cudgel gave up after a few wasted months, but the scratches from that dreadful stick remained.

Back in his cage, the dragon gave a shudder.

Don't think about it, he told himself. *Not this close to sleep anyway.*

Whitestaff scratched a niche in his straw, ready to doze at last, when he heard a noise.

'Psst.'

He waited silently for a minute or two, then shook his head and rested it down on the straw.

'Psst. Whitestaff, it's me, Mollie.'

This time the dragon knew the sound was real and his head shot back up. He smiled at the familiar voice.

'Mollie! You came back.'

The girl was wedged between a large tree and the outside wall of Whitestaff's enclosure. She'd waited until Cudgel was attending a customer then stealthily cut behind him and into her hiding place.

The man would never look in her direction because he was only interested in guarding the viewing platform, not the area around the cage. Why would he look for people on the ground when no one could see inside from there, only from above?

Mollie, however, didn't need to *see* the dragon or the unicorn to speak to them. She merely had to be close.

'Of course I came back,' she said. 'Didn't I tell you that I was going to help?'

Whitestaff brightened at her touching words. 'You did indeed.'

'Well, this is what friends do,' the young girl insisted. 'They help each other.'

'I'm sorry for doubting you, Mollie. It's just I've never had anyone count me as a friend before, unless you count Wendy.'

'Me neither,' Mollie admitted. 'But I'm sure you would help me the same way, right?'

The dragon answered straight away. 'Yes, I would. I definitely would.'

'Well, tell me what you want me to do again. What about those voices?'

The beast took a deep breath. 'I think the voices I hear are coming from Cudgel's van—the one with the painting of me and Wendy on the side.'

'Uh-huh.'

'Well, I want you to find the source of the voices. Find out who is calling me and why. Can you do it?' His words came out in a rush.

Mollie's legs and stomach shivered with excitement. 'You bet,' she said.

And with that, she crept away.

Chapter 5

By now it was getting late. Parents were taking their yawning children away from the dazzling fires of the Gibbon Fair and into the less interesting night. The din was dissolving, and the smells of the fair were being carried away by a frigid wind. Everything was slowing down. Most of the stalls were being packed away, but some were giving last customers a chance to test their skill.

'Leaving so early?' Cudgel called as the people left. 'Why not spend yer last few coins on a once in a lifetime spectacle. Roll up and see Cudgel's Wonders.'

Mollie's long black hair was perfect for hiding in the night. She teased the strands and let her locks fall about her, hoping they would provide her with some camouflage.

There was about a twenty-yard gap between her and the brightly painted residence of Cudgel.

Mollie took a sharp breath and held it while she scurried over to the rear of the van. The first twenty paces went by in a blur, but the last ten took forever.

She could see Cudgel out of the corner of her eye. He was trying to convince some more people to part with their gold and was about to turn around and point out the enclosure. He began to turn his body in her direction. Five yards to go and he was nearly facing her, two yards and she could see the side of his face, one yard and Mollie dived behind the large wooden wheel attached to the van. Once there, she slowly let out her breath.

She waited for Cudgel to shout out, or worse, to run over and catch her, but he didn't.

She was safe. For now.

With her back pressing firmly against the thick spokes, Mollie turned her head and looked for a door or a window. She found one of each. The door was closed and padlocked, but the shutters on the window were open a fraction.

Mollie tiptoed over to the shutters and pulled them back as gently as she could manage.

The left shutter gave an awful screech, so she left it alone. The right one was stiff but silent, so she pulled it out as far as it would go and poked her head inside.

The first thing she noticed was the stench. The smell was a blend of rotting fish and stale bread.

Mollie wrinkled her nose in disgust.

It took her eyes a moment to adjust to the gloom. She could see a table with only one chair, a dinner plate with scraps still on it and a heavy-looking chest that was clamped shut with a sturdy lock.

The most peculiar thing in the van was a giant egg sitting on a furry mat.

Mollie could see it had been broken in half, a sign that something large had hatched out of it years ago. The egg's surface was gold, flecked with a deep green. But the strangest thing was that in the middle of the egg, was a floating mist, like a sphere of hovering dew, with a rainbow of colours shimmering through it.

Mollie gaped in wonder.

I bet this has something to do with those voices. I have to tell Whitestaff!

She ducked back to her wheel and peeped through the spokes. *Where is he?* Mollie thought when she couldn't see Cudgel. *Oh well. Better hurry before he comes back.*

Mollie made a mad dash over to her hiding spot between the tree and the mobile barn.

'I saw it,' she said, brimming with excitement.

'What was it?' asked the dragon.

'It was an egg—a gorgeous, broken egg with a kind of watery ball floating in it.'

The dragon thought about this.

'Are you sure, Mollie? Do you think that's where the voices are coming from?'

'I'm positive. It was really the only thing in the whole van,' she said. 'Apart from a bad smell.'

'I must see it for myself,' Whitestaff said. 'The voices keep telling me to come home, so the egg must have something to do with getting there. Don't you think?'

'Yes, I'm sure you'll know what to do when you see it. It looks magical and wonderful.'

Whitestaff nodded to himself.

'Mollie,' he said. 'Do you think that, um, it is my egg?'

'What do you mean?'

The dragon looked up at the moon for a moment, lost in thought. 'Well,' he said presently, 'maybe it's the egg I came out of. Maybe Cudgel kept it.'

'Yes. You could be right. Do dragons come from eggs?'

'I guess so. I can't remember being around other dragons. I must have come out of the egg, alone.'

In the distance, the sounds of the fair were all but gone, and the chirping of crickets was louder.

'I have to get near that egg, Mollie,' the dragon said. 'If I have to be locked up in here for much longer, I'll go crazy. I'll begin to believe in the magic butterflies Wendy sees.' Whitestaff paused for a while and gave a deep sigh. 'Plus I'll never see you again, either.'

'What do you mean?' asked Mollie.

'Cudgel will take me to another town soon, to another fair. We only stay in the one place for a day or two. I expect we'll leave at sunrise, or a bit after.'

Mollie realised he was right. Her insides suddenly went heavy and her face sagged.

'Just when I find someone who'll talk to me,' she whispered.

At that moment something yanked the hair on the back of her skull so hard her head snapped backwards.

'Gotcha, yer little mullytill!' a voice shouted from behind her.

It was Cudgel who had grabbed her and swore.

'What the Latos do yer think yer doing?' he shouted, his mouth right next to her ear. 'Trying to steal my animals no doubt!'

Mollie was too petrified and in too much pain to answer. She couldn't even shake her head.

Cudgel didn't care anyway. He was pulling her towards his van, yelling and cursing all the way.

Chapter 6

Mollie became suddenly aware that nobody was around—everyone had left the grounds and all the fires had been put out.

Mollie felt like she was having one of those nightmares where it's impossible to wake up or scream. She tried to yell once, but her lungs seemed to have no air in them so only a rasp came out. The van was getting closer, and Cudgel's grip was getting tighter.

She took a deep breath, ready to squeal as loudly as she could, then *wham*!

They hit something very tough.

Cudgel fell to the ground and rolled like a large ball. Mollie spilled out of his grasp and smashed her new bracelet on a rock.

What was that? She looked up to see her mother.

Esmae stood over the two. Her face was grim and her jaw was set tight.

'Just what do you think you are doing, manhandling my girl like that?' she demanded.

Cudgel was slow to regain his wits. 'Where did you come from?' he asked groggily.

Instantly, Esmae was three inches from his face, without appearing to have moved her body.

Cudgel took a frantic step back.

'Answer my question,' Mollie's mother commanded; her voice was poisonous.

'S-she,' he pointed to Mollie, 'was near the, um, the, um… my creatures,' he finished.

'Did she pay you?' asked Esmae, moving closer to the back-stepping man.

Mollie had never seen her mother like this. Sure she'd seen her angry before, like whenever Mollie gave cheek when she was younger, but this was something else. Her mother was moving like a sleek cat, ready to maim her prey.

'Yeh-h, s-she paid.'

'WELL?' Esmae yelled.

But Cudgel didn't answer. He was cowering on the ground, unable to move. Mollie knew why.

Her mother was using a powerful magic on him. She made the earth suck the little man to the ground with enormous gravity, but that was not all. Mollie could see Esmae blending fire and water to create an energy blast that would blow Cudgel to the other end of the showground if it hit him. She was poised to deliver the magical blow when a speaker interrupted, and the beam of energy disappeared into the air.

'Are you ladies all right?'

Mollie looked over and saw Terry, the man who had generously allowed her and her mum to ride with him to the fair.

Nobody spoke for a while then Esmae said, 'Yes, we are fine.' She released Cudgel from her invisible hold. 'Come on, Mollie.'

Mollie ran over and took her mother's hand.

When Cudgel realised he was free, he unleashed a torrent of abuse, calling Esmae and her daughter witches and mullytills, and promising that someday they'd pay.

Esmae shot him such a threatening look that Cudgel scampered back to his van, his stumpy legs almost blurring with speed.

'What was that about, my ladies?' Terry asked, clearly puzzled.

'Just a misunderstanding, that's all.' Esmae turned to her daughter, 'Are you fine?'

'Yes, Esmae.'

'No you're not, you're shaking. Come here.' Esmae took Mollie in her arms and held her until she was still.

'Listen, I'm heading back to Danmurk,' Terry said. 'I could drop you off home on the way if you like.'

Esmae gave her daughter a soft kiss on her forehead.

'That would be lovely. Thank you, Terry.'

Terry took Esmae's arm and led the two to his small cart.

This time, Esmae allowed Terry to help her on.

The two chatted away, making small talk while Mollie listened, her head resting on her mother's shoulder.

'You two really should get yerselves a horse,' Terry said. 'Not that I mind givin' you a ride at all, just the opposite.'

'Mollie would agree with you there, Terry. She was saying that very thing on our way to the fair. Maybe we should get one after all, if we can save enough. It is a good idea.'

'Why is it a good idea if someone else says it?' Mollie asked.

'Now, Mollie, don't be rude. As I was saying, Terry…'

Mollie rolled her eyes and decided not to listen to the rest.

She looked to the starlit sky and saw a large group of bats flying silently overhead. The bats made her think of Whitestaff and how much he would love to fly free in the night sky.

Sorry I couldn't help, Whitestaff.

After a long time travelling, they arrived at the intersection of the road that would lead the two Adkins women home.

Chapter 7

'Well, goodnight ladies,' Terry said as he slowed the cart to a halt.

'Goodnight, Terry,' Esmae said.

'Night,' mumbled Mollie.

'You're welcome to stop by for dinner anytime you like, Terry,' Esmae added.

Mollie's eyes went wide, as did Terry's.

'That'd be lovely, Esmae,' he said. 'I just might do that. And by the way, I only live a step away from here, in the house with the red coloured roof. So if you ever need anything,' he winked at Esmae, 'you've only to ask.'

'Come on, mother,' Mollie said, yanking the older woman's arm. 'I'm tired.'

'I bet you are. Thank you, Terry. You are quite the gentleman.'

'Not a problem. Hoy, Bramble, let's get home ourselves.'

The horse nodded politely to Mollie as if apologising for his former rude behaviour, then clopped off. Mollie and her mother watched them until they were out of sight.

'I was so scared when I saw that man grab you,' Esmae said as soon as they began the walk home.

'Me too.'

'Why was he mad with you, daughter?'

For the rest of the journey Mollie told her mother about Wendy and Whitestaff, the voices calling him and the egg she had found. Her mother listened and didn't interrupt once, unless it was to ask for more details or for clarification.

The story finished as the two neared their small cottage in the woods.

Inside, Esmae lit some candles and Mollie scrubbed her teeth with soot from the fireplace. They both sat on Mollie's bed and talked.

'Sounds like you and this dragon got on well,' Esmae said.

'Not as well as you and Terry. I still can't believe you actually invited someone over!' Mollie said with a shake of her head. 'But as for Whitestaff, he didn't think I was strange or weird at all. I feel sorry for him, all alone and trapped like that. Was he really a dragon though? I didn't think they were real.'

'Oh, they are real,' her mother answered. 'Or were. You see they disappeared a long time ago. No one knows where they went, but most people were glad to be rid of them.'

'Why?' asked Mollie in surprise. 'Whitestaff was so nice; he wouldn't hurt a baby bird.'

'Well,' Esmae said as she considered the question. 'Dragons were like people, like men.'

'How?'

'Some men,' Esmae continued, 'are nice, while others are not.'

'And?'

'Let me give you an example. Take Terry—'

'Do we have to?'

Esmae gave her daughter a smirk.

'Take Terry. He knew that the townsfolk call you and me witches, but he didn't care. He did the right thing by us anyway.'

'He looks funny, and he needs a bath,' Mollie insisted.

'Yes, he may look funny, but he showed us he has a good heart. He didn't care about who we are; he just did the right thing.'

Mollie nodded. 'It *was* nice of him to drive us around.'

'Now about Cudgel. He is also a man, but he is a cruel one. He keeps those animals all locked up just so he can get rich. And he hurt you.'

'So what you're saying is that some men, no matter how they look or smell, have good hearts, while others are bad.'

'That's part of it, yes.'

'And you think dragons are the same?'

'Yes I do. You see, you can judge a person by their deeds. Terry showed us a good action, while Cudgel showed us a horrible one. I suppose dragons are just the same.'

Mollie yawned. 'I can see your point. But I think I might get some sleep now. Can *you* start the fire tonight?'

'Of course. But one more thing…'

'Hmmm?'

'If our actions tell what sort of people we are, you need to think about your actions. You are getting older now—as much as it pains me—and, it's time to become the person *you* want to be. The person you will become will be defined by the things you do, see?'

With that, Esmae blew out the candles, shut Mollie's door, and made her way in the dark to the fireplace.

Mollie thought about her mother's words.

What sort of person do I want to be?

She rolled about in her blankets.

I want to be brave. No more being scared of people.

She thought about Whitestaff in his enclosure, looking at the world through his tiny peephole. *I want to help those who need it, and I want to be a good friend.*

She tossed her pillow over, and imagined Wendy thrashing about and singing to herself and getting worse each day. The more she thought, the less sleepy she felt, and slowly as the hour passed, a plan formed in her mind.

I know what I have to do.

Mollie snaked off her bed so as not to make a noise, and with a new determination, sneaked out of the bare little cottage. She made her way along the dirt path she'd trodden not long before, hoping to be back before the sun rose and woke her mother.

Chapter 8

Whitestaff didn't sleep much either. He was sure one of his two hearts had broken at the sound of Mollie being dragged away by Cudgel. He had not been within earshot when Esmae interrupted, so he didn't know if Mollie was safe or not.

That poor girl.

He rolled on his back and watched the grey clouds drift past the black sky, and gave a loud sigh as some bats flew overhead.

'What's the matter with you?' Wendy asked from her side of the wagon. 'I can't sleep with you making all that noise.'

'Here we go again,' Whitestaff groaned. 'We had this same conversation about an hour ago, Wendy. Don't you remember?

'No'

'Well, nothing is wrong. Go back to sleep.'

'Something is the matter, I can tell. Plus, you're lying on your back; you're sad again.'

'You got me. Something *is* wrong.'

'Is it that child, that girl? I guess she was nice. Pretty too, like me.'

'Yes, Wendy, like you. We've said all this before.'

'So why are you so sad?'

Whitestaff yawned. 'It's not her that upsets me. It's me.'

'What do you mean?'

'Cudgel got her and I couldn't save her. I'm just stuck in this stupid cage. I made a friend and let her down in the first five seconds.'

'Don't worry,' Wendy said. 'Even if you weren't in the cage, you could hardly save anyone. You're too weak, remember?'

Whitestaff pursed his rough lips. 'Thanks a bundle, Wendy.'

'No problem. Now you can be quiet and go to sleep.'

But of course, he couldn't. His mind was cluttered with too many thoughts. Was Mollie fine? Would he ever see her again? What was the egg she saw, and would it somehow take him home?

He didn't know the answers, so he just kept asking the questions over and over until exhaustion took him to sleep.

Chapter 9

Mollie Adkins ran towards the main junction. The night, which had started off very cold, was now positively freezing. Mollie wished she'd thought to wear shoes. Her feet were sore from slapping the packed dirt and the cold was beginning to make them tingle.

I could go back for my shoes, but I really don't want to waste any more time.

She jogged on. The junction came into view, and after a few moments she was in the middle of the crossroads.

She looked toward Gibbon, then to Danmurk Shire.

After some thought, she headed south to Danmurk. She remembered that Terry had said he didn't live far from where he'd dropped them off, so she ran along the main road to look for a house with a red roof. It wasn't long before she did find such a house and, sure enough, the wagon they had travelled in was stationed in the yard.

Bramble was dozing in front of it.

'Bramble,' Mollie said gently as she approached. 'Wake up.'

'Huh? What?' Bramble shook his head to wake himself.

'It's me, Mollie.'

'Oh! What are you doing here, girl? Get back to your own house before I make a noise and wake my master.'

Mollie had expected Bramble's less than warm reception. 'I've come to help a horse,' she said.

'I don't need help, now go home.'

'Not you,' Mollie said as she moved closer. 'Another horse. And a beast. They're being kept in a cage at the fair.'

'Another horse you say?' asked Bramble.

Mollie knew this would get his attention. Horses always looked out for each other.

'Yes, she's being kept hostage in a cage, and she's gone mad. I want to help her and the, um, animal in the cage across.'

'She? Latos, child! Why didn't you say so?' At once the horse stood up and lifted his chin. 'On my back and let's get moving. A gentleman always rescues a lady.'

Mollie climbed on, grinning eagerly.

'Just get me to the Gibbon fairgrounds before the rooster crows, Bramble. I'll do the rest.'

The two made madly their way through the dark. The icy wind stirred behind them, flapping Mollie's clothes and rustling the leaves in the trees.

'So who is this horse to you?' Bramble asked as he galloped.

'Well, I made friends with her while I was at the show. Her master has her all dressed up like a unicorn in this tiny cage. The cage is a wagon with no windows, only bars on the roof.'

'You made friends with her, you say?'

'Yes, she was quite friendly really.'

There was an awkward silence as they travelled.

'I'm sorry I was rude when we first met. It's just strange talking to a human. I wasn't ready for it, that's all.'

Mollie suppressed a smile. 'That's okay.'

'You said there is another animal that needs rescuing. Is it a horse?'

'No, it's not a horse.'

Bramble ran on.

'What is it then?'

Mollie hesitated. 'It's a dragon, and it's in a lot of misery.'

'It can't be a dragon,' the horse said, 'they don't exist anymore.'

'This one does. But he is very lonely and very sick. I promised I would help him.'

'And what of the horse? We are going to help this horse, aren't we?' Bramble's voice became very stiff.

'Yes, we will help her too.'

'Because, child,' Bramble continued, 'if you tricked me into helping you and this, this dragon… you will find me less than amused.'

'Bramble, I did promise to help the dragon, but they are in the same wagon. We can save Wendy as well.'

The horse's body suddenly went rigid beneath Mollie's hands and he made no further attempts at conversation. The only sound was the steady rhythm of hoof on dirt and the wind shaking the trees.

Mollie could see the fairgrounds before too long, and she was glad to be at their destination.

'I'll wait here,' Bramble said, stopping short of the low wooden fence that surrounded the grounds. 'Bring her to me when you're done.'

Chapter 10

Mollie slid off Bramble and made her way to the back of the fair.

All the vans and stalls around her were silent, apart from the odd cough or snore. Mollie felt as though she was creeping between sleeping dogs and that any minute one of them would wake up and attack her. She shuddered at the thought. *What would happen if someone did find me?*

Mollie had a vision of the fat lady with the mole finding her and taking her to Cudgel. He in turn would drag her around the yard by the hair, swearing at the top of his voice. Then all the people from the vans would come out and laugh or throw things at her.

This thought gave Mollie pause. She hid at the base of a thick tree and gathered her wits.

Don't be silly, Mollie, she told herself. *You have friends in trouble, and if anyone does find you, bite them and run.*

She looked up and saw the picture of Whitestaff and Wendy painted on the side of Cudgel's van.

They're the reason you're here. If you were trapped and alone, you would want someone to free you. So stick to the plan!

Head down and feet light, she skulked past the van and over to the enclosure. Mollie climbed up the ramp and onto the viewing platform so she could see the captives inside.

'Whitestaff. Wendy. I've come back!'

Wendy woke from her sleep and blinked at Mollie casually, as if the young woman had always been there.

Whitestaff rolled onto his stomach and opened his green eyes. He gave a small shout when he saw his friend through the iron bars above.

'Mollie, you're okay! That's fantastic! You have no idea how glad I am to see you!' he said.

'It's good to see you too, Whitestaff. I had to come and see you to say goodbye.'

'Goodbye?'

'Yes, I've come to break you both free!'

Whitestaff cheered but Wendy snorted gruffly.

'What if I don't want to be free?'

'Why would you want to stay all cooped up like this?' asked Mollie in wonder.

'Well, for starters,' replied Wendy, 'I get all the food I want. Also, people come from everywhere to stare at my beauty. I will not leave this place. It is my home.'

Mollie's mouth was agape. 'You can't possibly want to stay here, Wendy. Horses are meant to run wild and—'

'WHAT DID YOU CALL ME?' Wendy shrieked. 'I AM NO COMMON *HORSE*.' She spat the word as though it were a dirty thing that had crawled into her mouth.

'I AM THE VERY LAST UNICORN.' She huffed loudly and turned her back on the both of them.

'Don't mind her, Mollie. You know she's…' Whitestaff didn't know how to finish, but Mollie knew what he meant. Any animal would go crazy if it were locked up in a cage for years on end.

'Whitestaff,' said Mollie, putting Wendy temporarily out of her mind, 'how can I get you closer to the egg?'

'You're not going to, Mollie,' answered the dragon.

'What ever do you mean? I'm sure we can think of something.'

'Of course we can think of something. All I do is think of ways to escape this prison, but not if it means risking your safety again.'

'And why not? I came all this way to help.'

'I know,' the dragon said patiently, 'but last time Cudgel caught you, and I thought something terrible had happened.'

'I don't understand.'

'Look, Mollie. I'm stuck here with nothing to lose. If Cudgel catches me breaking out, he won't do anything he hasn't done before. But what if he catches you? What if he learns you are special? He'll put you in a cage for sure then you'll be stuck like me.'

'And you don't think I've already thought of that? I know this is dangerous, but we have one chance at this, Whitestaff. Tomorrow you'll be gone and there'll be no way I can follow you. Now are you going to accept my help or not?'

'What if it all goes wrong and you get hurt? I'd never be able to forgive myself. Friends don't put each other in harm's way.'

'True, but if I were stuck in there without any chance of going home, how do you think you would feel? Rotten, that's how. And wouldn't you be doing the same thing, I am right this instant?'

Whitestaff thought for a moment.

'Yes,' he said to her through the bars. 'I would do the same thing you are doing now.'

Mollie nodded. 'Good. Now stop worrying and tell me what to do.'

'Okay, here is my plan,' the dragon said.

Mollie leaned closer.

'I'll get Cudgel to come out here, when he does— you sneak in and get the egg. Then, when Cudgel goes back into his van, slip me the egg then run away as fast as you can. Hopefully you'll be gone before he notices the egg is missing.'

'How will you get him to leave the van?' Mollie asked.

'I'll pretend I'm sick. Or better yet, I'll pretend someone is stealing me. That would bring him out.'

'Okay,' Mollie said. 'I'll wait behind his van.'

She turned to walk away.

'Wait, Mollie. Before you go… I might not see you again and, well, I don't know what to say.' The dragon stared after the girl with his massive eyes. 'Thank you, you have been kinder than anyone I have ever met.'

35

Mollie gave him a smile and wiped her eyes with her sleeve. 'Good luck,' she said. 'I hope you make it home.'

Chapter 11

Mollie quietly made her way to the back of Cudgel's van. She looked anxiously at the sky; sunrise was still a long way off. She drew her clothes tighter around her when she realised she was shivering.

Am I really that cold?

Before she had time to think, there came a deep, heart-wrenching moan from Whitestaff's cell. Mollie was about to get up and investigate before she caught herself.

Don't be daft, Mollie. That's the signal!

The next series of events happened in a slow moving fuzz to Mollie. As she was trying to gather her wits, Cudgel came bounding out of the van with a thunderous clatter and raced over to look on his precious animals.

'Help! Thief!' he yelled.

Mollie was crouched behind the van. She could see Cudgel's bare feet kicking up dirt as he ran.

In a nervous rush, she dashed around to the front of the van and leapt in the open door. The egg was exactly where it had been when she had spied it through the window earlier. She picked it up hurriedly, not even smelling the filthy odour around her, and hopped out the door and back behind the van.

From there she searched for a place to hide.

Thump, a heavy hand landed on her shoulder. Mollie looked up to see the round face of Audrey, the woman from the hoop-throwing game. Her mouth was grinning and her fingers tightened around Mollie's collarbone.

'Cudgel,' she shouted. 'I've got her. Come quick!'

Mollie hugged the egg tight, and twisted out of the women's grip. She ran blindly towards Wendy and Whitestaff.

It was too late when she realised this was a big mistake. Cudgel was of course still in there, tending to his dragon, and she was heading right for him.

With Cudgel in front and Audrey behind, Mollie had nowhere to go but up onto the viewing platform.

She bounced up the flimsy walkway and looked down. Cudgel was about to enter the moaning dragon's cage when he heard Mollie coming up the ramp. He craned his neck to see her through the bars and met Mollie's eyes with his own.

It took Cudgel a second to realise what was happening, and when he saw the egg in Mollie's arms, his face burned red with anger.

Whitestaff stopped mid-yelp, and Wendy, who was wondering what all the commotion was about, batted her eyelids and clopped up and down nervously.

Mollie could hear Audrey puffing and panting behind her. She was hopelessly trapped. Her mind raced for a solution. Thankfully, one came.

'Butterflies!' she shouted.

Cudgel, who was about to come out of the enclosures and nab the girl hesitated at the word.

It was a big mistake, for upon hearing it, Wendy went into a kicking frenzy. Just like before, she kicked and brayed in a crazy fashion, convinced the dreaded butterflies had returned to thieve her beauty.

One of her kicks went though the bars and into Cudgel's thick skull. The hoof sent him sailing forwards so fast his head became jammed between two bars on Whitestaff's cage.

Seeing that Cudgel was stuck, Mollie jumped onto the roof above the dragon and pressed the egg through a gap between the bars. It landed lightly on his straw.

The dragon could hear the voices clearly now, as could Mollie. *'Come home,'* they were saying in a far-off call, *'Come home, young dragon.'*

The aura of light between the two halves of the egg radiated brightly and grew larger.

Mollie and the dragon locked eyes.

About them was pandemonium, Wendy was bucking, Cudgel was swearing, and Audrey was on the viewing deck making high-pitched screams.

Despite the racket, Whitestaff's voice was clear in Mollie's mind. 'I'll never forget your bravery, or your friendship, Mollie. Thank you.'

With that, he reached out and touched the egg. Mollie watched in awe as the dragon was sucked into the moist rainbow at the egg's centre.

There was a slurping noise—then nothing.

The dragon was gone.

When Wendy saw the dragon disappear before her eyes, she went even madder. She doubled her kicking and barging until...*crash,* she made a horse-size hole through the wooden wall.

Wendy was free and running fast into the breezy air. The horn that Cudgel had glued to her head lay crumpled on the straw; it was the last he would ever see of his false unicorn.

With Whitestaff gone, Wendy free, and Cudgel stuck, Mollie was eager to go. Audrey was too unfit and slow to catch her, so Mollie slipped off the roof, landed on the ground gracefully, and left the fairgrounds behind to find Bramble.

I did it! She thought to herself as she ran. *I can't believe I really did it! I hope you're safe Whitestaff, wherever you are.*

Chapter 12

Whitestaff couldn't see a thing. He was lying on his back, confused and disorientated.

Wendy's mad sounds and Cudgel's foul language rang in his ears, and then faded into silence, leaving him alone in quiet blackness.

'Where am I?' he asked aloud.

'Home,' a voice answered.

The dragon gave a start.

'I know your voice! You called to me from the egg. Who are you? Where is this place?'

'Don't be afraid, young dragon. You are in safe company.'

A faint glow floated into the dragon's view.

'I can't see who you are,' said Whitestaff as he shuffled about in the murk.

'Your vision will come back soon. Try blinking.'

Whitestaff followed the suggestion and, bit-by-bit, the world around him became clear.

He judged by the dirt roof that he was in some sort of cave. He couldn't be sure, because against every wall were books leaning steadily on glass shelves. The books looked thick and heavy. He could smell thousands of ageing pages. A massive, circular rug covered most of the floor, at the centre of which was a sphere of glowing light.

Next to the light was a woman. She was the most enchanting human he had ever seen. She had black hair like Mollie's, long and swishy, and her face was white and delicate.

The room looked brighter now and Whitestaff could see her clearly. Above her full and red lips was a thin, straight nose. Her eyes were almost as black as her hair, but they sparkled with warmth.

'Can you see now?' she asked.

'Yes, I can,' replied the dragon. 'Where am I?'

The woman smiled at him. 'I told you. You are home. This is Sorteya—the Dragon Planet.'

'Dragon Planet?'

'Yes, this is where the dragons came to live, long ago.'

'You mean there are more like me?' Whitestaff asked hopefully.

The woman nodded. She was wearing a yellow robe with a hood that fell limp at the back.

'Hundreds,' she said. 'Just like you.'

Whitestaff cheered and punched the air. 'Thank you, Mollie! So, I am really home?'

'Yes dragon. You will meet the rest shortly. But tell me, what is your name?' The woman walked over to the dragon and looked in his eyes.

'Whitestaff,' he said, sniffing the woman lightly.

'I am Susset the Sorceress,' she gave a curtsy before him, spreading her robe wide.

'Pleased to meet you, Susset,' the dragon said, backing away as the woman advanced even closer.

'Don't be nervous, I mean you no harm,' she said. 'After all, it was my magic that brought you here.'

Whitestaff stopped moving away and stayed still, allowing Susset to brush his nose with her hand. He looked past her and at the bright light in the centre of the room. *That's where I must have come from,* he thought.

'Whitestaff is a strange name,' the sorceress said as she stroked him.

'Why?' he asked. 'I always thought it suited me.'

Susset laughed merrily at his question. 'Because you are gold, silly.'

'No I'm not, I'm white as a—'

He broke off as he looked down at his scales. They were indeed gold. They sparkled like treasure. Gone were the semi-transparent flakes of white that had covered him before. These scales were sturdy thick armour. He gazed at them in wonder.

'How did this happen?' he gasped.

'Hmmm,' said Susset as she smoothed her robe. 'That is a long tale.'

'A very long tale,' agreed an older voice.

Whitestaff looked over to the cave's entrance and saw a spectacular dragon flapping effortlessly in the air. The dragon was green and very big. It made a ducking swoop and landed lightly next to Susset.

'Allow me to introduce Olfar, your uncle.'

Olfar nodded his great, green head. 'How do you do?'

Whitestaff collapsed before he could answer.

Chapter 13

Back on Earth, Mollie had found Bramble where she left him. He was shifting from hoof to hoof, unable to remain still.

'I saw her. She ran down the road.' Bramble indicated with his head. 'Jump on, I can catch her.'

Mollie did as she was instructed and the two dashed along the road.

The young Adkins was glad to be off her feet. She buried her head in Bramble's mane and let her legs fall loosely around his body. Her arms shook as she clamped them around his neck.

What if they caught me? What if they took me away? What if I never saw mum again?

She had a vision of Esmae finding her bed empty, then pictured her running out to the lake behind their house, calling for her, panicking.

She shook her head and thought of Whitestaff instead. She imagined him home and flying through the air with other dragons. In her mind they were all small and white.

Her eyes closed themselves and her head rolled to the side.

Bramble galloped on.

She was suddenly aware he was talking to her. He said something about 'not believing her' and that he was 'sorry'. His voice changed when they came to the intersection Mollie had travelled to so many times in one evening.

'Get off here,' the horse said. 'You go home and I'll keep going. I can smell her just up ahead.'

Mollie half slid, half fell off his back, too exhausted to argue.

She made her way home in a daze, crawled into bed not caring about the noise she was making, and fell into a deep, dreamless sleep.

Chapter 14

Whitestaff awoke to find himself in the same room. He was sprawled out on the terrific woven rug, belly up. Susset was standing over him, her brow wrinkled.

'Do you feel all right?' she asked.

Whitestaff sat up and looked about. There was no sign of his uncle.

'I'm still here,' he announced to no one in particular.

'Yes. This isn't a dream or anything like that. I know it's strange but try to remain calm.'

She began fussing about him, checking his eyes and scales.

'Crossing through portals can sometimes make one sick or dizzy. Are you sure you feel normal?'

Whitestaff considered her question.

'No,' he replied. 'I do not feel normal. In fact I feel fantastic.' Whitestaff stood and flexed the muscles in his front legs. 'Look, I can stand. I can walk. I can... jump,' he gave a mighty leap upward and nearly hit the roof. 'I don't understand. I'm so *strong*.'

Susset nodded.

'Yes, you will be much stronger here than you were on Earth. More powerful than two dragons put together, actually.'

'Really?' asked the golden dragon. 'Why is that?'

'Well, let's see, how do I put this?' As Susset walked around the dragon, her voice took on a serious tone. 'Your essence, your spirit, is trapped between two planes: here and the Earth you came from.'

'Why?' asked the dragon as he stretched his enormous wings in delight.

'Hmmm,' Susset said as she combed her fingers through her hair. 'When you were just an egg, you were sent to earth through a portal. That portal was trapped inside your egg, so as you can see, the portal went through itself, with you.'

There was a long pause.

After a while Whitestaff said, 'That makes absolutely no sense at all.'

The sorceress forced a laugh. 'You're right, it doesn't. But it's the truth. It's a very complicated magic. When one opens the fabric of space one has to become comfortable with things that make no sense.'

Whitestaff just nodded his head and pretended he understood.

'Let's just say all dragons have an inner spirit. Yours is split so that you can live here or on Earth. When you are on Earth you have only a tenth of your spirit. That is why you are so weak there. When you cross over to Sorteya, you bring all of your spirit here, along with the tenth you have on Earth. That's why you're so big and why you're so strong.'

Whitestaff gave his head a little shake.

'I still understand. Why was I on Earth in the first place if this is where dragons live?'

Susset's fingers played with the fringe of her hood.

'Perhaps that question would best be answered by your uncle.'

'Where is he anyway?'

'He left when you passed out. He said it was probably too much for you to take in all at once so he gave us some space. He'll be back soon though.'

Whitestaff nodded. *A lot to take in, right enough.*

'Nice view,' he said after a moment of silence.

'Yes.'

The two walked over to the cave's wide entrance. The first thing Whitestaff noticed was that the cave was very high up, so high the clouds were actually *beneath* them.

It appeared that the room he was in was carved out of the side of a mountain. In the distance he could see many tall, pointed mountains. They looked like thin cones, or giant thorns coming out of the ground. The entire horizon was covered with them. Sorteya appeared to be a giant spike ball.

'It all looks so strange,' Whitestaff said, indicating with his claw.

'Yes. Nothing like this on Earth is there?'

'No. What are all these spiky things?'

'We are in one now. Sorteya is covered in them; we call them spires. They are a natural formation of this planet, likes trees on Earth.'

Whitestaff marvelled at the sight.

'Come over here,' Susset said.

She led the dragon over to the side of the wall. 'Feel it.'

Whitestaff patted the wall. It was made of a rich soil that moved beneath his claws. It was cool and moist.

'Dragons find a nice spire, dig out a home like the one you are in now and live in it.'

'Amazing.'

'You can see dragons flying in and out of them if you look closely.'

Whitestaff squinted his eyes. She was right. He could make out great winged beasts zooming in and out of the spires, like bees in a hive.

'They call their houses dugouts.

'What is that purple stuff on the side of the spires?'

'Oh, that,' she followed the dragon's gaze to see what he was looking at. 'It's balefruit. Look down.'

Whitestaff peered over the edge of the entrance. On the side of the spire's face he could see large purple welts sticking out.

'It's dragon food. Taste it.'

Whitestaff eased a front leg over the edge and grasped some of the balefruit with his sharp claws. He put it to his nose and sniffed. Tentatively, he stuck some in his mouth and chewed.

Juice exploded in his mouth and dribbled down his chin.

'It's fantastic!' he slurped. More fluid drooled out when he spoke, 'It's wonderful!'

'Well, get used to it,' she said dryly. 'It's all there is to eat around here.'

Whitestaff enjoyed another mouthful before swallowing hard and licking his lips. 'It's better than what I ate on Earth.'

'Oh? What was your life like on Earth?'

Whitestaff told her of his travels with Cudgel and Wendy as a sideshow attraction, and how Cudgel used to poke him with his stick when he was unable to do tricks.

He gave her a brief overview of his short but unhappy life in a cage, and how his days were spent travelling from town to town locked in a stinking wagon with Wendy. He spoke of how at each new town children would come and see him and laugh, jeer, or throw rocks, depending on the day.

He told her a voice used to call him from his keeper's van, but he didn't know what it all meant until he met a wonderful young woman with strange powers, a true friend who risked her life to make his better.

Susset listened with interest as the dragon relayed his story, her eyes growing wider with each sentence spoken. She was quiet for a very long time after he finished.

'I am so sorry,' she said in a whisper. Sh placed her hood back on her head.

'What for?' asked the dragon. 'You didn't put me in a cage.'

Susset raised her head and met his eyes with her own. 'I put you on Earth. I foolishly thought humans would have some respect for a dragon. I was wrong.'

'Well, it's over now.'

The sorceress gave a heavy sigh. 'For now. But you'll have to go back someday.'

'GO BACK.' Whitestaff hollered. 'No, you can't mean it! Why?'

'I explained before. You're essence is here and on Earth. You are strong now, but slowly your spirit will leak back into Earth and you'll be weak here. Please try to understand. The longer you live on Earth, the more spirit you have here. You may not have noticed, but you are about twice the size of your uncle, and I bet three times as strong.'

Whitestaff looked down at his body. He was indeed very large. Susset would have fitted into one of his paws. He felt strong also, as if he could break steel with his front legs.

'I don't know what to say. Why did you do this to me?'

'I thought it was best.'

'Best?' spluttered the dragon. 'Best to make me live on Earth with no dignity? Best to bring me here only to tell me I can't stay?'

'I told you before. Your uncle can explain it. Things happened before you were born. Things that you don't understand.' Susset turned her back on the dragon. 'Wait here for Olfar.'

The dragon watched as Susset cast a spell and disappeared.

'Don't go,' he said.

But it was too late; the sorceress had vanished. Whitestaff was left alone.

Chapter 15

Mollie awoke to find her mother sitting on the edge of her bed. Esmae was wearing an expression she had never seen before.

'Good afternoon,' her mother said in a prim voice.

'Afternoon?' She sat up with a jolt when she realised why she had slept so late.

'Ahh,' said Esmae, 'she remembers.'

Mollie rubbed her eyes and tried to control her breathing.

'The fair must have really worn me out, huh?' she said, testing her mother.

'Don't even try.' Her mother raised a thin finger and pointed it at Mollie like a weapon. 'I know *exactly* what happened last night so don't you try to deny it.'

'What happened?'

Esmae sniffed derisively and readjusted her black skirt. 'What indeed! Rescuing those animals, that's what.'

'Ohh,' Mollie said. She averted her eyes from her mother's gaze.

'Since when do you sneak off in the middle of the night like a thief? What if you had been caught? Or worse, hurt yourself where nobody could find you? How do you think I would have felt finding your bed empty in the morning and not knowing what had become of you?'

Mollie kept her eyes low.

'I'm sorry, mother. I should have told you what I was up to. I just wanted to help them so much and...' Mollie's head shot up. 'Wait! How did you know I rescued those animals?'

'I heard you go and I followed you. Turned myself invisible. But that's not the point. The point is you should have told me. I could have helped.'

'Helped?'

'Yes, helped. Don't be surprised. I didn't like the idea of those animals being cooped up either.'

'You mean, you think I did the right thing?'

Esmae sighed and rubbed her temples.

'The right thing in helping the downtrodden—yes. The right thing by sneaking off on your own—no. Why do you think I asked you about the sort of person you wanted to be and what actions you needed to take? I was hoping you'd come and get me and ask me to free the horse and the dragon. As it turned out, you didn't need your mother. But you should have at least written me a note.'

Mollie nodded. 'You're right. I only thought about that on the way home...'

'Oh, Mollie. Why do you think I'm always pushing you to learn more magic? It won't be long now until you're out on your own, and I'd feel much better about it if I knew you could at least defend yourself.'

Mollie didn't say anything.

'Daughter, I know sometimes you wish we weren't who we are. I know that if you had your way, you wouldn't have sorceress blood. You think that life would be so much easier if we were normal.'

'At least people wouldn't cross the road if they saw me coming.'

The two didn't speak for a while. Then Mollie suddenly asked, 'Why didn't you stop me last night if you heard me going out?'

Esmae shrugged. 'You haven't seen yourself lately. You're getting older. I have to let you find your own way. Bit by bit. Last night you showed me you are a person who helps those in need, and if you are going to make a habit of adventure, you should at least let me teach you a few defensive spells.'

Mollie shook her head. 'I can't believe you were watching me.'

Her mother leant over and kissed her smooth nose.

'I will watch over you for a while yet. Until some dashing young prince comes to sweep you off your feet.' They smiled at each other. 'Let me fix you a breakfast fit for a heroine. Just promise to tell me where you're going in future.'

Mollie agreed then watched as her mother fussed over the cooking food in the kitchen. Every now and then she would throw her daughter an approving look and nod. Afterwards, they ate breakfast in peace, each enjoying the moment.

Esmae became more serious when breakfast was over. She cleared the table and gestured for Mollie to remain seated.

'I've wanted to talk to you about this for a while, but I was waiting for the right time. Now is that time.'

Mollie leaned closer.

'You see,' Esmae began, 'magic is a powerful tool that most people can't perform or understand. It is very powerful and should be held in awe. Magic could make you richer than our king or more beautiful than you could hope. But...' her mother took a deep breath, not knowing how to continue. 'If you use it all the time, you will suffer the consequences.'

'I know your rule, Esmae. We can't use magic for personal gain. That's why we can't get a horse, or have nice furniture, or buy firewood instead of chopping it by hand.'

'Yes. But there is a reason for that rule. A reason I haven't told you before. We don't live rich because the last sorceress who let magic do her dirty work was burnt by an angry mob, not too far from Danmurk Shire. That unfortunate lady was a great aunt of yours.'

Mollie put her hand to her mouth.

'Listen, if you and I made ourselves gorgeous, rich and well known, what do you think would happen?'

'We'd be happy and I wouldn't have to chop firewood,' Mollie replied, liking the idea.

'No, think about it long and hard.'

Mollie did as she was told. She sat very still for several minutes and closed her eyes.

'Well, women would be jealous because all the men would like us.'

'Yes,' her mother urged.

'The poor people would hate us because we wouldn't have to work.'

'Keep going.'

'And the king would hate us because we'd have all the gold.'

'That's right,' Esmae said, clearly proud. 'All of what you have said has happened before.'

'To my great aunt?'

'Yes. I didn't know her very well and it was a long time ago. But still…'

'I think I understand,' Mollie said. 'If you use magic all the time you forget what it means to live normally. Plus, if you use it to be better than other people you get burnt by an angry mob.'

The two laughed at that.

Esmae was the first to compose herself.

'Well, yes, not that we should laugh about it. Let's just agree it's dangerous, mobs aside.'

'So what are you trying to tell me?'

Esmae drew another deep breath. 'I'm trying to say that last night you achieved something without using magic; you proved you didn't need it. So now I want to teach you how to cast some very powerful magic. Some potent spells, such as invisibility and levitation.'

Mollie closed her eyes again.

'Think about it, daughter. I saw how close it was last night, so close that I very nearly revealed myself. I'd feel better knowing you could protect yourself, and I know deep down you'd feel better too.'

She's right, Mollie thought to herself. *Last night would have been so simple if I knew the right spells. And, when Audrey caught me and Cudgel was right beneath my nose…*

Mollie lifted her lids and folded her hands in her lap.

'Esmae,' she said with a tiny grin. 'I'm ready to learn everything you have to teach. When do we start?'

Chapter 16

A gentle flapping roused Whitestaff from his thoughts. He turned his back on the shimmering arch in the centre of the room to face his uncle who touched down next to him.

'Feeling better, Nephew?'

Whitestaff shrugged.

'Where is Susset?'

'I think I offended her,' he said with discomfort. 'She, um, disappeared.'

'Don't get too upset, Nephew. She calms down as quickly as she heats up. All of us offend her at sometime or another. Now tell me, Nephew, what should I call thee?'

'Whitestaff, Uncle.'

'Quite a shock we gave thee, hmmm? Bringing thee here to this strange world.'

Whitestaff nodded and said, 'Yes, in more ways than one. I'm *gold* for starters.'

'Indeed. Big too. Strong looking. I expect Susset explained why?'

Whitestaff told his uncle all he understood about his growth and how it related to his essence existing in two places. Olfar stroked his grey beard and listened without comment.

'I asked the sorceress why she did it, Uncle. Why she sent me away like that. Why she denied me time growing up with you. She told me to ask you about it, and--I--I kind of lost my temper.'

Olfar put a front leg around his nephew's shoulders and began patting the younger dragon with his tail.

'I'm glad she didn't tell thee, Whitestaff. It is my place to let thee know what happened all those years ago. But listen, thou had no right to be angry with Susset. As thou will soon see, she did her very best.'

Olfar rested on the mat and curled his hindquarters around so his tail was under his chin. Whitestaff had seen cats lay the same way back on Earth. He followed his uncle's lead and made himself comfortable.

'One hundred and seventy-nine years ago, when I was barely a hatchling, the dragons lived on Earth with the humans. The Chin dragons, the Nazoor, and us, the Palal.'

'You mean there are more types of dragons?'

'Yes, Whitestaff. We all lived together for many centuries. The humans are a crafty bunch, they taught us many things about the world in which we lived. In return, we offered advice and wisdom to their leaders. Sometimes we offered protection.

'Those were good times, or so the chronicles say.' Olfar shifted on the mat and brushed his fuzzy, grey eyebrows out of his eyes with a hooked claw.

'Then things began to change. The Nazoor are a power-hungry breed, for they began to, shall we say, assert themselves with force. They wanted to rule over the humans, and so a war started.

'The Nazoor are quick and strong; therefore, they won the first few battles. Humans, however, are cunning and smart. They made weapons of tremendous destruction, and they had numbers. For every human killed there were ten more shooting arrows or catapults of fire. The Nazoor dragons dwindled.

'The Palal, that's you and me, didn't know what to do. We wanted to live in peace with humans, but the Nazoor are dragons like us, and they were getting slaughtered. We...'

Olfar broke off and wiped his forehead with his tail.

'We didn't need to choose, for the humans turned on *us*. They began to see all dragons as cruel, and they killed a few of the Palal. We retaliated and for years human and dragon blood was spilled; one sensless attack answered with another. Finally, a powerful sorcerer opened a gate to whole new world. A place where dragons could live away from humans and their weapons.'

'Sorteya?' asked Whitestaff.

'Yes, Sorteya, our home. We call the day we left Exodus Day. It's a very important day in our calendar. All our Sorteyan years start from that day. This is the year 176 AE—*After Exodus*. We all came here to live except the Chin, who asked to be sent elsewhere.'

'Chin?'

'Another race of Dragons. Tiny in number but colossal in physical form. I never had the chance to meet one, though I read all about them. I'm not surprised they didn't want to share a planet with the rest of us.'

Whitestaff thought for a moment then asked, 'What about me? Why was I left on Earth.'

'In good time.'

'Sorry, Uncle.'

Olfar smiled and cleared his throat.

'We were all very happy when we arrived in Sorteya. This place has everything a dragon needs and more. For years life was peaceful, but the Nazoor, in the year 155 AE… well, old habits die hard.'

'What do you mean?'

'The Nazoor wanted to rule us. To rule the Palal. They wanted to claim Sorteya as their own. Needless to say we didn't agree. We fought another war, dragon against dragon this time!'

Olfar's voice quavered.

'Are you okay, Uncle? Can I get you a drink?'

Olfar shook his head and took a moment to steady himself before carrying on.

'The war was terrible, as you can imagine. Many dragons died on both sides, including thy father and mother.'

Whitestaff jolted as if he had been hit.

'My parents? The Nazoor killed them?'

Whitestaff closed his eyes. It was the first time he had allowed himself to think of his mother and father. He knew of course that he had parents somewhere, and in truth he never expected to find them, but to be told they had been killed struck him coldly in the chest.

Tears came to his eyes.

Olfar allowed his nephew time to deal with the revelation.

'Should I continue?' he asked after a while.

Whitestaff nodded dumbly.

'Thy father was the king of the Palal. That is why thou are gold by the way, but we'll get to that later. He felt if the war went unfavourably all the Palal would be killed. His one hope for survival was thee, his son. But of course, thou were still an egg.

'He asked Susset to send thee back to Earth, thinking that at least one of the mighty Palal might endure the scourge of the terrible Nazoor. He asked her to make sure no dragon could follow thee, and that thou had to be the only one who could use the portal.

'Susset agreed and hid the portal in thy egg. The other end she hid here.' Olfar pointed to the shimmering arch in front of them.

'No one can go through there except thee. And no one but thee can use the egg.'

'But the Nazoor didn't win, did they? Otherwise you wouldn't be here.'

'Very good, Nephew. No, they didn't win. Thy father, whose name was Frendrek by the way, killed the Nazoor Queen, Mezelga. We had lost our king, and they, their queen. The Nazoor called a truce thereafter. Now we settle things a different way. But that's enough for tonight, thou are getting tired.'

Whitestaff agreed and closed his eyes to sleep.

'What are thou doing, young one?' Olfar asked in surprise. 'We aren't sleeping here. We are going to my place, my dugout.'

'Errm, how do we get there?' Whitestaff asked as he opened a big eye.

Olfar tugged at his beard.

'Well, we fly.'

Chapter 17

Terry allowed himself an extra hour in bed. The Gibbon Fair had kept him past his usual bedtime, so he didn't mind sleeping in.

He lay stretched out on his mattress, looking at the blank ceiling. He was thinking of the Adkins woman. He could still see her face, clean and elegant. He found himself wondering where her husband was.

He'd heard the rumours, of course. The Witches of Danmurk apparently cut men up into small pieces, then use these pieces in their potions. He didn't believe a whit of that nonsense, but still, where was he?

Surely that little one must have a father.

Terry suddenly felt a twinge of sympathy for the two.

Forget the rumours; it's most likely he just left them. Or worse, died of some fever.

He had seen Esmae in Danmurk a few times. Once, he nearly introduced himself, but something about the woman made him think twice. She possessed an inner strength, a self-sufficient spirit that told him he wasn't needed. Esmae looked as though she didn't require friends, or approval, or a man in her life.

Until last night, he thought.

He remembered how Esmae had let down her guard in his rickety cart. She flattered him a little, but not so much as to embarrass him—more to put him at ease. She spoke to him as though she hadn't had a proper conversation in years. It reminded him that Esmae Adkins was like any other woman, despite the rumours.

'A woman who just might be interested in a humble man, such as myself,' he said aloud to the empty room. 'She was certainly interested on the trip home.'

Terry leapt off the bed with new resolve.

'I'll do it,' he announced to no one at all. 'I'll call in on them this very morning.'

Terry made a living hunting wild fowl and pheasants. He was a keen shot with a bow as well as a skilled huntsman. He sold his poultry for a modest price to the cooks in Gibbon, who in turn prepared the birds for the nobles' dinner.

'I could stop by an' politely ask if I can hunt in their yard.'

He chuckled and then added, 'I could also inquire about Mr. Adkins.'

Terry went to the backyard and drew some water from the well. He washed his skin with it as thoroughly as he could. He then took some water inside and heated it over the fire. When it was hot enough, he mixed in some soap, pulled out a long blade, and began to shave.

Afterwards, his face was fresh and his skin smelt clean. He pulled on a shirt and some trousers, and made his way out the front door, whistling as he walked.

He gave a small yelp of surprise when he saw, next to Bramble and munching peacefully on some grass, a bright pink mare.

'Well now,' he said rubbing his chin, 'that *is* a horse of a different colour.'

Chapter 18

'I can't fly,' Whitestaff told his uncle meekly.

'Nonsense,' the older dragon replied. 'Dragons can fly the same way they breathe. Trust me; thou won't even have to think about it. Didn't thou ever fly on Earth?'

Whitestaff shook his head and explained he was too weak.

'Of course, of course,' said Olfar. 'There's nothing to it, Nephew, just… fly.'

Olfar spread his wings and Whitestaff followed suit.

'Whoa, quite a span you've got there, boy. Most impressive.'

Whitestaff bent his neck around to look at his wings. They were indeed massive. They nearly spread across the whole room.

The dragons walked to the opening of the dugout and looked out over the Sorteyan landscape.

Whitestaff looked out over the edge and was about to take a step backwards when Olfar gave his golden nephew a nudge, forcing him off the edge of the dugout.

Whitestaff's mouth sprang open as he fell off the spire. He wheeled his legs as if trying to run on the air and he clawed at the empty sky around him, all the while falling like a stone.

'Use thy wings, Whitestaff,' Olfar called after him.

Whitestaff looked frantically from wing to wing as if they were strange creatures he'd never met before. He closed his eyes and concentrated, and for the first time in his life, Whitestaff could actually feel strength in his wings. He could feel the air rushing over them and the urge to stick them out was strong. Slowly, like a flower opening with the dawn, Whitestaff spread his massive wings until the fall had almost stopped. He beat them up and down with little effort.

Whitestaff's hearts thumped furiously in his chest, with fear at first, then exhilaration.

He found his uncle was right; flying came naturally. He slowed his fall some more and straightened. Above him he could see the green shape of his uncle. He beat his wings harder to move upward and fell in line next to the older dragon.

'This is unbelievable!' he shouted. 'I'd always dreamed of doing this, Uncle, but I never thought if would feel so…'

'What did I tell thee?' Olfar asked with a grin. 'We are born to reign over the sky. Follow me.'

The two dragons flew side by side, laughing as they went. Whitestaff noticed he wasn't as nimble or graceful as Olfar, but he put that down to practice. He soon relaxed into the glide and enjoyed the scenery.

Sorteya was indeed a heavenly place. The air was moist and clean under a heavy sun. The balefruit reflected a purple light that made the spires they clung to glow.

Below him, dragons of red, green, and blue flew from one place to another. On closer inspection, he noticed each spire had about five caves carved out of the surface. The caves that served as private dwellings were higher. Those for public use were lower to the clouds.

Whitestaff flew past what looked like a library. A huge opening in the spire revealed about twenty dragons, all sitting and reading large books bound by leather. Hundreds more books were stacked along shelves. Whitestaff saw a dragon take one off, leaf through then return it to its place before deciding on another.

To his left he saw a small cloud sitting higher than the others. He was tempted to fly right through it, but didn't in case he lost Olfar.

'What does thou think, my boy?' called the green dragon. 'Wonderful, yes?'

But Whitestaff didn't answer, as he didn't hear the question. All sound had left him. His world had become the hush of noise you might find in the hollows of a seashell. In fact, time itself stopped, and Whitestaff was floating, weightless in the glorious sky. It was a beautiful moment.

I am free, Mollie, he thought as tears dripped down his scaly cheeks. *I really am free.*

He followed his uncle downward in a daydream. The purple haze, the towering spires, the freedom of flight, all evoked feelings of splendour and awe. He knew he had at last found his home.

He spiralled around after Olfar until the large green dragon hovered in front of a rather fat spire.

'Here we are,' Olfar said as he gestured with his front leg. 'My humble abode.'

Whitestaff swooped into the hollow and landed— right on the tail of his uncle.

'Not so close behind, Nephew,' Olfar suggested as he withdrew his tail from underneath Whitestaff's heavy paw.

'Sorry, Uncle.'

Olfar turned around. 'No need to cry, my boy. I know thou didn't mean to.'

Whitestaff held up his paw in a dismissive gesture and gave a grin.

'It's not that, Uncle. It was just so amazing and wonderful! I never imagined I'd ever…'

He wiped some tears from his snout and let the thought go unfinished.

Olfar nodded and played with his beard.

'I understand,' he said.

'So this is where you live?' asked Whitestaff, hoping to change the subject.

'Yes. Actually, it's thy home too. Until we carve out a home for thee, that is. I'll show thee where to sleep.'

Whitestaff followed his uncle. The first room looked like a greeting area. There was a fluffy rug on the floor, on top of which sat a chess table made of wood. Past this room was a huge hollow.

'This is the main room,' Olfar said.

Whitestaff was impressed. There were paintings on the walls showing great dragons in flight or in combat. On the floor were large cushions, big enough for a dragon to snuggle into. A fire burned brightly at one end.

'Where is the smoke?' Whitestaff asked.

'That's an enchanted fire. Susset conjured it for me as a gift. It never gives off smoke or needs fuel. Great, yes?'

'Yes,' agreed Whitestaff.

'Thou can sleep up there,' Olfar said.

He pointed to a large gap near the roof. It had another monstrous cushion on the floor for Whitestaff to sleep on. There was a mirror on one wall and a chest for storage.

'Thank you, Uncle. It looks very cozy.'

'Well, thou are welcome to stay as long as thou like. I've kept that room spare in hope that one day thou would hear my call and come home.'

'You mean that was your voice I could hear on Earth?'

Olfar nodded. 'Susset and I spent a few hours each night calling into the portal in her study, praying thou would hear us and come though.'

'I would have come sooner, Uncle,' said Whitestaff. 'I was desperate to,' he spread his front legs in a gesture of helplessness. 'But I was being kept in a cage. This stupid cage by this stupid tooker—'

'Come now, Nephew. It's been an eventful day and thou look worn out in the body and mind. Thy whole world has been changed in the space of a few hours, and thou should get some rest,' Olfar said.

Whitestaff let Olfar guide him up to his nook where the gold dragon collapsed on the cushion, unable to keep his eyes open.

'Thank you, Uncle. I want to stay awake but everything feels so heavy.'

'Thou are home now, Nephew. That is what matters. Rest, for tomorrow I have a big surprise for thee. Thou thinks today was special, wait and see what the new dawn brings.'

But Whitestaff didn't hear what his uncle had said. He'd already fallen into a deep sleep.

Chapter 19

Whitestaff awoke to hear Susset and Olfar talking in the massive chamber below him.

'I would like that too, Susset. However, Whitestaff needs his sleep. Thou should have seen him yesterday; he barely made it up to his room.'

'Olfar, you are as aware of the importance of today as I am. If one is to make a good impression, one must be prepared.'

Whitestaff yawned loudly and stretched. He flew down from his nook to say good morning.

'Before you start,' the sorceress said, halting his greeting with her palm, 'let me apologise for being rude yesterday.'

'No, please—'

'Let me finish,' she said. 'I was out of line. I should never have left you alone in a strange new world. My temper always gets the better of me and I'm very sorry.'

Whitestaff let her scratch beneath his chin, glad to be friends once more.

'Thank you, Susset. But *I* should apologise to *you*. Olfar told me how you saved me as my father wanted. You did the right thing. You had to send me away. Yesterday everything just came as a shock, that's all. It was too much too soon.'

Susset accepted his apology with a bow of her head. She was wearing a hooded blue robe today, and Whitestaff noticed she smelt like lavender.

'That bed you prepared for me, Uncle, is the most comfortable thing I have ever slept on. I feel like I've slept for a decade. Sure beats mouldy straw, right enough.'

'Glad to hear it, my boy.'

'What are we going to do today? Can we go for another fly?'

Olfar and Susset exchanged glances. 'Yes, well. That's why Susset came. Susset, would thou care to enlighten him?'

'Well, yes. You see... Actually, perhaps your wise uncle can explain better than I. Olfar?'

'Susset, we both know thou are much better at explanations. I tend to ramble, I've been told.'

Susset narrowed her eyes. 'Well, one must need more practice, and what better time than now?'

'Would someone just please tell me?' Whitestaff asked.

Finally, Olfar scratched his beard and spoke. 'Remember how I told thee that thy father was the King of Dragons, Nephew?'

Whitestaff nodded.

'Well, how should I put this? You have a... certain claim to the throne, see?'

'Claim to the throne!' Whitestaff spluttered.

'Yes, well, it's all complicated. Thou are Kai'dahl.'

Whitestaff gave him a blank look.

'Well,' Olfar began, tugging at his beard, 'when we were flying yesterday, did thou notice the other dragons?'

'Sure I did. They were everywhere.'

Whitestaff looked at Susset for further explanation. She just made a face and looked away.

'Hmmm, did thou observe what colours they were?' Olfar persisted.

Whitestaff thought hard. He closed his eyes and tried to remember.

'There were green ones, like you.'

'Yes, go on.'

'Red ones.'

'Yes.'

'And blue ones.'

'Is that all?'

'Yes, but what does that have to do… oh. There were no gold ones, Uncle,' he said, almost in a whisper.

'That's right. There were no gold ones.'

Whitestaff flopped on a cushion. 'What does that mean?'

It was Susset who answered this time, giving a textbook lecture on dragonology.

'Dragons are typically four different colours: green, red, blue and gold. Each colour has its own representatives in the King's Court. Six of each colour, except gold because they are quite rare.'

'Why are they—' Whitestaff broke off to correct himself. 'Why am *I* rare?'

'I'm getting there, be patient,' she answered softly. 'Each colour performs a certain role in the dragon community. For example, all female dragons are blue.'

Whitestaff's head jerked in surprise. 'Really?'

'Yes,' the sorceress continued. 'Males are red, green, or gold. The green males like Olfar here are wise and usually perform diplomatic roles. Your uncle sits on the Gra'dahl Council in the King's Court. He is a very important member too.'

Olfar drew himself up with pride. 'It's true. I should interrupt here to clarify something though. The word *dahl* means *the colour of* in our ancient tongue. Re is red, bo is blue, gra is green and kai is gold. So a blue dragon is formally known as a Bo'dahl, green are Gra'dahl, red are Re'dahl while you are a Kai'dahl.'

Susset continued. 'Green dragons are responsible for organising events, making policies… you get the idea. One can see them as the brains, so to speak.'

'Fascinating.'

'The Re'dahl are your best fighters. They are brilliant strategists and noble defenders of your breed. Though sometimes they do come across as aggressive.'

Olfar hummed into his chest at that remark. Susset carried on as though she hadn't heard him.

'The females take care of the young and matters of education. They also provide a valuable balance between the reflective, thoughtful greens and the forceful, insistent reds.'

'And the gold?'

This time Olfar answered. 'The gold dragon is usually the King, Nephew. In the old tongue Kai *leader* and *gold* meant the same thing.'

'Kai'dahl then means the colour of the leader?'

'Precisely! Gold dragons are our leaders. And that explains what the plan is for today,' said Olfar. 'We are going to present thee to the current King and his Council.'

'Why?'

Again, Susset and Olfar engaged in some silent duel.

'For heaven's sake, just tell me,' said Whitestaff.

Susset brushed the front of her robe and spoke. 'The King's Court must be notified of your presence because if anything happens to Cracone the Re'dahl—the current King—you would have a legitimate claim to the throne.' Then in a hurried voice she said, 'Plus you have to nominate for Dragon Champion because you're the only gold dragon on Sorteya.'

Whitestaff let the words sink in. That he could be the king of a race of dragons one day was too extraordinary for him to comprehend, so he didn't even try.

This other thing though, this, Dragon Champion…

'Susset?'

'Yes, Whitestaff.'

'What is a Dragon Champion?'

Susset winced and put her hood on her head. 'Each colour nominates a Contender to become Dragon Champion. Because there is only one Kai'dahl, that being you, you are automatically nominated to participate in the Dragon Champion trials, or the Tournament, as we call it.'

'They are all nominated today,' Olfar added.

Sensing there was something more he wasn't being told, Whitestaff asked, 'What is a Dragon Champion? What does one do?'

Susset rolled her head and took her hood back off.

'The Dragon Champion is the Palal chosen to face the Nazoor in combat.'

Chapter 20

The sun was pulsing heat down furiously on Mollie's pale forehead. Her hair of darkest black absorbed all of the sun's rays, causing her scalp to sweat and itch. She absently gave it a scratch as she listened to her mother, whose voice was being partially drowned out by the nearby gurgling stream.

'This is a fireball,' Esmae said as she pulled at the elements around her.

Mollie could see the magic being threaded together around the older woman. It wrapped about her like a spring. Esmae was lifting red, glittery heat from the ground and the air, and condensing it into a fiery sphere.

'As you can see,' her mother continued, 'I'm gathering all the heat I can from around me. You need to focus it all into a ball, then,' her face contorted with concentration, 'you push it where you want it to go.'

Esmae let the powerful orb blast off into the water, causing a geyser of steam to boil up higher than the treetops. It made a hiss so loud that it threatened to pierce a hole in Mollie's eardrums.

'Wow,' the younger woman said.

The water came back down as heavy rain, and Mollie watched the droplets fall with quiet reverence. She thought she saw a fish splash down back into the water.

Esmae panted and began to summon another ball.

'This one,' she said, 'is a blend of fire *and* water.'

Mollie could see the fire element being mixed with the blue watery haze around her mother.

'You mix the two like this.'

Fire and water clashed furiously in the space in front of Esmae.

'The two elements cancel each other out, so you're left with neutral energy. See?'

Mollie did see. The ball stretched out into a longer shape, like an arrow.

'It's called a Magic Missile. Much bigger than the fireball, twice as powerful.'

Esmae's breath was short, as though she was sprinting.

'It's the one you were going to use on Cudgel!' Mollie exclaimed.

'Yes, it is,' her mother huffed. 'If you don't want to burn someone's skin off, you'll use this one.'

Whooomp! Esmae let the missile fly—*Smash!*

It rammed into an old fig tree, blasting bark off in all directions and shaking lizards and bugs from the branches above. Birds flew out and upwards, chirping madly as the tree shook. Leaves fell steadily for minutes afterwards, making a carpet at the base of the fig.

Mollie was impressed.

'How the Latos did yer do that?'

The Adkins women turned to see Terry standing behind them. His eyes were as wide as tankards and his jaw hung as if dislocated. He was pointing at the near ruined fig with a shaky but well-washed hand.

'Lightning?' Mollie suggested.

The three of them slowly looked to the sky, which was clear and blue.

'Erm, would you like a drink, Terry?' Esmae asked, breaking the silence.

Still in shock, Terry let himself be guided into the kitchen by the older Adkins. He knew what he had seen, but his mind still couldn't accept it as reality. He had seen Esmae throw some invisible object then…

First a pink horse, now an exploding tree. What a morning!

He sat loosely on a wooden stool and watched Esmae boil some water over the fire.

A disengaged part of him wondered if the attractive lady and her sprightly young daughter were going to chop him up and use him in their spells.

Chapter 21

Olfar was polishing Whitestaff's scales with vigour. At first, the golden dragon protested at having clear glob rubbed onto him, but Olfar insisted. 'Thou are about to present thyself to the entire court,' he said fretfully.

He leaned in close to his nephew's scales and sniffed. 'When was the last time thee bathed?'

"Never" was the answer, but Whitestaff was too embarrassed to give it. Cudgel gave Wendy a rub down every three days—after he painted her, that is.

The only time Whitestaff had ever been in water was when rain came down through the roof of the wagon. He couldn't remember feeling self conscious about his appearance before and had never even tried to keep himself clean. Who worried about baths when standing was near impossible?

After much puffing and exertion, Olfar could at last see his reflection in his nephew's broad scales.

He stood back to admire his work. 'Much better.'

'Err, thanks.'

Whitestaff admitted to himself that he did look fabulous and clean.

What would the children on Earth think if they saw me in Cudgel's cage now? he mused.

A sinking feeling suddenly hit him in the stomach. He remembered Susset's rule about returning to Earth. He *would* have to go back to Cudgel one day, and he would have to be weak again.

'Cheer up,' Olfar said. 'Going before the King isn't that bad.'

'No, it's not that, Uncle. I was just… Never mind.'

He could see his uncle wasn't listening anyway.

Susset had gone to prepare the court for Whitestaff's arrival. The green dragon kept craning his neck around to the greeting room, then popping back to check Whitestaff was still there.

'Is something wrong, Uncle?'

Olfar pulled back into the room and shook his head.

'Are you waiting for someone?'

He gave Whitestaff a sheepish grin and pawed at his beard.

'Actually, I'd better tell thee,' he said with a resigned sigh. 'I have invited my daughter over to meet thee.'

'Daughter? You mean I have a—'

'A cousin,' Olfar finished. 'Yes. Her name is Luzahmin, and she should have arrived by now. Susset went to see her this morning while thou were still asleep. She said she would be overjoyed to meet thee.'

'That's fantastic!'

'I was going to save it as a surprise but after yesterday… you fainted…'

'Yesterday was different,' Whitestaff asserted. 'I promise I won't pass out ever again.'

He crossed his heart with a golden claw, then did the same for his second heart.

'Will she like me, do you think?'

'It depends, Whitestaff,' said a female voice from the entrance.

Whitestaff and Olfar spun around to see two dragons at the door. One was red, the other blue.

The blue dragon was an elegant looking creature. Her dull scales drank the light, making her green eyes appear brighter than sunlit jewels. She had a narrow face that was topped with three short spikes.

Whitestaff thought she looked a bit rigid, but pretty nevertheless.

She glided over to a smiling Whitestaff and brought her tail around to shake with. 'Hello, I'm Luzahmin.'

Whitestaff stared blankly at the upheld tail, which was pointed at him and waiting.

'It's polite to shake tails,' scoffed the red dragon.

'Oh,' said Whitestaff. He quickly brought his own tail around ready to shake. Unfortunately he was too eager, and his tail came from behind so fast that it jabbed Luzahmin in the snout and got stuck in her left nostril.

Luzahmin gave a yelp of pain and threw her head back theatrically. She put her front paws to her nose, wincing and sobbing. The red dragon dashed to her side to see if she was all right.

'Are you, er, good?' asked Whitestaff, wishing the dugout ceiling would collapse on him.

She shot him a glare through watery eyes as a reply.

'Sorry,' he said as he put his tail behind him. 'I'm really new at all this.'

Olfar patted his huge nephew and gave his daughter a forced smile.

'I'm Nap, by the way,' said the red dragon with a sneer. 'But I think we can go without the tail-shaking formalities—I want my nose to remain attached.'

'Hi, Nap,' Whitestaff said feebly. 'It's good to meet you both. It's great to find out I have family here.'

Luzahmin and Nap pointedly ignored him. They stood, tails linked, heads together, as if they were the only ones in the room. Nap whispered to her as she buried her head in his chest. It made Whitestaff feel very awkward.

'Nap is Cracone's son,' Olfar said, changing the topic diplomatically.

'That's great,' said Whitestaff. 'You'll be King next then, right?'

Nap ignored the remark, but Whitestaff could see him stiffen.

Something about Nap made Whitestaff uneasy. His very appearance was off-putting: wiry with blood-red scales and a permanent scowl. He also had a barb on his tail that looked like it was made from steel.

'Ahem, well,' said Olfar, breaking the silence. 'I have to go and take my place in the Court.'

Whitestaff made a desperate face at his uncle, who pretended not to notice.

'Do you have to go now, Uncle?'

Olfar gave a small chuckle. 'Thou will be fine with these two,' he said. He turned to the other dragons. 'I'll let thee all get acquainted, thou don't need the likes of me here,' Whitestaff was about to differ on this point, but controlled himself. 'Bring him along in an hour, yes?'

Nap nodded and Olfar flew into the blue sky.

For a long time nobody spoke.

The Last Dragon Home

Chapter 22

'Why don't you sit down and relax?' offered Whitestaff, pointing to a cushion.

Luzahmin huffed. 'If I want to sit in *my* father's house, I will. I don't need your permission.'

'Look, again, I'm sorry. I only got here yesterday and...' He let the sentence go unfinished as neither dragon was listening.

After a few minutes of being ignored, Whitestaff tried another tack.

'So, Uncle was telling me about the Dragon Champion Tournament. Sounds exciting. How does it work?'

Luzahmin rolled her eyes, but Nap answered.

'It's a tournament we hold to see who battles the Nazoor.' Then with a hint of self-satisfaction added, 'I'm the chosen Contender for the Re'dahl.'

'I'm confused,' admitted Whitestaff, causing his cousin to snort and mutter something. 'How can one dragon fight the entire Nazoor?'

Nap rolled his eyes. 'Our Champion fights the Nazoor Champion,' he explained, as though speaking to a child. 'Whoever touches the ground first loses.'

Whitestaff nodded. 'So we pick our best fighter, they pick their best fighter, right?'

'Right. That way we avoid a war.'

'Yes, Olfar told me about that. The Palal had a war with the Nazoor many years ago. My father killed their Queen.'

Nap let go of Luzahmin's tail, and began scratching noisily at the ground with the end of his.

'That's correct, I suppose. Since that day, we've settled our differences with the Tournament. If they win, they control Sorteya. If we win, things stay the same. We do this every ten years. There is much honour to be gained by competing.' He put a paw to his chest and drew himself up. 'I'm just glad to be nominated.'

Luzahmin snuggled back into Nap's chest. 'You're so brave,' she said.

'How do you know you've been nominated?' Whitestaff asked. 'Uncle told me that happens today.'

'His dad is the King, silly. Of course he knows before anyone else.' This earned her a peck on the cheek from Nap.

'So let me see if I've got this right. We Palal have to pick one dragon of each colour. These dragons compete against each other; the strongest one fights the Nazoor Champion. Is that it?'

'It's more complicated than that, but yes, that's the gist of it.'

'So, you and I will be competing against each other, right?'

'What?' cried Luzahmin as she pulled her head away. 'You can't compete, you have no right!'

'Who told you to compete?' asked Nap, aghast.

Suddenly, Whitestaff wished he'd never mentioned the whole championship. 'Olfar told me. He said one of each colour, and there's only one gold so I'm told.'

Nap's jaw set and his claws bunched into fists. 'Dad says you Kai'dahl are all the same. You think you're entitled to everything. Well, not this. Luzahmin is right; you have no place in the Tournament. I'll make sure of it.' Here he looked at Luzahmin. 'I'll bet your father put these silly ideas in his head. Olfar the Interferer strikes again.'

'He can't help himself,' Luzahmin agreed.

'I can just hear the old fool now, with his *thees* and *thous*.'

'It's embarrassing. Why can't he talk like everyone else? He reads too many of those old books. That's his problem.'

Nap laughed. 'His problems go deeper than that.'

'I like the way he talks,' Whitestaff said, closing his claws into fists.

Nap snarled at him. 'You would. And I meant what I said—you will not compete in this Tournament.'

'And why not?' Whitestaff shot back.

'Because, Kai'dahl, the future of the Palal is at stake. We can't afford to lose.'

'What makes you think I'd lose?'

'Have you ever fought before?'

Whitestaff didn't answer he just stared right into Nap's eyes.

'Ha! Didn't think so!' Nap slowly moved Luzahmin out of the way and took a step closer to the golden dragon. 'Tell you what, Whiteworm, you fight me right here, right now. If you win, I won't say a word to my father. If you lose, you agree not to nominate yourself for the Tournament. What do you say?'

'I say you're being ridiculous, both of you. Luzahmin, how can you poke fun at your own father? And as for you, *Red*,' he turned back to Nap, 'you need to stop acting like a tooker and lose that chip off your shoulder before another dragon knocks it off.'

Nap's already surly face grew even darker. His brow wrinkled with hate.

'You Kai'dahl dragons think you're so special. My dad is King now, and he's Re'dahl. If you think you have any chance of being King just because of your colour, you're wrong. I will be the next King, and my first order will be to have you put back where you came from.'

As he spoke, Nap got down from his hind legs onto all fours. He crouched down and swished his tail from side to side. Luzahmin backed away, sensing a clash was coming.

'Send me back? Just you try,' Whitestaff said.

With a fast spring from his hind legs, Nap leapt at Whitestaff's chest, teeth bared and claws outstretched.

Whitestaff was ready for this attack and threw a wild slap, but Nap was too fast.

The red dragon blocked the swinging claws and used his momentum to knock Whitestaff backwards. The golden dragon fell back with Nap on top of him.

Whitestaff suddenly realised this was a good thing. When the two were fighting in the open space, speed was better than strength, but with Nap on top of him in close quarters, strength was all that mattered.

Whitestaff threw his front legs around Nap and drew him in even closer, binding Nap in a crushing hug. The red dragon's forelegs were pinned to his sides, useless. Nap writhed his body and tried to escape the powerful grip. The Re'dahl's breath dried up, and his lungs were too squashed to get more air. Whitestaff's muscles were like stone; he applied even more pressure to Nap's struggling body. Behind him he could hear Luzahmin begging him to let go.

Nap gave one final fruitless kick then drove the silver spike on his tail into Whitestaff's back leg.

The pain made Whitestaff release his hold just enough for Nap to gasp in more air. He kicked away from the bigger dragon, and collapsed on the ground in a wheezing, coughing mess.

Luzahmin scurried over to him and cradled his head in her lap patting him softly with her tail. Whitestaff moved forward to make sure Nap wasn't too badly hurt.

'Get away! Get out!' Luzahmin screamed at him.

He saw anger in her eyes, and fear. Too exhausted to argue, Whitestaff left the massive hall and stood at the opening of the dugout.

A cool breeze caressed his face. He was aching after the fight, but he didn't care. He looked out over the landscape and forced his shaking body to relax.

After a while, Luzahmin came out to stand beside him.

'I will tell my father about all of this so he knows what kind of dragon he has brought home. You'd better pray that Nap doesn't tell his.'

Whitestaff shrugged his gigantic shoulders.

'Don't care if you do. Tell them all if you want.'

'You have no idea about the enemies you are making,' she hissed.

'You're right. I don't. But I do know that for the first time in my life I can fight them back. That's the only difference between here and Earth.'

He turned to face her. 'You and Nap showed me that. In a way, I'm grateful.'

Chapter 23

After a hot drink and some homemade cakes, Terry Gritbole felt much more at ease in Esmae's presence. Her mature charm and genuine nature had also settled his nerves, and now he was ready for the truth.

'I know what I saw,' he said. 'I just don't know what I saw, do yer see?'

Esmae patted his hand and Mollie tried to hide her smile.

Mollie thought he looked completely out of place at the table. But maybe that's because she'd never seen a man in her home before. The modest, almost bare cottage had only ever housed Adkins women. They kept it neat and respectable, and usually male-free.

'Yes, I know what you mean,' said Esmae. 'I will not lie to you, Terry, for I can tell you have an open mind and a good heart.'

Terry beamed at this and looked at his shoes.

'It is true what you saw. I did damage the tree, and I used magic to do it.'

Mr Gritbole ran his fingers roughly through his hair. 'Real magic? I never believed it existed. So you *are* witches?'

'No,' Mollie said, almost in a shout. 'We are not witches. Tell him, Esmae.'

'That's right. Witches are something else.' She turned back to Terry. 'We go by a different name.'

'What are yer, if yer aren't witches?'

'Sorceresses,' Mollie chimed in.

'So,' he said cautiously, 'Yer don't... um... put things, people let's say, in spells?'

Esmae stifled a laugh. 'No, Terry, we don't chop people up for potions, if that's what you're asking.'

Terry slumped back in the chair. 'That's a relief.'

Then a new thought occurred to him.

'Not to be rude, but whatever happened to Mr Adkins?'

Esmae looked pained at the question and Mollie stood and put her arms around her.

'Sorry, sorry,' Terry said as he bounced his hands around. 'That wasn't a good question—'

'It's fine, Terry,' Esmae assured. 'We don't talk about him often, that's all.'

She looked at her daughter and gave her a loving grin.

'Oh, I shouldn't have—'

'No, no, I'm all right. It is quite a long story. I suppose you've heard the rumours around Danmurk. They say horrible things.'

'I never believed 'em!' Terry declared, pointing at himself for effect.

Esmae smiled at him and patted his hand again. 'I bet you didn't,' she said. 'The truth is Mollie's father is a very special man.'

'Very special,' Mollie said with a nod. She knew all about her father. Esmae explained it all to her a few years ago, when she was old enough to understand.

'Mollie's father is a sorcerer,' explained Esmae, 'a very powerful one at that.'

'Ahh,' said Terry. 'He knew magic too, did he? Where is he now?'

Esmae took a deep breath. 'I don't know where he is, or when.'

'Hey?'

Esmae played with her sleeves, trying to figure out a way to describe something so mind-boggling. After some deliberation, she decided the best course was brutal honesty.

'You see, Terry, he is an extraordinary man capable of remarkable things. He can actually travel through time.'

'Time, you say?'

'Yes,' said Esmae. 'You know how you and I can move backwards and forwards through the air, through space?'

'Ye--ss,' said Terry, his forehead wrinkled.

'Well, Mollie's father can move through space *and time*, backwards and forwards.'

Terry looked as though he didn't quite believe her, so she continued.

'I met him a long time ago and we lived together for a short while. He was always doing new and wonderful things with magic, things even I could hardly believe. He was amazing.'

Mollie listened with a smile. 'One day, he told her that he'd found a way... Sorry, Esmae. You tell it.'

Esmae nodded. 'One day, he told me he had found a way to go into the past and into the future. He was so excited about his discovery. He talked about changing events in time, making up for man's mistakes. He said he'd like to go into the future and fix all the wars, stop all the diseases, and save mankind. I told him to go and do it, after all, who else could?'

'Very good of you,' Terry said, feeling he had to say something.

'After that, he would vanish for days on end then return with the most fabulous stories full of bizarre inventions and scandalous ways of living. I missed him when he went, but I couldn't ask for him to stay, for he loved travelling through time so much.'

Terry found this all hard to believe, but he was enchanted by the story nonetheless. He rubbed his nose and leaned forward.

'Keep going,' he said.

'Once, he went for a whole year.' A far-away look entered Esmae's eyes. She was silent for a while, then shook herself and continued. 'He thought he'd only been gone a day. That's when it became apparent it would never work, we could never be together, as normal couples could.'

Mollie shook her head glumly. This was the worst part of the story. She'd heard it before, but it still made her sad. It made her mum sad too, judging by the wetness in the corner of her eyes.

'So what happened then?' Terry asked.

'We had one last night together then I told him to go. Save the world in the future, fix mistakes in the past. I told him his work was too important, too many people needed him. He didn't want to leave me, but he knew I was right.' Esmae let out a dreamy sigh. 'I didn't know I was pregnant with Mollie until six weeks after he left.'

Terry didn't know what to say. He clumsily got out of his chair and bent over Esmae. He put his arms tenderly around her neck. He then rubbed Mollie on the head as he sat back down.

'Now yer don't know where he is. And he doesn't know he has a young 'un.' He shook his head with pity.

'What is his name?' he asked after a pause. 'Who is this sorcerer who moves through time?'

Mollie took her mother's hand, knowing how hard it would be for her to say his name.

'Merlin,' said Esmae. She sighed once more and looked out the window. 'His name is Merlin.'

Chapter 24

'Follow us,' said Luzahmin, not even meeting Whitestaff's eyes. She strode past her cousin to the spire opening, her muscles tense and her head tilted back.

Nap shouldered Whitestaff on his way past.

Nap and Luzahmin leapt off the edge of the hollow in unison, leaving Whitestaff with no alternative but to follow.

The skies were relatively dragon free. The few that Whitestaff did see were all heading the same way as him.

The sun was low behind the three as they flew in the cool morning air. Whitestaff still marvelled at his innate ability to fly, and he noticed it felt more natural than the day before. Nap though, he observed with a pang of envy, flew in a graceful, stylish way that made Whitestaff look like an airborne slug.

He found he breathed easier at this height, his blood circulated better and his body was loose and relaxed. He was also more aware of the things around him. Small, tawny birds scattered at his sides. Partially formed clouds carried the scent of moisture to his snout. It was as though living up in the sky made him healthy and fit and enhanced his senses.

Even if the company was poor, Whitestaff could love this place just for the stunning landscape. The towering spires and the thick fog below obscured the ground so he wasn't sure how high up he was.

The only things wrong with the scene were the two dragons he was chasing.

The fight with Nap was still fresh on his mind. He could even feel Nap's armoured tail digging into his leg and hear the throaty noises the dragon had made as he struggled for air.

Worse, his cousin's pretty face, darkened by seething anger, burned in his head. It made his stomach tighten.

Maybe I shouldn't have fought, Whitestaff thought. *But what else could I do? Let them make fun of Olfar? Let Nap tell me what I can and can't do? That would be no better than Cudgel's cage. As for Luzahmin, Mollie was kinder to me and I wasn't even related to her.*

They flew on. Whitestaff began trailing behind. He thought of asking them to slow down, but made his wings beat faster instead.

Luckily, as he was about to lose sight of them, they stopped and hovered outside an enormous cavern. The entrance hole was shaped to resemble a dragon's head with its mouth wide open. It had emeralds for eyes and its fangs were made of silver. The scales were a dazzling gold. It looked fantastic yet menacing at the same time.

Whitestaff watched as Nap and Luzahmin swooped into the dragon's jaws and into the room beyond, not even turning to see if he was still coming after.

That must be the Court of the King, thought Whitestaff. *I wonder what Cracone will say when he finds out I fought his son.* He pushed the thoughts out of his head. *He can't do anything to me, if he tries, I'll fight him too.*

But when he came close to the tall spire and its ominous hollow, he stalled.

'So, you're the golden boy I've heard so much about.'

Whitestaff flapped around to face the dragon who had spoken. He found himself gazing at a sleek green dragon. His face was wide and pleasant, and his body thin and stretched. He had strange legs that looked too long by a half, but he zipped through the air with ease.

'I'm Graggy,' he said. He zoomed around Whitestaff and looked him over. Whitestaff turned in frantic circles, trying to introduce himself. It was like chasing his own tail.

'I'm Whitestaff—' he tried. But Graggy whizzed behind him before he could finish.

'Would you stay still!' he bellowed.

Graggy threw his wings forward and stopped short. 'Sorry,' he said as he hovered in front of Whitestaff. 'I'm just curious. I didn't really believe my dad when he said Frendrek's boy was back.' He stuck out his tail and smiled.

Whitestaff presented his own tail, with more care this time, and the two shook without any mishaps.

'I'm Whitestaff.'

'Yeah, I know. Dad told me all about it. The whole court is in there waiting for you, you know. Can't wait to see the looks on their faces, especially Nap. He'll be furious.' Graggy's speech was like his flying style; quick and blurry.

'I've met Nap already,' said Whitestaff in a regretful tone.

'What happened? Did he try and fight you? He can't stand any colour other than his own, you know. He'd prefer Luzahmin much better if she were red. Ha.'

'Yeah,' Whitestaff agreed and gave a little laugh.

'So?'

'So what?'

'Did he have a go at you?'

Whitestaff's guilty look was all the answer Graggy needed.

'He did! What a Re'dahl. Not even on the planet five minutes and he picked you for a fight.' He rolled back in the air and chortled. 'How'd you do? Did you beat him?'

Whitestaff gave a non-committal shrug.

'You did! Good for you! I fought him once, you know. Fun too, it was.'

Whitestaff laughed despite himself. 'Finally, I meet someone on this planet with a sense of humour.'

'Ha! Well, come on. Can't fly out here all day talking. We'd better get you in.'

Whitestaff agreed, feeling more confident now he had someone with him.

Side by side, the two dragons soared towards the open mouth of the King's Court, and landed inside with a gentle flutter.

Whitestaff's hearts raced at the sight that greeted him. He never expected to see *this*.

Chapter 25

Mr Gritbole's fingers drummed on the old wooden table. 'It's grand that yer can both do these tricks and I thank yer both for showing me. But how do yer do it?'

'Magic has always been around us, Terry,' Esmae was explaining. 'For some reason only a few can use it. It takes some inborn knack, if you like.'

'We call it *gathering*, don't we Esmae?'

'Yes. It's like gathering sticks for a fire, Terry. Imagine elements like air or water that are always around us. We can gather them together with our minds, the same way you'd gather firewood in a forest with your hands. Then we use the elements to do our bidding.'

'How many others are there like you two?' he asked. 'I mean ter say, what if everyone can do it 'cept me? The more yer show me, and the more I think about it, the worse it gets.

'Are folks in my house right now bursting a hole in the front door? Are there more then jus' us in this room?'

He licked his lips and his eyes darted everywhere.

'Calm down, Terry. It's just us, I promise. No one is in your house. Magic isn't something to be afraid of.'

'Unless yer a tree.'

'That was just for fun. I was showing Mollie a few things.'

'Yer, well, I think we have different ideas of fun. I think I'd better go.'

'Terry, please sit,' said Esmae kindly. 'We are the only two I know of that can do magic, and I promise we won't harm you.'

'How do I know that?' Terry asked, almost unkindly.

'I thought you'd just know. I thought you were…' She shook her head and her jaw set firm. 'Well, do what you like,' she said tightly. 'I can't convince you, Terry. You can leave if you please, I don't want to keep you here against your will.'

Terry watched as Esmae's whole body seemed to stiffen. He was reminded of the time he saw her alone in Danmurk—alone and unapproachable.

Oh, no, he thought. *I've ruined my chance.*

'No need to shut the door on the way out.' Esmae began to tidy the table where they had been sitting, assuming her company had already left.

Terry teetered between inside and out, hopping on his feet, not sure of what to do. He looked at Mollie, who was staring at him with those big blue eyes then to Esmae's back, which was rigid and tense.

He gave a resigned sigh.

'I'm sorry,' he said. 'My mind wasn't as open as we thought it was, an' maybe yer caught me when I wasn't ready. I had other things in mind fer today, an' magic weren't one of 'em. Can yer forgive a fool fer being a fool?'

Esmae's body remained stiff for a moment, then she relaxed and turned around.

'Forgive me?' he asked again. 'Please?'

'Yes, Terry. I suppose we can forgive a fool.'

Mollie grinned as Terry sat back down.

'I think I'm ready to listen now,' he said. 'Wait!' he stood up so fast his feet left the ground. 'I want to show you something first.'

He took each lady by the hand and led them outside. 'Look,' he said. 'She was in my yard this morning.'

'Wendy,' Mollie cried. She let go of Terry's hand and ran to her pink friend.

The sudden shout disturbed the horse and she went into a kicking fit. Bramble, who was tethered next to her, shied away from her lethal hooves, whinnying with fright as he did so.

Mollie took a few steps back.

'Help her, child,' begged Bramble in fear. 'She'll hurt herself.'

Mollie looked up to her mother. 'Is there something we can do? I hate seeing her like this.'

'Yes,' Esmae replied. 'But it's dangerous.' She gripped her daughter's shoulder.

'I don't care. She's my friend, we have to save her.'

'What's wrong with her?' asked Terry. 'An' why is she pink?'

'She's been driven mad, Terry,' answered Esmae. 'We can save her, but it's something I haven't done since Merlin was around.'

'Whatever it is, Esmae, I'll do it.' Mollie stated. 'She won't last long if she keeps that up.'

Wendy's fit was disturbing to watch; even Terry had to look away.

'If you really want to save her, Mollie, we have to go inside her head. Something which is very risky.'

'I don't care about the risks. We can do it.'

Esmae saw the determination in her daughter's eyes and knew she had to take the chance. 'Hold onto my hand. When I say so, focus your mind on Wendy, I'll do the rest. Oh, and Terry?'

'Yes, m'lady?'

'Don't touch us, no matter what. Our bodies will be very still for a while. Just stand guard, all right.'

Terry nodded and touched his chest.

'Very well. Here we go.'

Mollie centred her mind around Wendy, her eyes shut tight. She could feel her mother's hand vibrating in her own. It shook so hard she thought she might lose hold.

Her head began to rattle, and a loud spinning noise penetrated her brain.

Then silence.

Mollie slowly opened her eyes and squinted through her lashes. As soon as the world around her took form, however, she wished she'd never opened them at all.

'What is this place?' she asked in wonder. 'I don't like it at all.'

Chapter 26

At that moment, on a different planet, Whitestaff was thinking the same thing.

I don't like this at all.

He was in the middle of an enormous amphitheatre. To his left were hundreds of green dragons, to his right hundreds of blue. Red dragons were in front, all ten levels high.

His uncle, with five other dragons of the same colour, sat in the front row of the Gra'dahl side. Six blue sat at the bottom of the Bo'dahl section. Whitestaff guessed this must be the Council.

Cracone was at the head of the Court, flanked by his Council, with three Re'dahl on either side. He sat on a throne of gold and held an ornate sceptre in his thick paw.

Whitestaff thought him a ferocious-looking Re'dahl. His left eye was patched with a flat piece of ruby, and a massive scar jagged across his chest, up to his ear. Susset was speaking with him, her back to Whitestaff.

The whole Court went silent as the two dragons landed lightly.

'You'd think they'd be used to me by now,' Graggy whispered as he waved to the crowd.

'Get to your house, Graggy,' ordered Susset, turning around and floating over to them.

He gave Whitestaff an encouraging nudge before flying to the top row of the Gra'dahl section.

Susset placed a hand on Whitestaff's front leg and walked him forward to the throne.

'May I present to the Court—Whitestaff, son of Frendrek,' she said with a bow.

After a split-second pause, Whitestaff gave a bow too.

'Hmmph. Frendrek's boy, hey? Big enough, I'll give you that.' Cracone's voice was a gruff rumble. He tapped the bottom of his staff on the ground. 'Rise.'

The two did so.

'Well, boy. Tell us your story,' the Dragon King ordered.

Whitestaff was puzzled. 'I thought Susset and Olfar told you all about me.'

The King bashed his sceptre on the ground. 'Impertinent Kai'dahl!' he bellowed. 'When your King gives you an order, you obey. Just because I've heard your story, doesn't mean the whole Court has.' He gestured at the surrounding dragons with the royal rod.

Whitestaff was unsure of whether to argue or not. All the eyes watching him, waiting to see what he was going to do and say next, made him feel like he was back with Cudgel.

'My story.' He cleared his throat. 'I was born on Earth, kept in a cage, and taken from town to town so people could look at me. Then I found the portal that brought me here. That is my story.'

'Any details you'd like to add?' asked the King roughly.

Some of the dragons giggled like hatchlings, Cracone silenced them with a scowl.

'I already gave you the interesting parts.'

This time more dragons laughed.

'The Bo'dahl Council welcomes you to the Court. Welcome, Whitestaff.'

The gold dragon turned to face the Bo'dahl and gave them a bow.

Olfar welcomed him in a similar fashion, speaking for the Gra'dahl.

Cracone drew out the bated silence. Presently he spat on the floor and welcomed Whitestaff on behalf of the Re'dahl.

The Court cheered and Whitestaff gave each section another bow. He caught Nap's eye in the red section and gave him a toothy grin.

Cracone broke the ovation with more rapping on the floor. 'Silence!' he shouted. 'Sit over there, Kai'dahl.' Whitestaff followed the point of the sceptre to a place high above the greens.

Before he could move, however, Olfar spoke. 'Hold it,' he said, raising his front legs high. 'Hold it there.'

'What is the meaning of this, Olfar?' asked the King.

Whitestaff wondered the same thing.

'The Gra'dahl Council wishes to move that Whitestaff be allocated a seat in the Council of Kai'dahl.'

Hundreds of dragons drew breath in unison.

'Explain this nonsense!' demanded the King.

'Well,' Olfar tugged his beard so hard strands began to come out. 'Since Whitestaff is the only Kai'dahl, he should automatically have his own Council. After all, who else would represent him? There are no other of his colour.'

The dragons in the Court began to murmur. Snatches of conversation reached Whitestaff. *He has a point,'* said some. *'Nonsense,'* said others.

Then the same blue dragon who welcomed Whitestaff spoke. 'The Bo'dahl will second that motion.' She gave Whitestaff a motherly grin.

The murmuring grew louder. Some dragons began to shout.

'Silence!' roared the King once more.

Red dragons began whispering frantically at him from both sides.

'This is a setup, you majesty,' one said. 'They have planned this in advance.'

Cracone growled agreement.

'Silence! Silence!' He rapped on the floor so angrily the sceptre vibrated in his grip.

'Let's vote. Those of you who think this *Kai'dahl,'* he said the word with obvious disapproval, 'should have his own Council, raise your paw.'

Whitestaff looked around and saw most of the green dragons with paws in the air. Graggy cheered from above, and Whitestaff gave him an exaggerated bow. This caused most of the Bo'dahl to laugh. They too put up their paws. Sensing his theatrics had turned the court in his favour, Whitestaff gave them the lowest, most dramatic bow he could muster, causing guffaws and laughter all round.

'Enough,' said the King before his own Re'dahl could vote. 'Enough. Let the Court recognise that Whitestaff has his own Kai'dahl Council. He will take his first sitting in three month's time.'

Some of the dragons booed this caveat, but shut up very quickly when Cracone gave them an evil, one-eyed glare.

'Until then, I suppose you can sit in the empty Re'dahl chamber.' Cracone pointed to a space next to the blues.

Whitestaff was about to make another bow, but decided not to push his luck with the Court. Instead he carried his massive frame to the bench and sat. He took up most of the seats just by himself.

'Now we've met Frendrek's boy and welcomed him, perhaps we could get some business cleared in this carnival. This gathering of the Court was meant to be a simple issue. We are here not to make a new member of the Council,' he gave Whitestaff a pointed stare, 'but to nominate the Contenders for the Tournament.'

The hall cheered.

'But first—all rise.'

Each dragon stood at once. Whitestaff looked around and got up from his seat.

'Just the first verse today,' Cracone ordered. 'Mariette, if you please.' He lowered his head towards a Bo'dahl Councilor.

Mariette smiled and began singing. After the first note, all the other dragons joined in. Whitestaff listened in wonder as the dragons filled the Court with their song. The Bo'dahl sang high and soft, the Gre'dahl deep and raspy. Whitestaff most enjoyed the singing of the reds though, powerful and bold.

They sang:

Soaring the infinite sky,
We reign.
Blue with heart,
Green with brain.
Defended by red's noble claw,
With one of gold,
To lead us all.

The dragons sat silently when the anthem was over, and Whitestaff wished they'd sing it again. But instead, Cracone got straight to the point.

'Firstly, let me say to those who are chosen that the entire honour of your family, and indeed your colour, rests on your ability to fight—and fight well.'

More cheers at this, mostly from the Re'dahl.

Cracone continued, 'Also, let me say that each Council has given much thought and deliberation into the choosing of their Contender. Respect their decision. I don't want a repeat of last time.'

He waited until the murmurings had finished. 'This year there will be four events testing agility, cunning, speed and brute strength. There will be cheating, that is allowed. There will be rough play; that too is called for. There will, however, be no quitters and no outside help—that we can detect.' The crowd laughed at this.

'To the Bo'dahl, who have only nominated once before, may I ask whom you have chosen to represent your honour?'

A tall blue dragon from the Council arose. 'We had only one worthy contestant this time, Your Highness. We have chosen Armay to carry our honour.'

High-pitched merriment came from the blues as a petite young dragon weaved her way to the Court floor. She was sleek and snake-like, with claws the colour of the sky. Whitestaff's hearts momentarily stopped as he gazed at her. She was pleasing to the eye, her body wonderfully smooth. He swallowed hard as she winked at him then bowed to the King.

'The Gra'dahl, always clever and wise, whom have you chosen?'

'Your Highness,' said Olfar with a cough. 'We had many great candidates. None of them, however, had the speed and courage of Graggy.'

Graggy swooped down from his perch to stand beside Armay. He waved to the Court and smiled, before remembering himself and giving Cracone a quick bob of the head.

'Fine, fine,' said Cracone, eager to move on to his colour. 'We Re'dahl have chosen none other than my lad, strong and smart: Nap.'

Nap took his time to find the floor next to Graggy, managing to fly a few rings around the Court before plopping himself into place.

'And there you have it,' announced Cracone, 'our Contenders.'

Nap turned and gave Whitestaff a sneer. Bile rose in Whitestaff's throat as he realised Cracone had no intention of letting a gold dragon compete.

We'll see about that, he thought.

Chapter 27

'We Kai'dahl have also nominated a Contender,' declared Whitestaff to the gathering.

'WHAT?' Cracone yelled. 'Learn your place, boy. You may have won a little victory before, but you are wearing out my patience and the patience of my Court.'

The jovial atmosphere of the surrounding dragons suddenly became tense. Cracone's outrage was obvious as his body shook with anger. His fellow reds made hissing noises in Whitestaff's direction.

He went hot under their glares and wanted to press on with his argument, but his voice had left him temporarily.

His uncle, thankfully, came to his rescue.

'The boy has a point,' Olfar said. 'It is the right of the sole Kai'dahl Palal to enter the Championship. It has been since Frendrek's death. We declared it so the following year.'

'That was twenty years ago,' argued a Re'dahl on Cracone's right. 'We haven't had a gold since then.'

'The tournament only started after Frendrek's death,' said Cracone, 'so how could that be?'

The crowd was silent, waiting for Olfar's response.

The green dragon pulled his beard and said, 'After Frendrek died saving our race...' he cast his eyes around the room, hoping the sentiment would sway them, 'we decided the best way to engage with the Nazoor is by a peaceful tournament every ten years.'

'Get on with it!' called a Re'dahl.

'I believe we stated that *one dragon from each colour* could enter. Seeing as though there is only ever *one* gold, he is automatically eligible to nominate.'

The Court again became rowdy, singing and laughing at Olfar's logic.

Cracone remained deadly silent. He knew if he called a vote he would be beaten again, but he hated the idea of a *Kai'dahl* just walking in to *his* Court and running the place. The Re'dahl Council would think him weak if he allowed it to happen.

What to do? he wondered.

Suddenly he noticed the dragons had all gone quiet. They were waiting for his response.

'You can participate,' he said icily, 'but hear this: being gold in colour does not grant you automatic honour. Your father died fighting the Nazoor, yes, but he also touched the ground before he died.'

The Court shrieked as though Cracone had said something horribly rude. Nap sniggered with the rest of the Re'dahl.

'Court dismissed!' announced Cracone over the noise and babble. With that, he withdrew through a door behind him, followed by his smirking Council.

Whitestaff didn't understand why everyone was so upset, but guessed it had something to do with the King's remark about *touching the ground*.

He shrugged to himself. *What do I care? At least I can become Dragon Champion and show Nap and Luzahmin a thing or two.*

The dragons began to fly out of the Court, chattering to each other in disbelieving tones. A few of them gave him sympathetic looks as they passed. Whitestaff just nodded at them dumbly.

Graggy bounded over and smiled. 'Great work there, buddy. Announcing you'd chosen yourself. Well done. I'd never have thought of that. You must be as crazy as me.'

Whitestaff raised his front paws. 'Maybe I'm not that bad.'

The two laughed then Whitestaff grew serious.

'It means I have to compete against you in… whatever it is we have to do.'

Graggy slapped his forehead. 'You mean you have no idea what the competition is, and you nominated yourself anyway? How mad are you?'

Whitestaff thought for a bit. 'I guess I just did it to spite Nap. Pretty stupid really.'

'No, not stupid at all. That's the same reason I entered.'

The two dragons laughed and threw a leg around each other's shoulders.

'Come back to my dugout,' Graggy said. 'I'll explain the competition there.'

'Yes,' said Whitestaff. 'And maybe you can also explain why everybody is looking at me as though I've just been spat on by the King.'

Chapter 28

Mollie and Esmae were in the middle of a bizarre forest. The trees that surrounded them were thick and slimy, with branches that looked like tentacles of oil and mud. There was no sun overhead, but the forest housed a dreary light which ebbed and flowed like water.

A foul-smelling fungus covered the ground and tickled Mollie's ankles.

'I don't like this either,' Esmae said. 'It's horrible.'

'It's so hard to breathe in here. And it's so hot. What is this place?'

Esmae looked around and screwed up her face. Wet slurping noises could be heard nearby. 'We are inside a very sick mind, Mollie. This is how Wendy sees the world: distorted and ugly.'

Something slithered past Mollie's ankle. She yelped and jumped sideways.

'It is also a useful defence,' Esmae said, peering at the ground. 'Wendy knows we are here, and she may not like it.'

'What do we do?'

'We learn some magic. Firstly, do you remember how to make a fireball?'

'Yes.'

'Good. Make one and aim it at that thing.'

Mollie's eyes snapped to where her mother was pointing. She saw a thick tree with what looked like black snakes growing out of it.

'Are you sure?'

'Yes, go on. Don't be afraid.'

'How can I use magic in a horse's head?'

'The elements are everywhere, dear, inside us and out. We are *made* of the elements, trust me.'

Mollie did her mother's bidding and concentrated on the environment around her. Sure enough, she could feel the elements at hand, waiting to be touched. She gathered the heat from the ground and the friction from the air, squashing what she could into a luminous sphere in front of her.

This time, something touched the back of her leg— something cold and sticky.

She kicked at it in panic. The thing quickly slinked away and Mollie's fireball had vanished.

'Try again,' said Esmae sternly. 'Keep focused no matter what.'

Mollie repeated the process, making a larger ball this time. The heat of it breathed on her face. When she could hold it no longer, Mollie projected the ball at the target. With a whooshing sound, it speared towards the tree. It was quickly joined by another ball Esmae had conjured. Hurtling with precision, the two orbs of fire struck the tree together, splattering a rank liquid in all directions.

At once, the forest became wild. Trees squirmed frantically and tentacles came from the ground. The air vibrated in anger. A low moan came from everywhere, hurting Mollie's head and filling her with dread. She looked to her mother for reassurance, but couldn't see her.

'Esmae!' she called. 'Esmae? Mother?'

'I'm right here, Mollie, look,' Esmae said, appearing next to her. 'Hide yourself with the air, quickly, like this.' Esmae showed her daughter the invisibility spell. 'You have to use parts of the air to bend the light around you.'

Mollie quickly saw the trick to the spell and repeated it on herself.

'Can you see me?' she asked the empty air.

'No,' came her mother's reply. 'You did it perfectly.'

Mollie lowered her voice to a whisper. 'Why are we invisible?'

'Just stay calm, and no matter what you see, don't move. This could get dangerous.'

Mollie paid heed and stood still, trusting her mother's guidance. Her unquestioning obedience saved her life, for a fraction of a second later, something hideous broke through the forest.

It was a nightmare on legs: taller than any man Mollie had ever seen, with three eyes, and completely black. The creature walked on two legs and had arms that nearly touched the ground. Its massive mouth dripped black saliva, and it stank like a long-dead animal.

Mollie fought the urge to whimper and run. She knew if she made a sound the giant would have her. Instead she froze and dared not breathe.

The putrid thing lumbered towards her, looking for the culprit who disturbed the forest.

It stopped a pace from Mollie. Each of its three eyes flickered this way and that, searching but not finding.

It took a step sideways. This time it lowered its head; its blood-shot eyes continued to hunt.

It stayed that way for a very tense while.

Mollie couldn't stand it anymore; she slowly turned her head to the side. The creature looked directly at her and she fought down a scream. Thankfully, it looked away and took another step.

Mollie didn't know where her mother was. The monster could be standing right on top of her for all she knew.

It took another step away and Mollie began to breathe again, slowly and deeply. The monster ambled further still.

It's going, it's going, thought Mollie with joy.

But when she was just about to relax, the monster turned around and began to test the air with its nose. It bent right down low, almost to the ground, its nose twitching with each snotty sniff.

The monster's eyes brightened as it caught a scent. It took two quick steps back toward Mollie then stopped short.

Without warning, its long arms groped for the air a few yards away from Mollie.

Esmae suddenly became visible in the monster's grip, kicking and yelling. Mollie could see she was trying to cast a spell, but the giant was too quick. It caught her around the waist and held her up in the air over its gaping jaws.

'Run, Mollie!' Esmae screamed as she tried to summon a spell.

Mollie dropped the threads of air that cloaked her, and summoned water and fire just as she'd seen Esmae do earlier. She didn't have much time to gather energy, so she threw what she had: a smallish Magic Missile.

It raced forward as Esmae was about to be eaten alive. There came a splintery sound as the missile shattered the giant's knee.

Howling in pain, the monster let go of its prey and clutched its crushed leg. Thinking quickly, Esmae wove a levitation spell to cushion her fall. Before Mollie could gather to throw another damaging spell, Esmae had summoned a massive fireball. She hurtled it at the thing's head, engulfing it in flames and sparks.

The howl ended abruptly, and the creature shrank and vanished, leaving behind a steaming pile of muck.

Mollie ran to her mother and threw her thin arms around Esmae's neck.

'I'm fine, Mollie. I'm not hurt.'

Esmae let her daughter hold her a while longer, then unclasped the girl's arms and brought her face up to meet her own.

'You did very well, Mollie. That Magic Missile probably saved my life. I'm very impressed.'

'What was that thing?' asked Mollie, her voice quavering.

'Hmmm,' said Esmae. 'I think it was Denial. This whole forest is Wendy's view of the world around her. The monster was the thing that stopped all rational thoughts creeping into Wendy's conscious mind.'

Mollie looked confused.

'Let me put it this way,' her mother tried. 'Every time your friend had a glimpse of the normal world, the world you and I see, that monster attacked it and drove it out.'

'Like it tried to get us?' Mollie said.

'Yes, exactly. It was trying to deny us entry into Wendy's troubled mind.'

'I get it. That monster attacks the truth! Every time I mentioned being a horse, Wendy went mad. That was Denial at work.'

Esmae brushed some black muck off her dress. 'Yes. And now we've destroyed it, our journey should be a lot smoother. Come on.'

Chapter 29

Mollie took her mother's hand, and the two walked further into the forest.

The light around them had grown brighter and the trees looked less troubled. The tentacles growing eerily from the ground swayed groggily and shrank away as the Adkins women walked passed, and the fungus at their feet dissolved underfoot like spun sugar does when it gets wet. Mollie's breathing came easier as the air lightened around them.

The place was getting less scary the longer they travelled, and soon Mollie began to feel more at ease.

'How much longer, Esmae?' Mollie asked as her legs began to stiffen.

'Nearly there. See how the forest fades?'

Mollie looked around her and saw her mother was right; the forest was thinning out. She could see a clearing through the trees ahead, so she jogged a few paces to see what was on the other side. Mollie burst through the low branches expecting to see a large meadow.

What she saw was a large black wall.

It looked like a shadow that stretched so high and so wide it appeared to go on forever. Mollie waited for Esmae to catch up.

'What is it?'

Esmae huffed and looked up. 'This is our destination. This is Wendy's unconscious mind. Beyond here, I don't know what we will find. Take my hand again.'

Mollie did so and squeezed tight, wishing silently that there were no three-eyed giants on the other side.

With a breath, the two women stepped through the shadow and deeper in to Wendy's uneasy mind.

They walked and walked in the darkness. There was no ground below and no sky above; no light either. Mollie opened her eyes as wide as they would go, but still she could not see. It was as though she was deep underground, or worse, in an endless space.

They walked on. Mollie realised there was no air brushing her skin as she moved, no air currents or resistance. She was about to ask her mother why when she saw a light in the distance, a small round glow surrounded by the black void. Her mother saw it too, for Mollie felt their pace quicken.

'That's the problem there,' Esmae said.

'I see it.' Mollie tried to make her voice sound strong and confident like her mother's.

The light grew larger as they approached, and soon Mollie could see the outline of a unicorn, leaping and bucking in the middle of the shine.

The two made their way to the edge of the light and peered in.

Wendy was going mad inside, thrashing about wildly. She was pink and the cone was stuck back on her head. She looked as she did the first time Mollie had seen her in Gibbon.

It soon became obvious that the cause of Wendy's distress was the tinkling, shimmering lights that surrounded her. The lights were like little fairies—they'd flutter about Wendy's body, then dart in at her trying to rip off her horn or peel the pink paint from her flanks.

'It's the butterflies,' Mollie whispered. 'That's what she is so scared of.'

'What?' Esmae asked.

'The butterflies,' Mollie repeated. 'Wendy said butterflies came to steal her beauty. This must be what she meant.'

Her mother nodded in the gloom. 'They aren't butterflies though, my child. They are reality. See how they try to take off the horn and paint? It's just the truth—the real world—trying to sink in. She won't let it though.'

No, she won't,' Mollie said. 'She kicks them away every time. What do we do?'

The older woman assessed the situation and said, 'We have to subdue her, let the lights do their work.'

'What do you mean?'

'We could use gravity to hold her still. That way, she can't fight back.'

'No!' Mollie said aghast. 'Let me try something else first.'

Before Esmae could stop her, Mollie ran to Wendy's side. The dancing lights stopped their attacks and hovered in the air, unsure of what to do.

'Mollie,' said the horse nervously, 'is that you?'

Wendy didn't take her eyes off the lights above her. Her large lips were covered in white froth.

'Yes, it's me, I'm here to help.'

'Good,' Wendy squealed. 'Get them to leave me alone. They want to take my beauty.'

'No, no, that's where you're wrong. They want to make you more beautiful.'

'You lie. You're trying to trick me, I know it.'

Wendy blew white flakes from her nostrils and shook her head.

'Why would I lie?' Mollie asked. 'I want to help. Remember how I helped Whitestaff?'

'That silly dragon? Yes, I remember. I suppose you did help *him*.'

'Now I'm here to help you,' Mollie said gently.

Wendy's body sagged, but she didn't take her eye off the butterflies.

Mollie kept talking, sensing her words were having an effect.

'Aren't you tired of fighting it, Wendy? Don't you just want to rest?'

Wendy shook her weary head, still looking up.

'Well, now it's time, Wendy. It's time to become something else.'

Wendy became agitated again. 'A horse? I'll never be an ugly, plain horse.'

Mollie tried to calm her friend back down by stroking her mane.

'No, Wendy, not a plain and ugly horse. A beautiful, wonderful, noble horse. A horse who isn't lonely anymore. A horse who isn't afraid or tired or scared. That's what you'll turn into Wendy. And I'll be here when it's all over, still your friend.'

Wendy hesitated. Tears started to form in her big, scared eyes.

'I am exhausted, Mollie. I am…' She put her head on Mollie's shoulder.

'It will be all right, Wendy. You'll see.'

Wendy nodded and sniffed. 'If you promise me it'll be fine, if you stay with me, I won't fight.'

Mollie agreed she would stay. Then, holding Wendy's big head in her arms, Mollie beckoned the lights of reality closer.

They descended like a school of hungry fish, stripping the pink layers of paint off Wendy's coat. The horn was eaten up like a meal. The shimmering flyers hung around the two like a fog. Wendy cried harder in Mollie's embrace, jerking her whole body with each sob.

One such jerk caused the top of Wendy's thick skull to hit the bottom of Mollie's chin. Mollie saw a flash of white as her head was thrown back. Her jaw was slammed shut by the force, causing her teeth to bite down on her own tongue. Her mouth filled with the tinny taste of blood.

But still she cradled Wendy's head.

Then suddenly, it was over. The butterflies were gone; reality had seeped in, and Wendy was a horse.

Mollie gently let go and stood back.

'Wow,' she said, ignoring her own pain. 'You look wonderful.'

'Do I?' Wendy snivelled.

'Yes, you do. I don't know why you were hiding such a magnificent mare under the pink coat.'

'You mean it?'

'Of course. You will make many a head turn.'

Mollie wasn't exaggerating either, for Wendy did look truly splendid. Her coat was the colour of honey and her mane chocolate. She had one round, brown spot on either cheek, making her exquisite in appearance.

'I do feel better. Lighter, in some way,' Wendy said dreamily. 'Oh, look. That's pretty.'

Mollie looked around to see the darkness fading. She could see her mother walking over to them. Esmae joined the two as a marvellous forest of green sprouted up around them. Flowers quickly came into bloom and grass grew underfoot. Birds came twittering past as trees yawned up to the sky and stretched their branches.

The three watched in wonder as the forest was reborn.

'You should go now,' Wendy said after a while. 'I'll see you on the outside.' Mollie nodded as the horse galloped off into the peaceful wilderness.

Esmae looked down at her daughter and took her hand.

Mollie thought she could see tears in her mother's eyes, but couldn't be sure because her own vision was blurred by salty drops.

'Concentrate on your own body now, Mollie. We have to go back.'

Mollie did as she was told. She closed her eyes tight and held her mother's hand. Once more her whole body shook and trembled as she was whisked away.

At first there was only blackness and Mollie panicked, thinking her mind had got lost somehow—then a comfortable feeling spread through her. The kind of warm feeling one gets when one arrives home after a long journey. Mollie was glad to be back in her own skin.

She opened her eyes to see Bramble, Terry and Wendy standing in front of her.

'Will she be okay, Mum?' Mollie asked as she looked up at her mother.

The older Adkins was coming around, still blinking her eyes dizzily. 'Ask her, child,' she muttered.

'I'm fine, Mollie, thanks to you. You are a wonderful witch.'

'Sorceress,' Mollie corrected. 'But thanks.'

Bramble hummed and snorted. 'I want to thank you too, Mollie. I don't know what you did, but without your intervention, well...' He trailed off, shook his head, and began again. 'I was wrong about you. I see now you are a remarkable young woman. Would you still like to be friends?'

Mollie nodded and gave Bramble a pat on the head.

The two horses snuggled each other, cheek to cheek. Mollie walked over to her mother, hugged her hard and said thank you about a hundred times in her ear.

Terry blinked and rubbed his nose, looking from the horses to the Adkins women in utter confusion.

Chapter 30

Graggy's dugout was almost identical to Olfar's: spacious and homely, with many neatly-placed books. Everything was well ordered and organised, the artwork chosen with care and attention given to colour-matching and furniture placement.

The dugout was balanced and well kept, which was at odds with Graggy's loopy, carefree disposition. Whitestaff noticed this and told him as much.

'Well, green in colour, Gra'dahl in conduct, I suppose,' was Graggy's only explanation. 'Would you like a drink?'

The dragon didn't wait for an answer. He took two silver mugs from a shelf and proceeded to pour a slick, purple liquid into them.

'Smells funny,' said Whitestaff placing his muzzle to the brim.

'It *is* funny,' came the reply. 'Drink too much and you'll think the whole world is funny. Even Nap would look good after three of these. Ha!' Graggy downed the brew in one gulp.

Whitestaff did the same.

At first the drink was pleasant and sweet; however, as it sloshed down his throat, it began to burn like a torch.

'Ehem,' Whitestaff said, sucking in cool air and wincing. 'What *is* that?'

Graggy laughed at his friends screwed up face. 'Balebeer,' he said. 'Alcohol made from fermented balefruit. Want some more?'

Whitestaff grinned and proffered his mug for more.

'We should go easy on this stuff though, it can make you say the foulest things to the nicest people, or worse, pleasant things to tookers like Nap.'

Whitestaff nearly spilled his drink.

'I didn't realise you used that word here too.'

'Tooker? Yes, but it really isn't a nice word to say too often.'

'Too late. No wonder Nap wanted to fight me. Ohhh, and I said it in front of Olfar as well.'

'Ha. I'm sure he's heard worse in his time.'

The golden dragon swilled his balebeer, trying to finish before Graggy. He did empty his silver mug first, and immediately wished he hadn't. A powerful blast erupted in his skull, giving him an instant headache. He found his vision a little blurred and his stance became wobbly.

'Sheesh,' he said to no one in particular.

'Knocks your head off the first few times,' Graggy said casually, 'but you get used to it.'

He pointed to a big cushion on the floor. 'Maybe we should sit.'

Whitestaff clumsily collapsed on the cushion, glad to be off his unsteady feet.

'How many fingers am I holding up?' Graggy asked with a serious voice.

Whitestaff struggled to focus on the green dragon's paw.

'Four,' he answered hopefully.

'No,' replied Graggy.

'No?'

'No. I'm not holding up any fingers. Dragons don't have fingers. We have claws.'

Whitestaff snuffled, then burst with laughter at his friend's joke. His chortles came humming through his snout and out his nostrils. But his nostrils weren't big enough for the laughter to escape from, so his mouth opened wide and chuckled hard.

Graggy joined in, glad that someone found him funny.

Unfortunately, Graggy owned a snorting laugh that sounded like a cat choking on fur. When Whitestaff heard it, his peals of laughter doubled, making it so difficult for him to breathe that he was in fear of passing out through lack of air.

Eventually though, the two calmed down and were able to talk once more.

'So,' said Graggy, looking his friend in the eye. 'Now I have you sufficiently drunk and cheery, I can tell you how Cracone the Re'dahl made you the object of pity in his Court.'

Chapter 31

Whitestaff sobered at this sudden change of mood and shook his head in attempt to clear his mind.

At that moment, the pretty dragon who had been chosen as Contender for the Bo'dahl entered.

'Armay,' Graggy said in surprise. 'Come in and sit down.'

Armay slinked over to the two sprawled-out dragons and took a seat next to Whitestaff—very close to Whitestaff. Their tails touched.

'Hiya,' she said, giving the blushing golden dragon a wink.

'I was just about to tell our resident Kai'dahl about the meaning of our King's remark earlier,' said Graggy with a grin.

Armay wheezed through her dainty snout. 'A very mean thing to say. Very low.'

'I don't get it,' Whitestaff said loudly. 'What did he say that was so bad? I thought the whole thing went rather well.'

'Yes, well, it did kind of,' Graggy admitted, 'but it was the touching the ground comment that was... unfair.' Graggy glanced at Armay and continued. 'Maybe I should start from the beginning.'

'Yes, please.'

'Well, we Palal have a thing about the ground. We think it's unclean.'

'Actually,' Armay interrupted, 'we think we are too special to dwell on the ground like most creatures, hence the dugouts.' She opened her arms to indicate the space around her.

'Our kind loses much honour touching the ground, it's almost taboo.' Graggy checked his friend to see if it was making any sense. 'There are going to be some tremendous gaps in your knowledge, isn't there?'

'I don't see what that has to do with my father,' Whitestaff said, scratching his head.

'Well,' Armay said, shuffling closer to Whitestaff, 'your father battled fiercely on the final day of the War with the Nazoor.'

'Without him we could've been exterminated,' Graggy chimed.

Armay nodded vigorously in agreement. 'But, you see, when he took on the Nazoor Queen, well… they both went down.'

'You have to understand,' Graggy pleaded, 'there were Nazoor everywhere. They filled our sky like dark clouds. They are little, but huge in numbers. They just about suffocated us. Until Frendrek joined the fight. So the story goes.'

'They say he was like you, but not as big,' Armay said, shuffling closer. Whitestaff could now feel her scales were pressing against his.

'Yeah,' Graggy went on. 'He singled out their queen—Mezelga was her name—then went for her. About ten Nazoor protected her, but your father fought through them. Finally, he caught her around the neck, clamping down with his jaws,' Graggy mimicked the action, biting down hard.

'Then he dragged her down,' Armay said, her eyes aglow. 'They fought all the way. Mezelga's guards clawed at Frendrek, but he held tight.'

Graggy took a deep breath. 'Then they hit the ground. All of them. They didn't get back up.'

Whitestaff was silent for a while then said, 'I must be missing something. My father dies saving the Palal, and somehow this is dishonourable?'

'It's silly, I know,' said Armay. She patted him gently with her tail.

'It was poor form for Cracone to bring it up like that. But some dragons think he dishonoured us by, you know, *touching*.'

'It's the most ridiculous thing I've ever heard, right enough.' Whitestaff bellowed as he stood. Maybe it was the balebeer giving his voice extra boom, but the dugout echoed with his roaring. 'A dragon fights to save his race then is held in contempt for touching the ground? Stupid, stupid. I was born on the ground, what do you think of that?'

Both Graggy and Armay recoiled at Whitestaff's words. Armay shuffled away from him. This made Whitestaff even angrier. 'Go on move away so you don't touch the *unclean* one.'

Armay raised her head to look at him, but then stopped short.

'I was good enough for you before, Armay,' Whitestaff rumbled. 'But now you know I'm a ground-toucher, you've changed your mind?'

'It's not that,' Armay said in a whisper, still refusing to meet his eye. She turned around to leave but Whitestaff jumped over her, blocking her exit.

'Touch me then,' he demanded, sticking out his tail.

Armay stared at the tail that was being offered. She looked at it, then to Graggy.

'I'm sorry, I can't.'

At those words Whitestaff's anger seeped out of him. It was replaced with disgust—for Armay—and himself.

Twice today you've let your temper loose,' he thought. *'You weren't like this on Earth.'*

He shook this truth from his head and stepped aside for Armay to pass. She left quietly, with Whitestaff looking after her.

'I shouldn't have done that,' he said to the empty air.

'No, probably not,' said Graggy from behind.

Whitestaff spun around to look at his friend. 'You were right about the balebeer. I just said something horrible to someone nice.'

Graggy considered Whitestaff's words. 'Maybe she deserved it,' he said. 'The whole *touching the ground* thing makes no logical sense.' Graggy put out his tail and rubbed the top of Whitestaff head with it. 'Maybe they all need to hear how absurd it all is.'

Whitestaff slumped. 'Not like that, though. Not in that way.'

The two stood at the mouth of the dugout and watched the Sorteyan sun bow slowly over the spires into darkness. A cool breeze tussled through, making a low, mournful groan through the room around them. It sounded exactly how Whitestaff felt.

It had been another long, emotionally-charged day. A day that made him feel as if he'd never slept a wink in his life and the aches of his past would never leave his bones. Luckily for him, he was protected from the awful truth: tomorrow would be even worse.

Chapter 32

Although Terry Gritbole didn't know exactly what the Adkinses had done, he knew it had worked wonders. The mare was no longer thrashing about like a fish on a hook.

Instead, it was sweetly nuzzling Bramble while Mollie patted its cheeks. That in itself was sort of odd; weirder still was the outward transformation of the horse from wild pink—to honey! He could not fathom how a horse could be pink in the first place, let alone change colour before his eyes.

He forced himself to relax.

After all, he thought, *they helped the animal. They used those strange powers for a good cause because they have good hearts. Kinder hearts than anyone else I've met.*

Without warning, Esmae took his hand in hers and led him back to the cottage. Her face was red and so was Mollie's. It looked as though the two had just been jogging for the past hour.

They all sat at the table inside and sipped water, the two women catching their breath.

Esmae explained to Mr Gritbole the background of Wendy and her life as a unicorn in Cudgel's show. She went on to describe how Mollie saved her, as well as a sickly dragon—the last of his kind on Earth.

Terry listened in amazement, not doubting a single word they told him. At the end of the story, he found himself very impressed with the Adkins girl.

'Yer are brave beyond compare,' he said, smoothing the back of his hand against her cheek. 'Yer father, wherever he may be, would be proud of such a fine young woman.'

Mollie blushed at his comment and smiled at her mum, who nodded in agreement.

After another hour of pleasant conversation, Terry excused himself. 'I have ter hunt some game,' he said with an air of importance. 'Nobles gotta eat too, yer know.'

'Would you like to hunt on our land?' Esmae asked coyly.

Terry's eyebrows shot up in surprise.

'Why I was going to ask yer if I could. Latos! You're not a mind reader too, are yer?'

Terry looked so alarmed at the thought that Esmae let out a burst of laughter.

'No, Terry, I can't read minds. You just have a bow and quiver slung on your back, that's all. I don't need to guess too hard at what they are for,' she pointed at his trade tools, 'or why you brought them.'

'Of course,' he said, giving a forced chuckle. 'I knew that.'

He gave each Adkins an awkward embrace then left the cottage to earn his wage.

Esmae looked at Terry's retreating back through the window. She gave a sigh.

Mollie noticed her mother had a sparkling, dreamy look in her eyes.

'What are you thinking, Esmae?' Mollie asked.

'Many things, my dear.'

'Such as?'

Esmae turned her face towards her daughter. 'Firstly, I'm thinking that twice you have risked yourself for a friend and succeeded in saving them. You even managed to save me.'

Mollie gave her mother a hug.

'Look at you,' Esmae said as she held her daughter at arm's length. 'You've grown so much. You've shot up over these last couple of months.'

'I feel older,' Mollie said simply. Her face took on a more solemn expression and she said, 'What else were you thinking? About Terry?'

'Yes. I was thinking about him.'

Mollie remained silent, waiting for more information.

'I was thinking that despite his rough language and poor grammar, he is a man very much like Merlin.'

'Really?' asked Mollie, wide eyed.

'Yes, really. They share the same natural respect for the things around them—especially women.' Now it was Esmae's turn to become serious. 'When you start looking for a husband, try to find that quality in them. You'll live happily in that marriage if you do. A man can be tough and strong and at the same time tread gently for women. Find one like that and you'll never regret it.'

'Esmae!'

She put a hand on Mollie's shoulder. 'I know. Some conversations are awkward. But you are growing up and we have to have them. Actually, I've probably held it off for too long.'

'Are you going to marry him?' Mollie asked softly.

'That is a long way off yet. Let's just see how it all turns out, yes?'

'All right.'

'But how would you feel about it, Terry and me, if it does work out?'

Mollie thought for a while.

'Once upon a time I would have hated the idea. But now, I think it would be nice for you to have some company when I'm gone.'

'What do you mean, *gone?*'

Mollie shrugged. 'I have a feeling that I'm not going to be here for much longer. Like you said, I am getting older. It's nearly time for me to start doing things for myself, finding my own way. Find employment; earn a living, that sort of thing.'

'Ohh,' Esmae sighed. 'Where do the years go?'

She held her daughter's face in her hands.

'Esmae, look at me. If we're being honest, it's probably past time I found work for myself. If half of Danmurk Shire weren't too petrified to speak to me, I would have had a job long before now.'

Esmae dropped her hands away. 'You're right. But I don't feel like I've finished with you yet. Tell you what, let me teach you all the magic I know. When I'm finished, then you are free to do as you please. How does that sound?'

'That sounds perfect, because there is something I need to do with that magic. Something I left unfinished.'

'What?'

'I want to get Whitestaff's egg back off of Cudgel.'

Esmae frowned deeply and bit her lip.

'Why?' she asked.

'Well, the egg was some sort of doorway to another world.'

'Ah ha.'

'So, if Whitestaff had to ever come back, Cudgel would just put him back in his cage and all my work will be for nothing.'

Esmae nodded to show she understood.

'Well,' continued Mollie, 'if I get the egg back and we keep it with me, I'll know Whitestaff will be fine if he ever *does* come back.'

Esmae was silent for a while. Mollie held her breath and waited for the answer. Finally Esmae said, 'I think that is an excellent idea.'

Mollie let her breath out.

'But why not let me come with you?'

'Because I want to do it by myself. It'd be too easy if you were there. Plus, we were just talking about me going off on my own soon.'

'But I have to train you properly first.'

'How long will that take?'

'About a year,' Esmae answered.

'But—'

'The older woman held out her hand. 'No arguments. One year, or I'll keep you here forever.'

Mollie agreed to the terms, secretly glad. She never thought her mother would agree at all.

'Can we start the year from today?'

Esmae rolled her eyes in mock exasperation.

'I suppose. In about a year the fair will return to Gibbon and you won't have to go far. I'll let you see the rest of the world after that. I promise.'

'Great,' Mollie said as she headed for the door.

'Where are you going?'

'I'm going to ask Wendy if she'll stay here with us. She can be our horse. Don't you think it's about time we got one?' She gave her mother a wink.

Esmae smiled as her daughter scooted out of the cottage.

I haven't had a day this good since Merlin was about, she thought to herself.

She took a deep, lingering breath through her nose, savouring the smell of a perfect day.

Chapter 33

Elsewhere, Whitestaff was midway through his detestable day. He'd woken earlier to find himself in Graggy's main room and it took him a few moments to recall where he was.

The balebeer had fogged his mind and he thought for sure he would open his eyes and see the familiar surrounds of Cudgel's jail. But of course, he was millions of miles away from that place, a fact which made him curiously glum.

He and Graggy ate some balefruit for breakfast and made some easy conversation (neither of them mentioning Armay or any other event from the previous night) and Graggy suggested a tour of Sorteya.

'I'll show you the sights of our fine city in the sky,' Graggy had said with mock theatrics.

Whitestaff agreed, hoping the rushing wind would clear out the fuzz between his ears left by the balebeer. He made a mental note to next time stop after one mug of the potent ale.

The first place they went to was the library, which didn't impress Whitestaff as he'd seen it before, and he told his long-legged companion as much. Not to be outdone, Graggy took his friend to an even more magnificent place: the hatchery.

It was a large cavern carved lower to the ground. Inside were hundreds of eggs, just like the one Mollie had tossed to him on Earth, only these eggs weren't hatched and didn't contain portals.

Surrounding these eggs were blue dragons. Some were gossiping others were sipping drinks round a large table. A cluster of blue dragons was clucking over hatchlings in the corner while sitting on their own eggs to keep them warm.

Whitestaff couldn't believe his eyes.

'Are you okay?' asked Graggy with concern. His friend had gone silent and looked almost petrified.

'They're white,' he whispered.

'Who are? The hatchlings? Of course they are; we're all born white. That's why we're called Lili'dahls when we eat our way out of the egg. *Lili* means small and *dahl* means *the colour of*. We don't colour for the first year. Didn't you know?'

Whitestaff couldn't answer; looking at the baby dragons was like looking into a mirror of his Earth-bound self. It was a shocking revelation. Susset had lied. He wasn't just weak on Earth, *he was a baby*! He nearly fainted at the realisation, indeed, he took a few backward steps, almost stepping on a fiesty little white creature.

'I was hoping you'd see all this.'

Whitestaff's head snapped up to the balcony above him where Susset stood. She was wearing a pink robe that complemented her rosy cheeks, and even in his state of distress, Whitestaff was struck by the woman's beauty. She levitated herself down to his level and patted his nose.

Whitestaff shrank away from her touch.

'I was a hatchling? A Lili'dahl?'

Susset nodded solemnly.

'Why didn't you say?'

'You fainted at the sight of your uncle. Plus, what I did tell you was true, about your essence existing in two worlds.'

'You left out something though, obviously. I've been living as a hatchling for over twenty years!'

Whitestaff heard his own voice rising. He struggled to remain calm. *Don't lose it again*, he urged himself. *Don't get angry before you know the facts*.

'Yes, I didn't tell you that on Earth your body hardly ages. Your physical spirit hibernates, which is why you are so strong here.'

'I don't understand.'

'Me neither,' said Graggy, who was trying hard to follow.

Susset grabbed her hood and pulled while giving Graggy an impatient glance.

'Remember I said I made the portal with another powerful sorcerer?'

'Yes, you said something like that.'

'Well,' said Susset in discomfort. 'That sorcerer has the ability to tamper with time itself. He said he needed to alter your body's sense of time so you could withstand the journey, being unhatched and all.'

Whitestaff shook his head. 'I still don't get it.'

'Me neither,' Graggy agreed.

'It is hard to explain,' Susset went on. 'Only Merlin really knows why we made the portal that way; *he* is the genius. I think that's why you have to go back to Earth one day. Here you age very fast; your body is super-powerful so you eat up much of your dragon essence. When you go back to Earth your body recharges the energy again, making it possible for you to return.'

'You tricked his dragon essence's sense of time? I think I'm starting to get it,' Graggy said with wonder.

'I'm not,' said Whitestaff. 'Where is this *Merlin* anyway? Maybe he can make sense of this.'

'He's not here,' said Susset. 'So you'll have to make do with my explanation.'

'Where is he then?' asked Whitestaff.

'He's not in this *time*, Whitestaff, and probably never will be.'

'You see,' said Graggy, catching his friend's weary look, 'Merlin the Magician can travel through time.'

'Yes,' said Susset. 'He brought me here to live when I was younger. He only showed up again as the Nazoor attacked and helped me make the portal in your egg.' Susset made a grim face as she remembered that day. 'No one really understands him or what he does, but we trust him, Whitestaff. *I* trust him. So even if you don't understand the unique predicament you're in, you will one day, and you'll probably thank Merlin that he put you in it.'

Susset's voice became angrier as she delivered her speech, so much so that Whitestaff almost stopped her in order to calm her down. When she did finish, she threw off her hood and flew away without as much as a goodbye.

'I have offended her again,' said Whitestaff gloomily as he watched her float off into the sky.

'Don't worry about her,' Graggy began.

'I know, I know,' said Whitestaff, cutting him off. 'She blows hot and cold quicker than Latos in a snow storm.'

Graggy continued playing the tour guide, showing Whitestaff the many levels of the hatchery and pausing to watch some Lili'dahls play. Whitestaff followed him, not really seeing anything.

'Do you see that curtain over there, Whitestaff? Behind that curtain is a very special portal. A one way trip. It's where we put our Alpos. We get one every generation, see. Be glad you're gold and not silver. Ha. We don't tend to talk about it though. Touchy subject.'

I was a baby, he kept thinking. *They mucked up my whole body, why? Why did they do that to me? Was it really so important to send me away? Who is this 'Merlin' anyway?* These questions kept forming in his mind and going unanswered, until at last Graggy's voice broke in.

'Look, buddy, I can see this has shaken you up a bit. I don't really know what you and Susset were talking about, but I can see you need some time to think.'

Whitestaff hummed in agreement, giving his friend an apologetic look. He'd only just realised that he hadn't shared his past on Earth with Graggy. Anyone else probably would have prodded for more information—especially a green dragon—but not Graggy.

He just accepted me for who I am, Whitestaff thought. *He didn't even worry about me or my father touching the ground.*

'Thanks,' said Whitestaff. 'I genuinely appreciate it. I'll finish looking around by myself and I'll find you when I'm in a better mood.'

Graggy clapped the large gold dragon on the back and flew away, leaving Whitestaff surrounded by pale yapping hatchlings. He gently lifted one off his foot, placed in with another on a soft mat then took to the skies, all the while wondering why fate had been so cruel to him.

Chapter 34

After flying around aimlessly for a while and thinking, Whitestaff decided to find Susset. So far as he could gather, Frendrek feared the Palal would be wiped out by the Nazoor, so he wanted to send his unborn egg back to Earth for safety.

Susset and this Merlin character hid a portal in his egg and sent it through itself, a task that required Merlin to meddle with time. This resulted in Whitestaff being weak of body on Earth and possessing tremendous strength on Sorteya.

Does that sound right? He was sure there was more to this story; certain Susset was keeping something back.

Maybe I should let her cool down a bit before asking any more questions.

He hovered in the air, uncertain whether to continue his search for the sorceress or to just go home and reflect on his life. *Maybe the answer is obvious and I just need some time to think about it.*

In the end he decided to go home. He flew languidly around, already familiar with the layout of his new environment. He flapped by the library, rounded a crooked spire, then flew left and down till he arrived at his uncle's.

He swooped, tucking his wings in a little to avoid scraping them on the walls, and landed lightly.

As he made his way through the greeting room, voices carried to him from the main room beyond.

He paused at the entrance to see whom his uncle was speaking to.

It'd better not be Luz.

And it was not Luzahmin he saw, but a very strange dragon. Actually, it looked like a lizard with wings. It was reclining on a cushion, casually conversing with Olfar. It was black all over, save for grey dots that freckled its skin.

Skin! No scales.

Olfar suddenly looked up and saw his nephew staring, mouth open in wonder.

'Come in,' Olfar said with a chuckle. 'Meet Cross. Cross, this is Frendrek's son, Whitestaff.

The lizard thing stood and, with horror, Whitestaff noticed he only had *one* pair of legs at the front—no back legs like the Palal.

Cross held out his tail, ready to shake. 'Pleasure to meet you,' the strange dragon said. His voice sounded hissing and slow.

Whitestaff shook back, trying not to let his discomfort show.

'First time you've met a Nazoor?' Cross asked.

'Nazoor?' Whitestaff shouted, throwing down Cross's tail. 'Uncle, what is this?'

Olfar jumped up looking worried. 'Please don't offend our guest,' he said. Then turning to Cross added, 'Forgive him, Cross. He is new to this planet. There is much he does not understand.'

Cross nodded and looked back to Whitestaff.

Whitestaff's joints went weak under the Nazoor's gaze. It was terrible. For one thing, Cross didn't have coloured eyes, just black pools that didn't reflect the merest speck of light. More worrying was his face. Cross didn't have a snout like Palal dragons, instead he had a wide, powerful beak. A black, forked-tongue squirmed inside it.

Whitestaff gave an inward shudder.

'So thisss is the Kai'dahl Contender?' Cross asked with a flick of his head.

'Uncle, I don't understand,' Whitestaff blurted before Olfar could answer. 'Why is he here if he's a Nazoor?'

Cross looked down at the dugout floor.

'Whitestaff,' said Olfar haughtily. 'He is here as my guest. Cross is one of our best allies with the Nazoor race. It was he who forewarned us of many Nazoor tactics during the Dragon War. It was he who alerted us to the very first battle. Without him, we would be many Palal fewer.'

'You do me honour with your wordsss,' Cross hissed, bowing at Olfar.

'The truth is just that,' Olfar said. Then to his nephew added, 'There are many things thou does not understand, Whitestaff. In fact, before thou interrupted us, Cross was telling me the Nazoor have already chosen their Champion, isn't that right, Cross?'

The black dragon nodded. 'Yess. Audgar is hisss name. He is our Alpossss. Though I know the Palal would prefer not to know about that ssssort of thing. Very tough, very strong.'

'Alpos?' said Whitestaff. 'Graggy mentioned that word at the hatchery. What does it mean?'

Olfar looked down at his paws and mumbled something.

'Perhapssss I should explain?'

The green dragon nodded, still refusing to meet Whitestaff's eye.

'Whitessstaff, a long time before the Exodus of Earth, the Nazoor and the Palal decided to create ssstonger ties with each other. One of the wayssss was through marriage.'

'You don't mean—'

'Yesss, one of your kingssss married our queen. It didn't last, unfortunately. And the process managed to contaminate the bloodlines of our racessss. When Palal and Nazoor have offspring, the resultsss are, shall we sssay, unfavourable.'

'So what is an Alpos?' Whitestaff asked, already fearing the answer.

'An Alpossss is born every generation or sssooo. It'sss the result of our bloodlines crossing. For the Nazoor, our Alpos are bigger and stronger than the rest of us. Not sssso smart though. Never even learn to sssspeak. Audgar is like that.'

'And for the Palal, Uncle?'

But Olfar didn't answer.

'Hold on! At the hatchery. Graggy said something about a one-way portal. We don't just get rid of them, do we, Uncle?'

Olfar finally lifted his head.

'It's not like that, Whitestaff. The Palal Alpos are mad. They only live to destroy. We tried to find a way for them to live with us, but the results were catastrophic. One Palal Alpos killed thirty-four dragons once. Since then, we use the portal.'

'But where do they end up? Where do these other dragons go?'

This time, Cross answered.

'The portal of which you ssspeak is a magical device that sendssss the Alpos egg to other places. Random placesss. We don't know where or even if they ssssurvive.'

Whitestaff was about to shout, but Olfar silenced him with his paw.

'Nephew, another time I will tell thee all about it. Maybe put thy mind at rest. But for now, Cross is telling us that Audgar is an Alpos, and that means they have a chance at beating our Champion next year.'

'And we can't have that,' Cross insisted.

'Why would you want us to win?' Whitestaff asked. 'Don't the Nazoor want to rule Sorteya?'

'Not all Nazoor are the same, Nephew. Cross here leads a small group of Nazoor who want to live in peace. They like this planet and want to live without wars, without bloodshed.'

Cross lifted his head. 'It'sss true. Not all Nazoor are the same.'

'It's the same with us, Whitestaff. Not all Re'dahl are the same, nor greens, nor blue.'

Whitestaff could see the logic in this; there was a great deal of difference between Graggy and Olfar, and they were both Gra'dahl.

'I'm sorry,' he said. 'I make a terrible first impression. Ask my cousin.'

Olfar laughed heartily, as did Cross, who didn't get the joke but joined in out of politeness, and the tension in the room eased a fraction.

'Mezelga won't be pleased to know about a new Kai'dahl dragon in your ranksss though, Olfar.'

The green nodded stiffly, his grin quickly falling.

'I suppose thou has to tell her?'

'It'sss my duty to tell her.'

'Wait,' Whitestaff broke in, 'Mezelga?'

'All our queensss are named Mezelga,' Cross said, guessing the reason for the question. 'This Mezelga is the sixxxx-hundreth and seventh. Your father killed Mezelga the sixxx-hundreth and sixth.' Cross's tongue flickered in and out of his beak, which was lined with needle-like teeth.

'Oh,' said Whitestaff, trying hard not to shudder as he looked at the guest.

'Well. I'd bessst be off. Good luck with your training, Whitessstaff. Much is riding on you.'

'Me?' asked Whitestaff with surprise. 'I may not even win. Nap might, or one of the others.'

Cross gave a lisping laugh. 'Not against a dragon your ssssize. Audgar is big, but you make him look tiny. I'm sure the othersss don't stand a chance.'

Whitestaff and Olfar walked with Cross to the mouth of the dugout, then watched as he flew away. His body moved like a whip, tail flaying the air around him in blurry strokes. He moved like a snake in the air and flew faster than Graggy.

'They were called *Wyverns* by the humans on Earth.' Olfar turned to face his nephew, his thick, grey eyebrows drooping down his temples. 'They all look the same, apart from those pale spots. Each Nazoor has a different pattern. That is how they can tell each other apart. The females are slightly smaller than the males.'

Whitestaff listened with interest as Olfar led them back to the main room.

'They aren't as strong as Palal, but they are twice as deadly. They attack in packs and with speed. Never underestimate their minds either. Sometimes I think they are much smarter than us.'

'Do you think our Champion can beat them in the Battle?'

Olfar sighed. 'Yes. I think our Champions always will, even if they do put an Alpos forward. In a war, the Wyvren are deadly, but one-on-one is a different story. But still, perhaps thou should start training now, with Graggy. The Dragon Championship is only a year away.'

'A whole year? That's plenty of time.'

'Well, the Tournament that decides the Champion is a full year from now, the Battle six months after, so I guess thou has plenty of time. But think of the stakes, my lad. All of this,' he cast his arm around him, 'under control of Nazoor.'

Whitestaff scratched his head. 'But I thought Cross—'

'Cross is one of only a few,' Olfar said. 'Not all of them are the same, but most are. I was only being diplomatic before. The important ones are always bloodthirsty, like every Mezelga that has ever ruled. Do you see?'

The thought of the Nazoor reigning over his own noble kind chilled him. It made him forget all about being a Lili'dahl on Earth and finding Susset. All that was important now was winning the Championship in twelve months, then beating this *Audgar* half a year after that.

'I'll start training right away,' he promised. 'I'll go find Graggy again. I won't let us down.'

Olfar tugged his beard and grinned knowingly. 'Of course thou won't. Of course.'

Renewed with energy, Whitestaff zoomed out into the sky to find his friend.

I'll train every day. I'll get even stronger, he thought.

Chapter 35

Many of the dragons that flew by waved their paws at him, even a few reds smiled in his direction. Higher he soared, up into the clear air. He hoped by flying higher he'd have more chance of sighting long-legged Graggy.

Down below and far off in the horizon, he thought he saw green. A flash, that was all, but a long way from anything. Whitestaff pulled his wings in and shot off after it, leaving the dwelling of the Palal behind.

Before him was endless blue, below him lay the permanent blanket of mist that hung high around the spires.

There was no green, no Graggy. *In fact*, thought Whitestaff with alarm, *there is no anything!*

He was right. There was no sound, no dragons—nothing.

Maybe I've come too far. Maybe I should just turn back.

Whitestaff was still deciding what to do when he had all the breath knocked out of him. Something tough had barged into his back at a terrific pace, sending his limbs flying and pulling his wings back.

He plummeted towards the ground as spots zigzagged across his vision. He didn't know which way was up or what had happened, and his lungs were too squashed to take in air. Things began to go black. With sudden panic, Whitestaff forced a ragged breath down his throat, taking it in with a rasp. He stuck his wings out to the side to slow his fall and gently steered himself upright, all with his eyes closed.

The world began to move at normal pace and his stomach settled with a queasy wave. He opened his eyes and saw Nap, grinning wildly at him.

Whitestaff put the pieces together quickly.

'You,' he said, still regaining his wits. 'You could have killed me. What for?'

Nap looked smug. 'Because I hate you. I hate what you Kai'dahl dragons have done to us.'

Whitestaff looked around him. Evidently he had fallen far from the sky because below him he could see the bare, brown ground. Above him was the blanket of cloud.

'We're a long way from help, dragon,' Nap said coolly. 'Under the fog no one can hear you either.'

'Why would I need help, Nap? I'm twice your size, remember?'

Shame flickered across Nap's face as he remembered his earlier loss to the golden dragon. It didn't last long, a mere second, then Nap resumed his icy composure.

'See that,' Nap said, pointing to the ground. 'That is why we have the Tournament. That is why we need a stupid Champion.'

Whitestaff remained silent, the uneasiness spreading through his body. *Where is this going?* he wondered.

'I don't suppose anyone told you, probably didn't want you upset. But I'll let you know. The Dragon Wars didn't end because your stinking father killed Mezelga. The Dragon Wars ended because our magnificent Kai'dahl King,' he said with thick sarcasm, 'touched the ground with Mezelga. Nazoor and Palal felt such great dishonour at their leaders touching *it*, that neither side had the pride to fight any longer.'

Whitestaff wanted to argue, to say it was all a lie, but he recalled Armay's reaction to him when he told her he was 'born on the ground', and somehow he knew it fitted— touching the ground really would have ended a War, not death. It explained Cracone's insult at Court, too.

'But can't you see if my father hadn't done what he did, you'd be dead?'

Nap huffed and bared his teeth. 'I'd rather be dead than belong to a race whose King caressed the dirt. Frendrek putrefied us all. At least he made Mezelga do the same to the Nazoor—speaking of which...'

Nap looked past Whitestaff, and a sour smile crept across his face.

'Good luck, Whiteworm, you're going to need it.'

With those words the red dragon shot up into the air like a rocket, heading for the fog above. A feeling of dread pressed upon Whitestaff like a mountain as he slowly turned around to see what had made Nap so happy.

He saw them, about ten in all. Nazoor. Coming for the kill.

They were moving fast toward him, in a 'V' formation. Whitestaff could see the dragon at the front clearly, small and black, with grey spots forming patterns on its leathery skin.

Like flying lizards.

They looked exactly like Cross, the same size, the same flying motion, and worse, they all had those black, empty eyes.

Whitestaff's legs jerked with fright as he began to ascend, towards the fog. He pumped his wings hurriedly, trying to find a hasty rhythm, but he was hardly moving.

It's no use, he told himself as he looked over his shoulder. *They're too fast.*

He was right; the Nazoor were moving on him like snaking darts. They would beat him easily; speed was not his strong point.

But strength was.

I'll have to fight, he thought grimly.

He stopped flapping and turned around, startled by the progress they'd made. He didn't have time to think of a strategy, for they met him like ants swarming on honey. The leading Nazoor came at him front on while the others surrounded his gold frame, jaws open, ready to bite.

Whitestaff pulled back his massive paw and clapped on the leader's beak-like snout, causing him to squeal in pain and drop away. That only made space for the next one though, who scratched at Whitestaff's face. Luckily,

Whitestaff's tough gold scales prevented too much damage, so he returned with a slap of his own.

More dragons piled on to him, biting and clawing. Whitestaff thrashed frantically at the horrid things that covered him like insects. A few of his blows connected, but he felt many more in reply. He was losing; there were just too many.

Olfar was right. One alone would be no bother. But this?

As he was being pummelled from every angle, he became strangely detached from the situation, as though it was all happening to someone else. Suddenly, the blows didn't hurt at all. Everything was numb.

He didn't know it, but he was losing consciousness.

Smack! A claw hit him roughly on the face, bringing Whitestaff back to reality. He gave a tremendous roar and doubled his efforts to fight back. He bit wildly at whatever was closest to his mouth. He heard more squeals as the terrible Nazoor fought on.

Whitestaff swatted, claws out, feeling skin ripping underneath his nails. But he knew it couldn't last. He was floating off again and seeing stars as something hit the back of his skull.

He thought of Nap's smug face. Nap, who had forced him down here. Nap, who had led him into this trap. Nap, who would be the next Dragon King, a reign of Re'dahl. Who would take over? Certainly no Kai'dahl. He was the last, about to die.

This thought made him furious. So mad, in fact, that he snapped back into the fight. He could barely feel the Nazoor now, but he could see them. They were all over him. Some would fly away then charge back, knocking him around the air like a sack of meat. His raged increased.

Nap will pay for this.

Mercifully, the Nazoor had paused their attack to regroup. Obviously this was harder on them than they thought it was going to be. One dragon versus ten should have been simple, but Whitestaff was stronger than anything they'd ever encountered. Many were sporting tears in their skin while others were nursing twisted limbs.

Only seven were left and Whitestaff wondered where the other three were.

He didn't have time to arrive at an answer, for without warning they flew at him again, shrieking like birds of prey.

Whitestaff knew he couldn't face another onslaught. At the same time, however, he knew he couldn't allow Nap to get away with this.

Anger burned away in his chest like molten lava.

I can't die here. I won't die like this.

They came at him.

Their claws outstretched like talons of doom.

Whitestaff inhaled as deeply as he could, then, with pure rage filling his lungs, he let out a massive stream of fire.

He didn't know how he did it or that such a thing was possible. It was just a natural reaction, like flying. Hot, burning air passed out of his open mouth and at the cluster of Nazoor, charring their skin on impact.

Still furious, Whitestaff belched more fire, burning even more of his reptilian-looking attackers.

Again he shot out flames, again and again—until the sky was clear.

The shrieking had stopped.

The Nazoor were nearly gone. Only one remained in the sky, flapping crookedly in retreat, smoke wisping from its hide.

No more fire came out of Whitestaff. He hovered lamely in the air, panting like a dog.

He let himself drift slowly down, down, just above the ground.

For an instant he wondered if he should touch it. It was supposed to be a shameful thing to do. But he brushed away the thought, thinking it a silly rule. Besides, he knew he'd never make it home in his current condition.

His paws hit the bare earth, followed by his stomach, then his whole body. He lay there, spread on the ground in utter exhaustion, until the darkness came.

Chapter 36

Whitestaff regained his wits several hours after his victory over the Nazoor. The warmth of the ground seeped into his muscles and the stiffness eased. He opened his eyes, sat upright, and checked his body for signs of damage.

There were many. Small cuts, large gashes, and a series of puncture marks on his hind leg where one of the filthy mini-dragons had chewed. He was mildly relieved to see his blood had clotted effectively over the wounds, so he wouldn't pass out from bleeding.

He gave a tentative flap of his wings and found the left one was torn.

No flying for a while.

He gently lay back down and stared at the dense fog that hovered hundreds of yards above.

I can't yell for help, because no one would hear me. I can't fly. What am I going to do?

He rocked his head to one side and saw a dragon-like figure lying motionless on the ground a short distance away. He was about to call to it when he realised it only had two legs. It was one of the Nazoor he had beaten—or was it one that he had burnt? In any case, it was dead. Whitestaff watched as a grey smoke drifted out of the body, and the skin of the Nazoor collapsed in on itself. The smoke drifted upwards and out of sight.

That must be dragon essence, he thought. *Gone now.*

He moaned with regret. Whitestaff had never killed anything before, not even the flies that annoyed him back in his prison on Earth. Granted, he never before had the strength.

And this is how you use it? he asked himself heatedly. *You find that you have all the muscle in the world and you use it to destroy?*

His anger died quickly though. Another part of him knew that without fighting, he'd surely be as lifeless as the Nazoor he was staring at.

With aching joints and tender regions, Whitestaff forced himself to stand and walk. He travelled shakily away from the body of the dead dragon. On and on he pressed, not even looking at where he was bound.

When you're lost, one direction is as good as another.

He eventually came to the base of a spire. This one was thin and shot straight up out of the ground, piercing the cloud above. Some balefruit bubbled out of the spire's sides, just low enough for Whitestaff to reach. Only this balefruit wasn't purple; it was a queer looking yellow—the colour of pus.

Whitestaff gave it a sniff. It smelled of citrus. He plucked one off and licked the skin. It was bitter but not unpleasant. He bit a small chunk off and chewed it thoughtfully.

He waited.

Nothing happened.

It hasn't made me ill, he thought, licking his lips.

Whitestaff decided it was safe to eat the whole thing. He plopped it in his mouth, suddenly ravenous, and juice squirted everywhere. He plucked another one from the growing dirt and ate it too. Some juice trickled down his chin and oozed into one of his deeper cuts on his chest, making Whitestaff yelp with pain.

It felt as though acid was eating away at his scales, then the pain abruptly stopped and his cut went very cold. He gripped it tight with his paw. Unfortunately, it was covered with more juice. Pain flared again and he took his paw away, cursing himself for his stupidity. The wound started to go cold again and Whitestaff watched as the most amazing thing happened. His cut began to heal. Not much, but enough to notice a difference.

He excitedly mashed some of the yellow fruit into a messy pulp in his paw. With a wince, he stuck the glob onto a gash on his shoulder and felt the familiar sting he'd experienced before. He took the poultice off when the wound went icy several seconds later. Sure enough, the gash had partially healed.

I bet I'm the only dragon who knows about this stuff, he thought. *The others wouldn't get this close to the ground to see any of it. Fools.*

Encouraged by his accidental discovery, Whitestaff mashed the fruit like mad, covering himself with yellow patches and eating to his heart's content.

He did this for the rest of the day and wondered if anyone was missing him.

Probably not.

Whitestaff scratched some dirt loose for a bed when it began to grow dark. He replaced all of his messy patches with new ones and closed his eyes to sleep.

Is this land any better? he wondered as sleep began to slow his mind. *Nap, Nazoor, fighting—even killing? Maybe I would have been better on the other side, with Mollie and Wendy.*

He began to dream. He saw himself back on Earth, Mollie patting him and Wendy talking about herself as usual. They were in a lush meadow. Birds whistled happy tunes in a spotless sky.

In his dream he was still gold in colour, still strong and big. He flew over the countryside with Mollie on his back. It was a blissful dream; one he'd never forget.

Chapter 37

The next day he peeled off the mashed fruit and stretched his wings. He felt much better than before and decided to take the chance of flying home. He flapped his wings unevenly, drifting up and to the left. His whole body hurt anew, but he screwed his face up tight and kept rising.

To take his mind off the pain, Whitestaff pictured Nap's face and imagined how the red dragon would look when he saw Whitestaff return triumphant.

But I mustn't tell them, he thought. *They'd never believe that the son of the King would set such a deadly trap. They'd accuse me of making it all up. It would just give Cracone an excuse to send me back home. But what should I tell them? How do I explain all the gashes and sores, not to mention the hole in my wing?*

He didn't have time to find an answer, for as he ascended through the fog, a glorious sight presented itself. Not one or two, but the entire population of Palal were flying toward him, spread out and searching.

'There he is,' shouted one, beckoning with his head.

'I found him first,' hollered another.

Several dragons looked over, and they too shouted.

'Over here.'

'He looks sick.'

'Poor thing.'

'Is he all right?'

'What happened?'

Once again Whitestaff found himself surrounded by dragons, though this time it wasn't terrible clawing enemies that swarmed him. It was friendly, concerned dragons of his own kind, patting him like a long lost friend and asking if he needed help.

A cloud of Palal encased him and soon Whitestaff began to feel claustrophobic.

'I'm fine,' he insisted, trying to smile and hide some of his fiercer wounds. 'Really, I just had an accident, that's all.'

He could hardly hear his own voice over the babble of the mob.

'Make way,' sounded a familiar tone. 'Let me see him.'

The dragons soon hushed each other. 'Make way for the Sorceress,' some said.

'Be quiet.'

'Let her through.'

The Palal parted like a coloured curtain to let Susset closer. Worry wrinkled her delicate brow as she floated over to Whitestaff, who could feel his face going red from all the attention.

The kindness and fret in her voice surprised the golden dragon. 'What happened, Whitestaff? Where did you get these wounds?'

He gave her an uneasy grin and cleared his throat. Everyone had gone silent around him, waiting for an answer.

'I was flying,' he said, trying to keep his voice steady, 'then all of a sudden I got ill, really sick, and I couldn't see where I was going.'

The blue dragons in the crowd made a collective 'awwww'.

'I hit that spire,' he pointed to the thin one behind him, 'then tumbled down it, nearly to the bottom.'

'Did you touch—'

'No I didn't touch the ground,' Whitestaff interrupted grumpily. 'I rolled down it and got wedged in a crevice. I called out for help, but no one came. I only just managed to work myself free.'

Whitestaff thought it sounded a plausible enough story, despite occurring to him only a second earlier. The other dragons thought so too, for they all made sympathetic noises and asked if there was anything they could do.

Three more dragons joined the pack: Olfar, Armay, and Graggy. Graggy bounded through the air with his usual haste and met him first.

'Are you okay? You had us all worried. How did you get *that*?' he pointed at the huge scab on Whitestaff's chest.

'He fell down a spire,' someone answered for him.

'Yes,' Susset agreed. 'Your body must still be adjusting to its new form. One should have expected this. Come back to my study and I'll fix you a hot drink.'

Armay came forward, and without speaking, inserted herself under Whitestaff's wing. She snuggled in close to his body and helped him fly on. Graggy took the other side, acting as an aerial crutch.

The three dragons flew pressed together in this fashion, and Olfar and Susset followed from behind. The crowd went along for a while, then seeing the excitement was over, lost their mob-mentality and went about other business.

When they were relatively alone in the hazy Sorteyan sky, Whitestaff turned his stiff neck to Graggy.

'How long till the Tournament?' he asked.

'A year,' said Graggy, 'why?'

'Promise me we'll train hard.'

'After you've recovered from your accident, we will train every day. Why? What's brought this on?'

Whitestaff thought for a while.

'Nap,' he said at last. 'I want to beat Nap in front of everyone.'

Graggy smiled. 'That's my buddy.'

'I'll help you train too,' Armay whispered from his side.

Whitestaff met her eyes. 'Good,' he said. 'I'm sorry for before. I shouldn't have said anything.'

'Yes, you should have. You were right. The truth just hurts a little, that's all.'

'It wasn't an accident, was it?' asked Graggy keeping his voice from reaching Susset's ears.

The Kai'dahl shook his head. 'No. And if I don't win this Tournament, I hope one of you will.'

'Don't worry, Whitestaff,' Armay said. 'I will do everything to make sure you win.'

Whitestaff had never heard anyone sound so determined in his life. He let his friends in closer under his wings and closed his eyes, letting them carry him to safety.

Chapter 38

Much can happen in just under a year. Esmae knew it, but still it struck her as odd that a short space of time can change so much. Mollie's body had finished its final growth spurt, and now the only difference between the two women was some wrinkles and choice of hairstyle.

Mollie's progress at the magical arts was astounding. In almost one year, Esmae had watched her daughter become a fully-fledged sorceress, able to conjure any spell Esmae could teach, and usually twice as fast and strong.

'It's the blood of Merlin,' she told Terry one day. 'That's why she's so powerful.'

'Yer mean, she's better at it than yerself?'

'I'm afraid so. She could drain the whole lake if she wanted to. Her fireballs are the size of this cottage, and she can levitate for hours without a rest. It's phenomenal.'

'Yer must be proud of her.'

Esmae bit her lip. 'I don't know. Maybe I've done the wrong thing.'

'What do yer mean? I thought yer wanted to teach her?'

'I did. I do. It's like this. When Mollie was four, I decided it was about time she learned how to swim. We have that lake right behind us, and I thought if I taught her to swim, I might save her from drowning.'

'That makes sense ter me.'

'Yes, however, Mollie took to the water with reckless abandon. She loved it. She put her head under, paddled out to the middle, threw objects to the bottom and swam down after them. She had no fear. And here I was, up to my knees watching her like a hawk, scared stiff that she wasn't going to come back up, pulling her out every minute or so to make sure she was fine. That went on for two summers in a row.'

'Must have been very tense for yer.'

'It was. And now I feel like that all over again. As though she's paddling out too far and I can't stop her.'

She often caught herself wondering if things would be different if Merlin were around. Surely he'd be a better teacher. He'd know how to control things.

Thoughts of the great, bearded man occasionally made her chest tighten, but time had changed that too, for those stings were becoming duller and less frequent, and were being replaced by flutters that laced her heart whenever she thought of Terry.

He'd taken to calling in daily, and stopped pretending he was only there to hunt. Terry had become accustomed to the magic weaving that occurred at the Adkins' residence and was no longer in fear of his innards being used in a potion.

He took to Mollie and showed her how to fish with a line and how to fletch an arrow so it would fly true. Of course he knew Mollie could use magic to fish or shoot, but Terry wanted to teach the girl *something*. And for her part, Mollie was a very attentive student.

Esmae stood up and gazed out of the kitchen window. She could see the two, shooting a bale of hay with Terry's bow. After several more shots they came inside, thirsty despite the return of cooler weather.

Mr Gritbole gulped down his drink, gave each Adkins a hug then bade them farewell winking to Esmae on his way out the door. The older woman was sad to see him go but forced a smile.

He'd been gone barely ten seconds when Mollie rounded on her mother.

'It's time,' she said.

'Time for what?'

'Don't pretend you don't know, Esmae. It's time for me to go and get Whitestaff's egg.'

Esmae's jaw set firm.

147

'Are you sure? I thought it was another two months away yet.'

'Quite sure. Positive actually.'

'There are still two months.'

'If I go now, you can spend some time with Terry. And you won't have to sneak kisses when you think I can't see.'

'What a horrid thing to say!'

'Don't be like that. It's obvious you two want to be alone.'

'I'd never want you to leave! How could you say that?'

Mollie walked over and laid a hand on her mother's shoulder.

'I know you don't want me to go. But I also know you and Terry need some time with just the two of you. I don't hate you for it; it's just a fact of life. Maybe one day I'll find a man I want to spend my days with, but for now I have something important to do, and you have Terry to think of.'

'You're right,' Esmae sniffed, her eyes tearing. 'You are old enough and I would like some time with Terry. But...'

'But that doesn't mean you love me any less, I know, don't worry. Please don't cry.' Mollie patted her mother as if *she* were the child.

Esmae straightened after a while, her face wet and red. 'Actually there are still...' she paused to blow her nose loudly in her white handkerchief, '...still four weeks left. I have been counting, so the fair won't be at Gibbon yet. It'll be on the other side, and you've never gone that far.'

Mollie frowned. 'I thought as much. That's why I should go now. Cudgel may very well be expecting me in Gibbon, so if I catch the fair in another town, I'll have the advantage of surprise.'

Esmae shook the handkerchief and blew again. 'I think--I think I knew you would go. At first I thought you might grow out of the idea, but no, not you. You'd never let a friend down. How can I hold something like that against you? Just promise me you'll wait till tomorrow, and promise you'll be safe.'

Mollie gave an excited laugh and embraced her mother once more. 'Don't worry about me I can take on a whole army of Cudgels. And look at you, crying away! Why, if men like Terry make us Adkins women soft in the head, I'm staying single.'

After another warm hug, Mollie went outside to find Wendy.

The horse was grazing contently in the yard, and she looked up with placid eyes as Mollie approached.

'Hi, Mollie,' she said as she munched.

'Morning, Wendy. How are things?'

'Fine.'

'That's good to hear.' Mollie patted the horse while she ate. 'Wendy, do you ever think about Whitestaff?' she asked, trying to sound casual.

'Why? What do you look so happy about? You've come to ask me something.'

'There's no fooling you, is there? Well, do you remember I told you one day I'd get Whitestaff's egg from Cudgel?'

Wendy shivered at the name. 'Ewww,' she said as she shook. 'Don't mention that wretched man to me.'

'Well, do you remember?'

'Yes, I do. What's your point?'

Wendy bent down to chew more grass, watching Mollie's feet shift uncomfortably as she did so.

'Well … um. I'm going tomorrow. I have to get the egg back, you see? Because poor Whitestaff will be trapped again if he ever comes back from wherever it is he went. Do you follow?'

'I follow.'

Mollie was practically dancing now.

'What is the point, Mollie?'

'The point is, er… I want you to come with me.'

Wendy's head shot up with a crack. Half eaten grass fell out of her mouth.

'You want me to lay my beautiful eyes on that stinking man again? After he locked me up? Are you mad?'

Mollie had expected this, and so came prepared with an argument.

'Firstly,' she said, 'Cudgel will not recognise you; you're not pink anymore. Secondly, you've seen what I can do with magic, I can protect you.' Wendy relaxed a little.

'True, you would be more than a match for him.'

Sensing she was getting through, Mollie continued. 'Thirdly, think of Whitestaff. You know how weak he is; he'd never be able to defend himself or fight back or anything.'

Wendy bit off some more grass and chewed it thoughtfully.

'Think of it as an adventure,' Mollie urged.

'I don't know. It does sound dangerous. Cudgel is a horrible man.'

'Yes,' Mollie said emphatically, 'he is mean, that's why we have to get that egg away from him. We have to help Whitestaff somehow. Plus,' Mollie added in a whisper, 'Whitestaff would do it for you, you know he would.'

That last argument brought the horse around. Wendy knew the girl had spoken the truth, and she was ashamed for not agreeing straight away.

'Okay,' she said. 'I'll go with you. Just let me go and say goodbye to Bramble.'

Mollie squealed in delight and grabbed the horse around the neck. She kissed one of the spots on Wendy's cheek. Wendy neighed in kindness, nuzzled the young woman's shoulder then trotted off to Terry's house to find Bramble.

Mollie walked back to the cottage and hummed a tune. She could not wait for the new day to bring her the adventure she'd craved for nearly a whole year.

'In a few days' time, Whitestaff,' she said aloud, 'I will have your egg. That is a promise.'

Chapter 39

Those long months had changed much on Sorteya too. Whitestaff had soon recovered from the injuries inflicted by the Nazoor, and true to his promise, Graggy had trained with him almost every day for the Dragon Championship.

Both dragons had the bulging muscles to prove it.

Not only was he even stronger, Whitestaff was also a faster dragon in the air now too, though he was still not a match for Graggy. If anything, Graggy had become even swifter than before, appearing as just a long-legged blur of green when he was at full pace.

The two had formed a solid bond of friendship over the long hours spent chasing each other or mock fighting in the sky. They had become like brothers.

Armay and Whitestaff had all but forgotten their feud, and they had become good friends also. Every now and then, the blue dragon would join in with the boys at their training sessions. She played as rough and as dirty as either of them, often using her agility to slip her body around the sky and catch them off guard with a thump to the head.

Luckily, Whitestaff and Graggy had thick skulls.

According to Graggy, there were three events in the Tournament. One was a time-trial flight through the skies of Sorteya. Its purpose was to test the candidates' speed. Graggy was unsure what the other two were.

They changed from year to year, so no dragon could practise for them. Only the Council knew, and even though Whitestaff was officially on the Council, he'd been barred from any meetings that discussed the Tournament, and rightly so. He did not want anyone to think he had an upper hand.

But, of course, he did have the upper hand. Whitestaff was an enormous dragon by Palal standards, and even though he wasn't that fast in the air, he was mighty strong. And he could breathe fire, which he still kept secret.

A few weeks after his dreadful encounter with the Nazoor, Whitestaff asked his uncle about flame-breathing dragons.

Olfar just chuckled. 'Why do thou ask, lad?'

They were sitting in Susset's study. The bookshelves surrounded them like a cocoon, and the white portal to Earth shimmered in front of them like watery froth at the bottom of a high waterfall. Somehow it all made Whitestaff feel very safe. It was, after all, the first dugout he'd ever been in. It was almost like home. He began to wonder if the sorceress had put an enchantment on the room that made visitors relaxed and comfortable. He was so at ease that his mind had drifted off. His uncle had to repeat the question.

'Oh, ahhh, nothing really. I just heard rumours on Earth about dragons who could burn things with their breath.'

Olfar smiled indulgently. 'Yes, humans do love their unsubstantiated gossip. But the truth is that no dragons alive can breathe actual fire. Not anymore. The last on record was a forefather of thine, many hundreds of years past. His name was Shale, or Shale the Fire Dragon as he liked it.'

'And no one since him?' Whitestaff asked innocently.

'No, not since then. I doubt whether any dragons will ever be able to do that particular trick again.'

'Why not?'

Olfar tugged his beard thoughtfully. 'I have a theory, you see. Long ago, many Palal could breathe fire. It's on record. Probably tells you the exact percentage in one of these books.' Olfar twirled a claw at the many tomes that surrounded them. 'But it didn't serve a purpose really. Sure, if we had a war it was a very handy weapon, but due to our size and strength those wars were quickly won, leaving us with no real enemies for many centuries. With no rivals left to fight, we had no use to waste energy belching fire all over the place. I think the skill just left us because it wasn't required.'

Whitestaff considered asking more questions. If he enquired too much, his uncle might get suspicious and start asking questions of his own. He decided to risk one more.

'Well, if the skill only left us because we had no need for it, do you think it would come back if we had more wars?'

Olfar's eyes popped open. 'I hadn't thought of that. Good question. Maybe, I suppose it's possible. Why do thou ask?'

Whitestaff cursed himself inside.

'Erm, just a fascinating subject, that's all,' he said with what he hoped was a nonchalant voice.

He had thought about telling his uncle everything about burning the Nazoor with his breath. Part of him wanted to reveal everything that had happened under the fog, but he held back.

He didn't want to be punished for killing the Nazoor, or blamed for starting wars. He *could* tell them Nap led him into a trap and that he killed only in self-defence and everything would be fine. That is, if they believed him. He knew Nap would deny everything anyway, and with no proof, the Palal would just think he was lying. He would probably be punished for that too.

He supposed he could tell his uncle about breathing fire. He could make up a story about accidentally burning something with his breath while asleep or something, but again he withheld the information.

If what his uncle said was true, and no other dragons could breathe fire, Whitestaff really did have a surprise advantage. He decided to keep his remarkable ability to himself. Besides, he didn't know if he could do it again even if he wanted to.

There were times during the past year when he had been tempted to try. The thought of spewing hot flame all over Cracone appealed to him on several occasions. The powerful Re'dahl had been so rude to Whitestaff in Council meetings that the gold dragon could actually feel hot lava boiling away in his chest. He wasn't sure if it was anger or fire burning inside him, but he kept it in just the same, telling himself that Cracone's days as ruler would come to an end.

Who would be King then? Whitestaff asked himself. *'Me? Will I ever be ready for such a responsibility? No, not yet. Let Cracone keep that job as long as he likes.'*

But a small voice inside him panicked. *Golds should rule*, it said. *A Red King is too dangerous.*

That little voice intruded more often as the year went on, and as Whitestaff readied himself for another Council meeting, it called to him again. He pushed it from his mind as Susset entered the dugout.

'Nearly ready?' she asked as she glided over to him.

He was still living with Olfar and was polishing his scales near the enchanted smokeless fire.

He noticed Susset was looking her best too. She wore an ornate hooded robe that was decorated with delicate swirling patterns. Small jewels were sewn into the hems; they sparkled in the firelight. The effect was dazzling, and it occurred to Whitestaff that Susset grew even more stunning every day. He wondered if she had enchanted herself with a spell of some sort.

'Yes, I'm nearly done,' he answered.

'Good. Something tells me one will not want to miss this one.'

'What do you mean?'

Susset dropped her head and motioned for Whitestaff to come closer. The two walked to the dugout mouth and stood. There was no breeze—all was still.

'I don't know. Just the way Cracone has been acting lately. He's up to something.'

'What?'

Susset shook her head. 'Best we go find out. Can I ride this time? I have a niggling suspicion I might have to save my strength.'

'Sure, hop on.' He crouched down low for her, which was a pointless gesture because she levitated herself onto his back anyway.

The golden dragon waited until his passenger was holding on tightly before leaping into the air.

For fun he let himself free-fall, diving towards the fog at a great speed. He could hear Susset whooping with joy as her stomach lurched. The air was no longer lifeless, it whipped about them, creating tears in their eyes and making their faces tingle. Down, down the dragon went, shouting and laughing like the sorceress.

When they were about to hit the fog, he spread his magnificent wings and swooped upwards. Susset clung to his neck, her eyes wide with excitement.

'You shall have to remind me to tie myself on, next time,' she shouted over the rushing air.

Whitestaff smiled and slowed his pace, giving Susset time to fix her hair and clothes before they made it to the Court.

Chapter 40

It wasn't long before they could see the great dragon-headed entrance, mouth open, waiting for the Council to arrive. A small stream of dragons flowed into the jaws, led by the Red King.

Whitestaff joined the line and landed inside.

'What's that around his neck?' Whitestaff asked, jerking his head towards Cracone.

Susset squinted. 'Oh,' she said in surprise. 'That's the royal medallion. A gift from Merlin himself. It grants the wearer immunity from magic.'

'What do you mean?'

'Well, if I cast a spell on him, that medallion will absorb the magic, cancelling the spell. I wonder why he's wearing it today?'

Whitestaff looked more closely at the item. It was a round gold talisman that hung on a thick chain. Embossed in the middle of the medallion was a rearing silver dragon surrounded by strange symbols. It looked a priceless and powerful piece of jewellery.

'Why would Merlin create such a thing?' Whitestaff asked aloud.

'Who knows?' answered Susset. 'Only the Great Wizard, I suppose. I still don't see why he's wearing it today.'

'Well, you did say something strange was afoot.'

Susset didn't respond. Instead they took their seats quietly and waited for the proceedings to start.

After polite mufflings of pleasantries, Cracone banged his sceptre butt and called for order.

'As you know,' he began, 'the Tournament is nearly on us. Next month is the due date to start.'

Whitestaff wiggled on his bench, wondering if he should be hearing this.

'I have decided to move it forward. It will begin in two day's time.'

This resulted in many urgent whispers among the Council, but before anyone could complain formally, Cracone went on.

'I do this because we have an urgent matter to discuss, that is, the Nazoor have moved to the edge of the Dire Channel.'

More whispers. Whitestaff looked to Susset for an explanation.

'The Dire Channel is what separates our side of Sorteya and theirs. After the Dragon Wars, both parties agreed not to live too close to its banks—a thousand yards, to be precise. It was meant to give the Palal and the Nazoor an extra buffer.'

Whitestaff nodded and looked back to the King.

'As you know, this goes against our treaty. I propose we Palal also expand our borders to live by the Channel.'

'To what end?' asked Olfar.

Cracone threw him a dirty look. 'If you haven't noticed, Olfar, our population is rapidly expanding. The extra land along the Dire Channel would suit us quite well.'

'I agree,' said a heavy-set Bo'dahl. 'Our hatchlings are too cramped. We need to spread out.'

'Why can't we move to the south?' asked a Gra'dahl.

A red dragon answered, 'No spires, no fruit. The best stuff is by the Dire.'

Nobody argued this point. It was true, all the tall spires and fat balefruit stood on the banks of the Dire.

'I'll give you some time to discuss the matter.'

Cracone reached to his left and grasped a massive hourglass. It was filled with red grains the size of peas. He flipped it, and all the dragons swooped to the middle of the Court, talking in heated tones.

'Why can't we find other land?' Whitestaff heard someone ask.

'It would give us more food for the Lili'dahls,' another said.

'What if we start another war?' one cried.

Cracone moved leisurely among the Council, offering his opinion, hoping to sway some members for an affirmative vote.

'That's why he wore it,' Susset said in Whitestaff's ear. 'It's a symbol of power, a reminder of his strength. He's hoping to intimidate others into voting his way. This is not good.'

But Whitestaff thought it *was* good. He too was strolling around the Council, listening to both arguments. Sure, the Nazoor might be angry, but broadening the ground of the Palal to include the rich riverbank was appealing. Besides, he didn't care if the Nazoor liked it or not.

After more open debate the last red grain fell to the bottom of the timer. 'Enough,' bellowed Cracone. 'Time is spent.'

The muttering Council members made their way back to their respective benches.

'A vote,' said the King. 'Should we do as the Nazoor have and use the good land on our side of the Channel as we see fit? Or should we stay put, crowding ourselves in while the dirty Wyvren do as they please?'

'Re'dahl Council, how do you vote?'

A wiry old red stood his voice high and slow. 'We vote unanimously for the affirmative. We take the land.' He sat back down. Cracone gave him a wink with his one good eye and a nod.

'Gra'dahl?'

'We vote five against, one for,' said Olfar.

Cracone shook his head and snorted.

'Bo'dahl?'

A heavy blue stood her voice hesitant. 'We vote two with, four against.' She looked nervous, as well she should have. The Council was hung.

'Kai'dahl,' shouted Cracone, his voice echoing through the empty chamber. 'That's nine on each side. It's down to your vote. Show some sense, boy.'

Whitestaff stirred uncomfortably, aware of all the eyes on him. Olfar gave him a pleading look, hoping to sway his vote against the move.

Cracone tapped his sceptre impatiently. 'Make the right decision, lad,' he said, his voice dripped with threat. Whitestaff knew if he went against the King, Cracone would make him pay. On the other hand, Olfar had voted against him, and Olfar was usually right.

What to do, what to do?

All members of the Council were growing impatient, so Whitestaff just started talking.

'As you know,' he began, 'I haven't been a member for long. I am leaning towards voting in favour of the land takeover,' at this point Cracone gave him a nod of approval, 'however, I'd like to survey the land before I cast my vote, with your majesty's permission.'

'Why?' barked the King.

'Well if it's as bountiful as I've heard, then I see no problem in moving there.'

'And if its not?'

'If it's not, then I say it's not worth causing trouble over.'

Some of the Greens nodded at this wisdom. Olfar tugged his beard while the blue dragons smiled at him kindly.

'Hmmm,' said Cracone. 'You leave us little choice. I assure you the land is all we say, so I guess there's no harm in letting you look first.' He scratched his neck and paused. Everyone was silent, waiting for more. 'Fine, so be it,' he said abruptly. 'We will meet back here on the first day of the Tournament to hear the Kai'dahl's vote.

'Meeting adjourned.'

He banged his sceptre three times on the ground and the Council left the Court, muttering and murmuring to each other on the way.

'You did well,' Susset assured her friend. 'You gave yourself more time to think it over, well done.'

'Yes, wise given the circumstances,' said Olfar as he approached. 'Of course, I wish thou had sided with me, but thou are thy own dragon. Thou should find out the facts for thyself. It's what Frendrek would have done.'

Whitestaff glowed at the compliment.

'Well,' he said, 'the Tournament is only in two days. There is nothing to do now but fly to the Dire Channel and look around. Care to come with me?'

Both sorceress and Olfar nodded, to Whitestaff's relief. In secret he had feared getting too close to the Nazoor by himself again. He knew from experience that they were not a force to meet alone.

Olfar said farewell to his fellow Council members, then the three set off for the restricted land

Chapter 41

'What a foul year,' whined Cudgel.

He was sitting in his van (which no longer stank) eyeing the heavy chest on the floor in front on him. He nervously eyeballed Audrey and wriggled on his stool. He sat on his hands. As soon as he said the words, he knew he was in trouble. He was right.

'Oh, so it's been bad having me for a wife, has it? I clean your wretched van, cook for you, help you all day, and the best way to thank me is to insult me. It that it?'

Cudgel bowed his head. 'S'not what I meant, sweet-pie,' he said in earnest. 'I jus' mean... you know... me money an' all that. No dragon, no unicorn. 'Ow's a fella supposed ter live?'

'We've been doing all right, ain't we?'

Cudgel didn't say a word. By Audrey's standards they were rich. By his own, however, they were paupers. He had to dip into his savings to afford the wedding, a fact that rankled him no end.

It all seemed a good idea at the time. He had just lost the wretched dragon and the foolish horse that had been part of his show for years. He was desperate for some money. He needed a new act otherwise he could not become the wealthy man he'd always yearned to be. So teaming up with Audrey sounded reasonable.

They decided to combine their stalls, hoop throwing and dragon egg viewing. But then Audrey wanted more. She wanted a husband *and* to be equal partners. What could a man do? He had no choice. He bought a ring (which he knew cost far too much), arranged a church, bought a suit, and married. And received nothing but grief ever since.

How he longed for the old days! Stupid children giving him gold to see a fake unicorn and a lazy, joke of a dragon—an over-sized lizard at best.

How he used to smile when that money covered his palm! It made him think of his future. It let him imagine buying a mansion, having a few slaves, living like a noble. He'd dream of buying fat pheasants and shooting them down just for fun. Oh, the life he would live.

But these were not the old days. Not at all. Audrey harped about him finding a new dragon (like they grew on trees) or some other attraction. And boy, could she spend money. Always she'd be asking for this, or needing silver for that. He sat by miserably and watched the booty in his big old chest drain away, like his dreams of living large.

And Latos, could that woman nag! She was always at him to fix this, or put that away, or eat these horrid green things. It was a nightmare!

As soon as I get a new act, I'll divorce her, he thought grumpily.

'What are you thinking?' she asked all of a sudden.

'Wha—? Oh nothin'. Just wonderen' 'ow we could get more dough, that's all.'

Audrey frowned. 'I'm glad to see you've finally decided to think straight. Why don't you sell that stinking egg for starters? That should fetch a pretty penny.'

Cudgel gave in inward groan. 'Because, dear, it's worth more to us if we keep it. If yer charge fools to look at somethin' without lettin' em 'ave it, yer can keep it and charge another fool ter look at it later. See? Yer keep maki'n money off the same stupid thing.'

Audrey huffed. 'Don't talk to me like a mullytill or I'll thunk your head with a frying pan!'

'Sorry, dear.'

'Now if you want to make more money off the egg, why don't you let the customer try and break it?'

'What?' shouted Cudgel in outrage. 'Why in Latos would I do that? If they broke it I'd have nothing.'

Audrey smiled smugly. 'Because they can't break it, can they? It's magical. You've tried to smash it yourself, remember?'

It was true. After Whitestaff had disappeared Cudgel took to the egg with a hammer. He was so furious he went into a frenzy; he thought if he smashed the egg he could somehow hurt the dragon, or bring him back.

'Yeah, I remember.'

'You couldn't break it, could you?'

'So?'

Again Audrey smiled, clearly proud of herself. 'So, you silly little man, you could charge a tooker a gold coin to have a crack at it, see? If they break it, they win fifty gold coins.'

'Fifty!' Cudgel spluttered.

'Yes. Fifty. You have to make it worth their while otherwise no one will part with their gold. Don't worry though, no one will break it. It's magic.'

Cudgel closed his eyes and pondered the idea.

S'pose it could work. Yes, I think it would work.

'So what do you think?' Audrey asked her voice sweet and high.

Cudgel shuddered at the sound.

'Oh, er, yeah. I guess we could give it a go. It might work. Of course, I'd need ter improve the idea a little, yer know.'

Audrey squeezed one of his fat cheeks between her fingers. 'Good boy,' she said with a wide smile.

Cudgel smiled back.

I'll get rid of yer yet, yer cow, he thought to himself. *Just yer wait.*

But to his wife he said, 'Dearest, while we are talking about money…'

'Yes?'

'Well I had an idea that could make us real rich.'

Audrey sat down opposite him and leaned closer. 'Yes?'

Then Cudgel explained his idea. At first Audrey was shocked then little by little, a thick smile oozed itself onto her face. She rubbed her hands with glee and thought about all the money they would make from Cudgel's clever plan.

Chapter 42

It was a haphazard day when Mollie said goodbye. The sun kept disappearing behind dark clouds, only to re-emerge later with a shining blaze that drained the colour from everything. The wind blew the first icy warnings of the approaching winter, and Mollie couldn't decide if she was cold or hot.

Esmae stood at the gate to wave her daughter and Wendy off. She never let go of Terry's hand.

'If something happens to her,' she told him, 'I'll never forgive myself.'

'And if you don't let 'er go, she'll never forgive *you*.'

Esmae wiggled her body closer to his. 'You're right, of course.'

'Plus,' Terry said with a grin, 'what could happen to 'er? She's only goin' ter the other side of Gibbon. Plus, I've seen what she can do. I don't know much 'bout magic an' all, but I do know she a right strong 'un.'

Esmae nodded in agreement. 'So strong, but such a young body.'

'Yer seein' from a mother's eyes. She ain't so young at all.'

'I know. But sometimes I like to pretend. Soon enough she'll come home and say she wants to marry. I don't think I'm ready for that yet.'

Bramble watched them go too. His big heart beat low in his chest, his attention mainly on Wendy.

'Don't take long, Wendy, and please be safe.'

'I'll be safe, Bramble. Besides, look who I have for company; the most powerful human ever!'

'Yes. Too powerful, I often think.'

'Don't be like that. Just be thankful it's she who can do magic and not someone like Cudgel.'

Mollie gave the little group one last wave and urged her horse forward. She instantly felt their watching eyes disappear as she rounded the bend.

'Here we go, Wendy. Off on our own big adventure.'

The horse sighed wistfully. 'It's good to be out. I'm excited and scared at once.'

'I know what you mean.'

They rode on in silence after that until they reached the crossroads. 'Here we go, no turning back now,' said Wendy as she headed for Gibbon.

The plan was to go through Gibbon and seek out the fair. Mollie guessed it shouldn't be too far away, because the fair was due at Gibbon in four weeks.

She'd spoken to Terry about this, and according to his calculations, he reckoned that there were only two places the fair could be, and the best bet was Quilshire.

Quilshire was much bigger than Gibbon, and it lay on the northern side. Terry had been there once and he'd told Mollie all about it; the fancy shops, the funny clothes, the beautiful people who always wore makeup no matter what day it was. Mollie couldn't wait to see the place.

But the road there was long and tiring, and they had only just begun.

Neither traveller spoke for a long time, each lost in her own thoughts. It was probably just as well too, for their voices probably wouldn't be heard over the din. Crickets and cicadas chirped noisily in the thick undergrowth at the roadside, birds called to each other and screeched overhead, and there was the constant clanking of supplies that came with each of Wendy's steps.

The horse was so burdened with equipment she looked like a moving storehouse. Pans and bedrolls, food and water, clothes and toiletries; it all weighed her down immensely. She felt like she was under one of Mollie's Gravity spells.

And so they plodded, with mouths shut but minds content, until they came to Gibbon.

'I don't really remember anything apart from the showgrounds,' said Mollie absently.

So they meandered through the streets until they found a ramshackle building that was painted pale yellow. It was called the Barren Arms, and it was Gibbon's only inn.

Wendy tipped up her nose and sniffed.

'Now, now, Wendy, don't be like that. Terry said this was the only place to stay in the entire village.'

She led Wendy to the stables and then double-backed to the entrance.

The door stuck halfway when she pushed on it, so Mollie had to squeeze inside.

She instantly wished she'd stayed out. The smell of tobacco was overpowering, the floor was covered in filthy sawdust that hadn't been changed for months, and through the gloom she could see a bunch of rough-looking men whispering at the bar. They stopped to watch her as she walked in.

She hesitated, then as confidently as she could, marched up to the bar.

'Bit too polished for ale aren't you, my lass?' asked one of the men, whose beard nearly touched his waist. The others laughed and winked at each other.

'Do you have room for me and my horse?' Mollie asked the stout man behind the counter.

He looked at her steadily. 'We don't have room for your type,' he said, his voice dangerously low.

For a while nobody said anything then the tough-looking bearded man spoke up.

'Jake, what do you mean *type*? Type of what?'

Jake didn't take his eyes off Mollie. 'That there is one of the Witches of Danmurk, boys. That's the youngest one.'

The man with the beard laughed. 'Jake, she's a paying customer, let her have a room.'

He then turned to Mollie and put a heavy hand on her shoulder. 'You're not a witch are you? You're too pretty for that.' Again he laughed at his own joke, his friends joined in once more.

'No,' Mollie replied primly. 'I'm not a witch, I'm a sorceress, and if you don't take your hand off me, I'll smash it into pieces with a wicked piece of magic.' She gave him a humourless smile.

The man took his hand off her shoulder as though it were on fire. 'Whooo,' he said, pretending he was scared. 'I like this one, Jake. She's got guts. Right boys?'

His friends nodded and cheered. 'Let her have a room, Jake. I'll pay.' He turned back to Mollie. 'It's the least I can do for making fun.'

Jake didn't say anything for a while; he was weighing up the risks. 'What if you pay for her room *and* any damages she does during her stay?'

The man at the bar grinned. 'Jake,' he said, 'Any damage she'd do would be an improvement on this dump.' This time, even Mollie laughed.

Jake nodded. 'Deal,' he said.

'Name's Bob,' said the bearded man. '*Blackbeard* to some.' He held out his hand and Mollie shook it. She saw his knuckles were covered with dull tattoos. 'Now my pretty sorceress, accept my apologies for being rude earlier. I forget my land manners at times.'

Mollie said that she would and gave him a smile.

'Now, excuse me and my crew. Come on lads, we got work to do.'

His mates groaned and followed him out the door, leaving Mollie alone with Jake. He was still glaring at her.

'Which room do I have, Jake?' she asked politely.

'Six,' he mumbled and threw her a large key.

Mollie forced herself to walk away slowly, up the stairs, down the hall, and into the numbered room on her left. She did not want Jake to know how much he had unnerved her. It was strange. She knew she could restrain anyone with a single finger, but she still felt vulnerable.

'It's because you're out on your own,' she said to the empty room. Well, the room wasn't so empty. She had many cockroaches and bedbugs for company.

At least I'm not paying, she thought. She sat on the rumpled bed and found her knees were shaking slightly.

She took some deep breaths and made herself relax.

'Don't worry about small-minded fools,' she told herself. 'You are here to help a friend. Now get to it.'

She put away her things and then went back to the stables to unload Wendy.

It didn't take long to relieve the horse of the supplies, and soon the two were back out on the grim streets of Gibbon.

Chapter 43

The Dire Channel was dead ahead, and much to Whitestaff's disappointment, it was flanked by magnificent spires covered with plump balefruit. The food enveloped the spires like a purple rash. The sight made his mouth water.

The channel itself was extremely wide and deep. Tall cliffs towered above the water on each side, and every now and then huge chunks of rock would slide down and land in the choppy waters below.

Spray shot high in the air. It tickled Whitestaff's scales.

He followed the channel back out to the sea where the water was madly splashing itself white. The roar of the waves made his insides vibrate. They slammed against the cliffs causing mighty geysers.

The tide was coming in fast; it rushed and churned through the channel.

'How far does that go?' asked Whitestaff as he watched more rock collapse into the Dire.

'Miles and miles,' answered Susset.

'Two hundred and sixteen, to be exact,' said Olfar.

They hovered in silence for a while, in awe of the ocean's power.

'Do you want to fly lower?' asked Olfar.

'I think I've seen enough,' answered Whitestaff miserably.

Susset flew close and patted his head. 'I know what you're thinking,' she said. 'You wish it weren't so good here so you'd have an excuse to vote against the move.'

Whitestaff nodded glumly. 'Yes.'

They flew down near the surface. It looked even better close-up.

The smell of fruit and saltwater gave the air a clean, energising scent. It was clear to Whitestaff that this was possibly the best land on Sorteya.

'We need the space and fruit,' he said aloud.

'At what cost?' said Olfar. 'See over there? On the other side of the Channel, can thou see?'

Whitestaff squinted through the watery mist. Small black shapes slithered through the sky in the distance.

'Nazoor,' said Whitestaff, his voice bulky with hate.

'Yes, so close. Too close.'

'Much too clossssssse,' agreed a familiar voice.

They all turned to their right to see Cross flying towards them. His black eyes gave away nothing but his voice was panicked.

'Too clossse for all of ussss,' he said.

'So why move here? It's against the agreement and it's asking for trouble,' said Whitestaff.

'Exxxactly,' Cross hissed urgently. 'It's a deliberate attempt to lure you into a fight. They're trying to provoke you.'

'Why?' Susset, Olfar, and Whitestaff asked in unison.

'Why would they want to do that?' Olfar persisted. 'The Tournament is only a matter of days away. It doesn't make sense.'

'Becausssse they know they won't win. Some of the Mazelga's Council have sssseen your Golden Palal here and they ssssay we have no chance againssst him.'

Olfar looked at Whitesatff. 'Sure he's big, but he hasn't even won the Tournament yet. The Champion could be anyone.'

Cross's beak twitched with irritation. 'He will win. Of course he will win. Any dragon who can breathe fire is absssssssolutely certain to win.'

Susset and Olfar looked at each other in surprise.

'Thou think my nephew can breathe fire?' He gave a laugh and stroked his beard. 'Thy spies must be mistaken.

No dragon does that anymore, it's common knowledge that…'

At that point Olfar recalled the odd conversation he'd had with the lad about a year ago. *Didn't he ask about breathing fire then?*

Olfar hummed into his chest and cleared his throat. He deliberately did not look at Whitestaff.

'Are you sssure?' asked Cross. 'Our Council is very concerned. They sssay with this golden dragon as Champion, the Nazoor will never win the Battle as he hasss an unfair advantage. They sssay we should have a war instead. At least we could win that.'

Whitestaff kept quiet through the whole thing. He remembered back to the fight with the Nazoor. The one he let get away must have told the rest what he'd seen. Now the Nazoor knew about his remarkable ability, but his own kind didn't. He felt sick with worry. He'd inadvertently set these nasty lizards off, and now he had to vote on whether to move closer to them or not.

'So what you're saying, Cross,' Whitestaff asked, 'is that the Nazoor Council thinks I can breathe fire, and so instead of letting Audgar face me in the Battle, they want to start a war by moving closer to the Channel?'

'Yessss,' said Cross. 'They realise they'll never win in a one-on-one Battle, so they move clossssser, hoping you'll do the same. Then Mezelga will claim you started a war by breaking the agreement. Don't you sssee? She's looking for an excuse to go to war again. If you move here you'll be giving her the reason she needsss.'

'Then we can't settle here,' said Whitestaff. 'It's not worth it.'

Susset and Olfar nodded in agreement.

'We will see the Tournament out, then Battle Audgar fairly, like we have done since my father died.'

'Good,' Cross hissed. 'My followers will be happy to hear that. We don't wish for war, you ssssee. When the time is right, the Party for Peace will overthrow Mezelga and we will never know war again. But for now…'

He didn't finish his sentence. Instead he bode them farewell and flew off, through the thin haze and to the other side of the Dire Channel.

'Cracone won't be happy,' said Susset when he'd gone.

'No,' Whitestaff agreed. 'But he'd be even unhappier with a swarm of Nazoor biting his neck.'

Susset and Olfar exchanged meaningful looks before following the Kai'dahl back home.

Chapter 44

Mollie and Wendy needed to find out if the fair was at Quilshire, or west at Lareborough. If it went to Quilshire, then Terry was correct in his guess and the two would keep going north. If Terry was wrong and the fair travelled to Lareborough… well, Mollie tried not to think about it. The way to Lareborough was through a mountain range, high and hazardous, and full of bandits and thieves.

She decided it was time to ask the locals, who would surely know.

'Excuse me,' Mollie said to a frail old woman who stood at a doorway.

The woman gave a jerk, clutched her heart and made a sign with her fingers, then went back into her house, clicking a lock behind her.

'Happen often?' asked Wendy.

'More than you'd believe,' Mollie replied.

'Why don't you let me try? Here…' Wendy trotted round a corner to catch a horse she'd spied.

On the horse was a rigid old man wearing a black suit with a purple vest.

'Hi,' Wendy said as she pulled alongside the horse.

The gentleman pretended not to see Mollie or Wendy. He too had heard of the Danmurk Witches and knew their inky-black hair was the surest way to spot them.

'Hellooo,' said the grey horse.

'My mistress here is searching for the travelling show that comes through every year. Do you know if it's at Quilshire or at Lareborough?' Wendy fluttered her eyelashes a little.

'My lady, I do know. And if you'd dine on some hay with me later, I'd be soooo happy to tell you.'

Mollie rolled her eyes, but Wendy agreed with enthusiasm.

'Oh my,' she gushed, 'do you really mean it? Of course I'd love to. So can you tell me where the fair is?'

'Well, we did pass them on the way here. It was north, my pet. It was sooo long agoooo, but I have a brilliant memory. I spoke to one of the horses myself and she... er... *he* said they were bound for Quilshire.'

'Oh, thank you so much. What a charming and helpful horse you are.'

Mollie dug her heels in Wendy's sides.

'What time tonight, my lady?' How about seven at my stables? It's the large one yonder. Is something the matter?'

'No. Just my mistress isn't good at riding.'

'Oh, some are never any good, are they?'

'No, some aren't. And if this one doesn't learn to trust me, I shall make her walk.'

Mollie frowned and tossed her head.

'So, tonight?'

'See you then.'

'Very gooood, my lady.'

Wendy stopped while the grey horse carried his master home. The gentleman gave a visible sigh of relief when Mollie and Wendy pulled away. He risked a quick glance round then seeing Mollie was no longer near, he spurred his horse to move faster.

'What was that all about?' Mollie asked angrily. 'You can't just get friendly with another horse! What about Bramble?'

Wendy snorted loudly. 'Well, Mollie, which horse I choose to keep company with isn't really your business. But seeing as though you're so concerned, I never intended to meet with that stuck-up fool at all. I just told him what he wanted to hear so we could find out where that stinking Cudgel is. I got the information for *you*.'

'Oh,' said Mollie in a small voice.

'And I meant what I said, if you don't learn to trust me you can walk.'

Without another word, she took Mollie back to the Barren Arms.

Mollie alighted at the Arms and quietly made her way back to her room. Jake eyed her with open suspicion on the way.

She flopped down on the small bunk and thought.

Wendy is right. I do have to learn to trust her. Of course she wouldn't hurt Bramble, and the way she swindled information from that snobby grey horse was smart.

Mollie decided she'd have to learn the lesson her mother tried to teach her; things are rarely what they seem.

You're going to have to stop being so naive, my dear, she told herself. *Or you'll end up being sailed down the river of deceit without an oar.*

Chapter 45

'I say we strike tonight,' Mollie told Wendy after midday. 'That way we can nab the egg, come back and sleep here, then be back home by tomorrow.

The horse chuckled. 'What happened to our big adventure? I thought you'd draw it out for sure.'

'Yeah, I know,' Mollie said, flopping her head forward and slumping at the shoulders. 'I'm not so brave after all.'

'Hey, I was just joking. You're the bravest person in the world.' Wendy nuzzled her friend's neck. 'I want to get out of here too. Let's eat first though.'

The two ate a hurried meal and were soon bolting on the wide dusty road to Quilshire.

The forest around them gradually thinned out, leaving large meadows of purple and yellow flowers. Hundreds of winged insects flew, jumped, and buzzed through the gorgeous smelling blooms.

After a while the wind blew more fiercely, pushing the two from behind and spearing them forward. Trails of dust loomed in their wake, and flowers swayed frantically on the side of the road.

On and on Wendy galloped with Mollie holding tight. Each time Mollie thought the horse was about to rest, Wendy would double her efforts to keep up the pace. She kept it up for a very long time.

Eventually though, the horse had to slow down and catch her breath. She was covered in a foamy sweat and wobbled as she walked. Mollie could feel the horse's ribs expand and collapse under her.

'Stop here,' Mollie suggested, pointing to a shady tree.

They took a break and drank some water from a bladder.

'Good going, Wendy. I'd say we're halfway there already.'

'Hmmm. Haven't had a run like that for a long time. I'd better not waste too much energy though, in case we need to get out quick tonight.'

Some other travellers passed them as they rested, and by the time Mollie was ready to remount, the road was steadily filling with traffic.

'Bound for the fair?' some would call out to her.

She'd nod and wave back, not wanting to talk, only wanting to get Whitestaff's egg.

They pressed on, trotting quietly until the day was almost over. They knew they were close to their destination when the traffic grew so thick around them they couldn't overtake anyone.

It frustrated Wendy, who kept prodding for space hoping to move up in the growing convoy.

'Looks like we're all trying to get to the one place,' a lady beside her joked.

'You bet,' replied a man.

They all had to shout over the sound of horse hooves clopping and cart wheels bouncing.

'Where you from?' called someone to no one in particular.

'Mordburg,' said one.

'Erodull,' said another.

Mollie ignored all the chatter around her and stood a little in her saddle to see if Quilshire was within view.

It wasn't. But she kept checking anyway.

Half an hour of slow pacing went by, and at last small cottages began to dot the roadside. People stood in their doorways watching the procession while others left their homes and joined it, ready for a night at the fair.

The houses grew bigger and the spaces between them grew narrower. Streets began to peel off at the sides.

After a few minutes, they passed under a massive sign that read:

WELCOME TO QUILSHIRE
TIDIEST TOWN IN THE NORTH

There was no need to ask for directions, Mollie just followed the throng right into the heart of the showground.

The Quilshire showground was about three times the size of Gibbon's. The fires were just being lit as the sunlight began to fade, and once again Mollie was surrounded by the noises, sights and smells of the travelling fair.

'We're here,' she said as she patted her horse. 'You did very well, Wendy.'

'Thank you. But I think I'll leave this next bit to you. I'll wait over there by the entrance.'

Mollie got out of her saddle and walked around to face her horse.

'Don't be frightened, Wendy,' she said soothingly. 'He can't hurt you anymore.'

Wendy shook. 'I know. But I don't know what I'd do if I saw him again. Just get me when you've have the egg.'

And with that she turned and left Mollie on her own in the crowd.

'Don't go,' said Mollie. But her voice didn't make it to Wendy's ears.

Terry had been right about Quilshire. It was so different to Danmurk.

The people wore frills and coloured clothes. Some of the men wore *earrings*, and she saw ladies in *boots!* Boys had long hair and girls were in shorts. Mollie forced her mouth to shut.

She made her way timidly through the people, trying to avoid eye contact. The only light now came from the lanterns that hung from poles or from the bonfire in the middle of the showground. The firelight dazzled and half blinded her.

All the sideshows and stalls towered over the young Adkins, and the fairgoers pushed her, this way and that, not even apologising for stepping on her toes or bumping her roughly. The noise of people shouting and children squealing banged on her eardrums, and she plugged them with her fingers.

There was strange music coming from a band. The smell of alien food, damp hay and too many people stuffed up her nostrils. And after more shoving and pushing, she found herself lost, disorientated and slightly panicked.

Mollie spied a narrow alley and dashed in, breathing heavily and shaking. She sat against the wall of a dirty old caravan and hugged her knees. The din, the strangeness of her surroundings, and the sheer number of people overwhelmed her. She had never seen so many unfamiliar people in the one place!

Keep strong, she told herself. *Nothing here can hurt you. Don't forget why you came.*

Remembering her own powerful magic soothed her, and the thought of Whitestaff gave her courage.

She stood herself up to try again and drew a deep breath.

'Let's get that egg!'

But before she had even left the alley, she saw something else that made her stomach queasy with dread.

Audrey, the terrible woman from the hoop stall, scurried past clutching a large black bag.

Mollie was sure it was her. She recognised the mole on her forehead and her matted, straw-coloured hair. Mollie wanted to go after her, thinking she might lead her to Cudgel, but her feet were rooted to the spot.

Come on, she commanded herself. *They are just people. You could blast this whole fair apart with one Magic Missile.*

But the thought of going out again amongst all those strangers made her sick.

'I know what to do!'

Mollie calmed her mind. She felt for the moisture and air around her, used them to weave a spell, and took off after the large woman, completely and utterly invisible.

Chapter 46

The sun glinted and glimmered off the polished scales of hundreds of Palal. Snatches of conversations held in excited voices drifted down to Whitestaff, who stood at the mouth of Olfar's dugout, watching the Sorteyan sky fill with his fellow dragons.

They were all flying in the same direction, and they were all moving quickly in eager anticipation.

'Nervous?'

Olfar's voice made Whitestaff jump. He turned around to face his uncle.

'Don't do that. You made one of my hearts stop.'

Olfar chuckled. 'Thou are coiled tight today, Nephew.'

'With good reason, right enough. Today is the big day. The first day of the Tournament. Not only do I have to compete, I have to face the Council too. My stomach feels like it's full of lead and it is making noises I've never heard before.'

Olfar huffed his eyebrows out of his eyes and rubbed Whitestaff's head with his tail.

'Thou will do fine on both occasions. Thou are a Kai'dahl, and as long as thou do thy best, thou can be sure Frendrek will look down with pride.'

Whitestaff didn't respond. He turned back to watch the flying parade. Two shapes zoomed out of the long line and plunged downward towards the dugout. Whitestaff could tell by the extra long legs that the one on the left was Graggy, and the one on the right, with the graceful movements of a swan had to be Armay.

His two training partners swooped down to hover in front of him.

'You're still here?' Graggy asked incredulously. 'What in Lato—' he cut himself short when he realised Olfar was standing a little further in. 'I mean, what are you still doing here? Plan on making a big arrival, huh? Stealing my thunder?'

Whitestaff grinned. 'No, nothing like that. Just taking it all in.'

'Ohhh, he's nervous,' teased Armay. 'Don't worry we won't beat you too badly.' She landed herself next to the Kai'dahl and wrapped her tail around his.

'Yeah, we'll make it look close,' agreed Graggy. 'You know, so you don't feel so bad. Ha!'

'How very kind of you,' said Whitestaff giving Armay's tail a little squeeze. 'But I think you'll find me way too far in front for any of that.'

Graggy snorted and flew a loop. 'Whatever, big boy. Last one there is a Nazoor lover.' And with that, Graggy became a green streak, quickly growing smaller as he headed away.

'Hey, wait,' shouted Armay, trying to untangle her tail from Whitestaff's. 'We weren't ready!'

She shot off after him like a blue bolt. Whitestaff turned around to look at Olfar, who was smiling broadly behind his mug of baletea.

'Go on, my nephew,' he said with a nod. 'Don't let them beat thee already. I'll be there soon.'

The massive golden dragon dived out after his friends, the rush of wind in his ears, the uncomfortable stomach forgotten.

Other dragons cheered as he flew past, even a few Re'dahl. The festive mood was contagious, and by the time he'd caught up with Graggy and Armay, Whitestaff was positively brimming with energy.

They flew on, calling to each other, doing tricks, flying upside down and acting crazy, only stopping when they reached their destination: the Stadium.

'This is it,' said Graggy. 'Impressed?'

Whitestaff could only nod his head. The Stadium was one massive spire that had the top half lopped clean off, leaving behind a round expanse of thick, rich dirt. The centre had been slightly lowered to make a natural amphitheatre. Around the edge of the Stadium there were pillars of pure gold that stretched to dizzying heights overhead. Between the pillars were grandstands lined with cushions for the spectators to sit on and watch the events in comfort. The cushions were nearly all full, and unlike the Court, Palal sat wherever they wanted.

A special place was made for the king.

Cracone sat in a high gold throne talking to those around him. The ruby slab that covered his bad eye glinted in the sun. He too was in high spirits, and Whitestaff could not recall seeing the vicious Re'dahl smile so much. He even caught Whitestaff's eye and waved with his tail. Whitestaff gave a hesitant wave back and Cracone resumed his conversation with those around him, which included Susset.

'Shouldn't we get a seat or something?' Whitestaff asked.

'No need,' said Armay pointing, her claw to the middle of the Stadium.

Whitestaff looked down, and in the centre of the ground saw four podiums: one green, one red, one blue and one gold. A place for each Contender.

Nap was already standing on his podium, waving to his friends and winking occasionally at Luzahmin.

'Let's go,' said Graggy. He bounded off and left his friends behind. He entered the large circle and made his way to the green podium. On the way there he did some tricks, twisting his body and spiralling forward, flying backwards, diving to the earth and pulling up at the last second. The crowd loved it. When he finally got to his podium, he hovered above it for a few seconds, making sure everyone was watching him. He folded in his wings and dropped soundlessly onto all fours at the same time.

The crowd gave a cheer as soon as his paws touched. Graggy did a few flips for good measure loving the attention he was being shown.

'Here goes,' said Armay. She took a deep breath and made her way to the middle.

More cheers from the spectators. Armay looked embarrassed and took her place on the blue podium without fuss. She was the complete contrast to Graggy, who was still showing off.

Whitestaff looked on from a distance, unsure of what to do. He knew he needed to fly to the middle and take his place next to his friends.

But what if they all laugh at me, or what if they don't cheer? Whitestaff didn't know if he could face the rejection.

'Off thou go.'

The sudden voice startled him. He turned to see his uncle coming up from the rear.

'That's the second time this morning, Uncle.'

Olfar chuckled. 'Take thy place, Kai'dahl. Thou has nothing to fear from thy own kind. I thought thou would have learned that by now.'

'I'm still scared, that's all.'

'Hmmmm,' said Olfar, smoothing his grey beard. 'A good leader presses on, especially when he *is* scared. And he never lets anyone else guess that his insides are churning like mad.'

'I'm not a leader, Uncle. That's Cracone.'

Olfar paused. 'True, but the Palal will look to thee some day. Not just because of thy colour either. Now go. Do thy best and have fun. The rest will take care of itself, it always does.'

Whitestaff nodded and made his way to the centre of the Stadium. As he did so, the strangest thing happened: little by little, the crowd hushed. It was as if a magic spell was clamping each mouth shut one by one. Whitestaff looked over his tail to see his uncle shooing him on.

He turned his gaze to Armay for reassurance, confused at the growing silence. He slowed his pace, feeling each eye on him. About halfway, and every dragon was still.

What's happening? Why aren't they cheering? Have I done something wrong?

Armay seemed to shrug her shoulders, but he was still too far away to see her properly. He thought of turning back and hiding in his uncle's dugout, but he forced himself to fly forward.

The podium was a long way off.

The crowd was so silent now that he could hear the sound of the wind, the flapping of his own wings, the beating of his own hearts.

What's going on?

On he flew, half hiding his face, half scanning the crowd. Maybe there was something he was missing, some great danger he couldn't see. At last the gold podium was beneath him and he flopped on it with complete relief.

A second more of silence.

He looked to Armay, to Graggy.

They stared blankly at him, not daring to talk.

Whitestaff looked up at the crowd. They were expecting something, but he didn't know what. He felt he had to do something, anything. So he gave a deep bow. Just like the one he gave on his first day in the King's Court.

There was another beat of absolute quiet then the crowd cheered with a force that nearly blew the dragons off their podiums.

How they hollered. They whistled, they clapped, they called his name and chanted '*Kai'dahl*' at the top of their lungs. They threw things in the air, they flapped their wings, some did a dance in the sky.

And Whitestaff laughed with relief. Armay and Graggy joined in. Even Nap grinned.

'You did steal my thunder, by Latos!' Graggy said, clapping his friend on the back with his tail. 'Looks like we know who the most popular dragon is.'

They waved to the crowd for a while longer until Cracone banged his sceptre on the ground and demanded silence. Susset had made the air amplify his voice, so that the King's deep growl carried easily to every ear.

'Silence!' he commanded. 'Silence!'

He waited until everything was hushed.

He cleared his throat. 'I, Cracone, King of our noble race, welcome you. Welcome, Palal. Welcome, Susset. Welcome, chosen Contenders. We are here to witness the best of the Palal compete for the high honour of becoming Dragon Champion.'

He was interrupted here by more cheering. He let the crowd show its joy before continuing.

'Contenders will be tested on their cunning, their speed, their agility, their strength, and most important— their wits—to see who will face a deadly Nazoor in combat.'

He thrust his staff against the stone ground for effect. 'On the shoulders of our Champion rest the hopes of peace and the pride of our race. It is a title that carries prestige and great responsibility.

'To the Re'dahl, Nap, Son of my own. May the red blood give you passion and cunning.

'To the Bo'dahl, Armay. May the blue blood give you courage and confidence.

'To the Gra'dahl, Graggy. May the green blood give you wisdom and speed.

'To the Kai'dahl, Whitestaff—' here he paused, causing the crowd to lean in intently. He cleared his throat, biding his time. He took a sip of water from a massive cup, licked his lips and continued. 'May the gold blood give you hope and power.

'Let the Tournament begin!'

The crowd went wild.

And Whitestaff wasn't afraid anymore.

Chapter 47

Mollie had become Audrey's shadow. She darted here and there, through the thick carpet of people. She carefully dodged her way in and around the crowd, anxious not to bump into anyone or stand on any toes.

Mollie knew even though she was invisible, she could still be felt.

Audrey was quick on her feet for a big woman. She scurried like a fat rat, and Mollie had to half run to stay close.

They wove through the fair and towards the back exit of the showground. Audrey knew exactly where she was going. Her head was down and her pace never slackened.

Out of the showground she went, down an unlit street, sticking to the darkest patches and always looking over her shoulder. Mollie had to stop whenever she did lest her footsteps be heard. They went over a little bridge that had water gurgling beneath it, then followed a narrow track for a long time. Mollie could just hear the sounds of the fair in the distance.

Eventually they came to the back of a row of houses.

Audrey swished quietly over a grassy yard until she made it to a large white fence. It was here she stopped for a few moments to get her breath. She crouched down low and waited. Mollie stopped short and held her breath, hoping the invisibility spell was still working.

Audrey's head moved this way and that, looking, scanning, making sure no one was watching. When she was satisfied that she was alone, Audrey lifted up a couple of fence palings and disappeared.

Mollie saw it all and sneakily made her way over to the fence. She waited for a bit, unsure of whether to follow or to turn back. She thought she heard rustling on the other side of the fence, so she stood still for a while longer.

What if she's gone? What am I doing? She's not taking me to Whitestaff's egg. Wait here or turn back? Decisions, decisions.

Just as she was about to lift the palings and follow, Audrey scampered back through on her hands and knees, crawling madly as though a pack of dogs was behind her. In her mouth, carried between her teeth, was the black bag.

Mollie quickly stepped to the side. Her hand jumped to her mouth to stifle a scream as Audrey had nearly bowled her over in her mad dash.

The large lady picked herself up, checked again that nobody was in sight, and once more set off hurriedly, this time back in the direction from which they came.

Mollie followed, trembling from her near miss and feeling the sudden urge to go to the toilet.

Audrey took the black sack from her jaws and carried it under her arm, still marching at a cracking pace. Mollie noticed Audrey clinked now when she walked.

What is in that bag?

Back to the fair they dashed, through the grass, over the bridge, down the dusty street. But Audrey was still careful. Whenever the moon reappeared from behind the clouds, she would leap for the nearest shadow and wait there until it was dark enough to continue.

Audrey rejoined the revellers at the Quilshire showground, tucking the bag further under her arm as she did so. She led Mollie round a few stalls, down a side alley or two, past a hall where a band was playing pipes. She finally stopped in front of a cabin on wheels.

Mollie recognised it immediately: Cudgel's van.

Audrey climbed the steps, knocked three times and waited nervously.

Mollie crept in closer.

A lock clicked from behind the door. It swung open and Audrey dashed in, leaving Mollie alone outside.

She could hear muffled voices from within, so she tiptoed up to the window shutters and peered through a gap in the slats.

She could see Cudgel's thick neck as he was sitting with his back to her. She could also see the top half of Audrey. She could hear them as though she were in the room. Nevertheless, the two spoke in hushed tones.

'Were yer followed?' Cudgel asked. His voice made Mollie shiver.

'Course not, you tooker! I wouldn't be here if I was followed, would I? What kind of question is that?'

'Sorry sweet-pie, sorry,' he said putting his hand up. 'Twas daft to ask yer. Jus' can't be too careful. I think folks is gettin' suspicious of us an all.'

'They ain't, you fool,' said Audrey, raising her voice a little. 'We been over this. We been careful. Don't get yellow!'

'Sorry, angel face. You know I jus' don't want ter get caught. Not when we've got so much.'

Audrey rolled her eyes and muttered something that Mollie didn't catch.

'I got something to shut you up anyway.' And suddenly Audrey grew quiet; a glaze came over her eyes. 'Look at this.' Her voice was sweet and velvety. She smiled lovingly at her husband and then at the open sack.

'Ohhh,' said Cudgel when he saw what was in the bag. He gave her a big grin in return. 'That'll do us nice. Fetch a pretty bit o' gold, that. Yer did good, dearest, real good.'

Audrey snapped the bag shut. 'Course I did, fool.' Her smile left as quickly as it came. 'I always do, don't I? Every town we go to I do good. While them tookers are busy throwing hoops and eating spun sugar and looking at fancy clothes, I'm taking what is in their homes. Serves them right. Fools.'

'Yes, dear. Yer do a great job,' said Cudgel and he took the bag from her. 'I'll put it with the rest.'

What Mollie saw next made her jaw drop.

Cudgel took a large key from out of his pocket and opened the door to the other half of the van. Through that door Mollie could see enough treasure to sink a small boat. Gold and silver jewellery spilled out of the doorway. There were coins of different shapes and sizes, pitchers of pewter, cups with precious stones along the rims, decorative candleholders, paintings, trophies, pocket-watches of fine quality and much, much more. Mollie only got a quick look, but she was staggered by the value of what her eyes had caught.

How many homes have they robbed? she wondered. *It looks like they raided a castle vault.*

Cudgel shut the door and locked it, then sat down with his back to Mollie again. 'I suppose we'd better do the egg,' he said.

Mollie ears pricked up.

'I wish we didn't have to do that stupid show,' Audrey huffed.

'Me too, my honeybee, me too. But we 'ave to keep it up for appearances. It's our, cover ain't it? If we didn't do a show, everyone would wonder where we got our money from.'

He stuck a stubby finger in his ear and pulled out something green, inspected it for a second, then stuck it in his mouth.

'I know,' said Audrey. 'I just hate working when we don't have to.'

She walked over to the large chest on the floor and opened it. Mollie gasped when she saw Whitestaff's egg inside.

It was just as she remembered. It was open in a clamshell way, gold like the sun on the outside and dotted with specks as green as emeralds. The portal still shimmered inside. The doorway to Sorteya.

Mollie's eyes narrowed on something.

That's Whitestaff's egg all right, Mollie thought to herself worriedly. *But what is that awful crack?*

Chapter 48

Susset was floating in front of Graggy, Whitestaff, Armay and Nap. She wore a robe of the deepest plum colour with silver dragons embroidered in the hem and cuffs. A hood hid her thick black hair, but she still managed to look breathtaking.

She had made her own voice louder so all in the Stadium could hear.

Cracone let himself relax back in his throne, an unnerving smile on his face. Re'dahls gathered around him and whispered excitedly as he scratched the heavy scar on his chest.

'Let me explain the rules of the Tournament,' Susset said, her voice as clear as a bell.

'There are three events to test you. Placing first in these challenges will net you three points. Coming second will earn you two, coming third will raise your score by one. Lucky last gets zero points.'

Nap leaned closer to Whitestaff. 'No points for you then.' He gave a nasty laugh and prodded the Kai'dahl with the barb on his tail.

Whitestaff ignored the insult and concentrated on Susset. He was new to all this and didn't want to miss any information he might need.

'Your first competition is a simple one. You will fly through these.' Susset waved a hand to her left and made large, shimmering rings appear in the sky. Each ring was big enough for a dragon to go through. There were twenty in total and they were located in different places around the Stadium. Some were up high; some nearly touched the

Stadium floor. Some were close to the grandstands and one was straight up, nearly out of sight. Everyone was craning their necks or looking from side to side, trying to take them all in.

'As you fly through a ring it will disappear. I will time your flight.' With this the sorceress conjured a massive hourglass and made it float above her head. It was filled with clear grains the size of giant acorns.

'The grains will stop falling as soon as all the rings are gone. We will weigh the grains that have fallen to the bottom of the timer. The dragon with the least weight will be the winner.'

Right, thought Whitestaff. *Whoever takes the longest will have the most grains to weigh. So it's just a test of speed. Fastest through the rings wins!*

'Whitestaff, you will be the first.'

The onlookers clapped and whistled, but the golden dragon barely heard them.

Armay and Graggy wished him luck. He gave them a wan smile in return.

'On my mark,' bellowed Cracone from his throne.

Latos! It's all happening so quickly.

Indeed it was. Cracone had banged his rod and shouted "GO" but Whitestaff was still trying to ready himself.

'GO!' yelled Graggy pointing to the rings.

The first clear ball had hit the bottom of the timer.

Whitestaff could hear Nap chortling.

'FLY!' hollered Armay.

Whitestaff shook his head, scrabbled and slipped on his podium in his haste to get airborne, then flew straight up to the ring at the top. It was the furthest away, so it gave him time to think.

Calm down, he told himself as his wings beat madly. *Just fly your fastest and hope for the best.*

He neared the first ring and tucked in his wings as he flew through. He heard a reverberating *pop* as the circle of light disappeared.

He looked down and could see the other rings quite easily. He chose the nearest one and flew through it.

Pop!

From the corner of his eye he picked out another ring. Pop. Past the King's throne he zipped, all heads following him as though he had them attached to strings.

Pop, through another circle.

Then more. *Pop, pop, pop.*

This was easily the fastest he had ever flown. His lungs ached for air and his giant muscles burned, but he surged faster and faster still. Pop, pop.

More rings. Faster and faster.

Pop.

Pop.

He was pleased with his progress, until about three-quarters of the way through when he realised his mistake. He had chosen a line of rings that took him away from the others. That meant he had to double back to get the last few. Without pausing for thought he wheeled himself around to the remaining rings, cursing himself for the lost time.

The journey back across the Stadium felt like forever. In his mind's eye he could see the bottom of the timer filling up.

He tried to pick up speed but he couldn't make his wings flap any faster. He was running out of energy and desperately needed to stop for breath.

I need more pace.

Pop.

Come on.

He strained his powerful muscles.

Pop.

Nearly there.

Pop, pop.

Faster, he told himself. But he had nothing left to give.

Reaching the last ring took a lifetime. Whitestaff had slowed right down as his wings beat out a jerky rhythm.

Closer and closer now, the crowd voicing their support.

Pop.

And it was all over.

The spectators gave him a rousing reception as he flew limply back to his podium, but he knew he had blown it.

It wasn't just a test of speed, he thought angrily. *It was a test of strategy too. I needed to think out the quickest path, not just madly dash for the closest ring.*

He flopped lifelessly down and panted his tongue out and his eyes closed. Armay and Graggy patted him with their tails and said nice things. But the encouragement was lost on him. All he heard was Nap's snorting laugh and his own criticisms in his head.

Stupid! Stupid! Stupid!

Chapter 49

Not only did Whitestaff's egg have a portal to the dragon planet in it, it was also given a very special protective spell by Merlin. He coated the egg with magic so it would survive the journey from Sorteya to Earth and be safe if it landed on hard sharp rocks, fell into a volcano, got crushed under a landslide, or worse.

And worse was happening right in front of Mollie's eyes.

'Step right up an smash the Egg,' Cudgel called as people went by. 'Fifty gold pieces to him what can smash the Egg O' Wonder. Jus' one gold coin per hit.'

Of course, many could not resist the chance to take the bet. The egg was large but it looked no match for the mallet Cudgel was holding.

One dark-skinned man gave over his gold and took hold of the wooden mallet. His arms alone were the size of Mollie's waist, and he used them both to lift the hammer. The man strained with his back, held the blunt weapon over his head then brought it crashing down on the egg with all his might.

SMACK!

The man yelped in pain as heavy vibrations were sent up his wrists. The egg hadn't budged at all, but the crack in Merlin's spell widened.

Cudgel blasted a laugh and clapped a hand on the man's shoulder.

'Another go?'

The stranger just gave him a foul look and walked away, massaging his forearms and swearing.

Cudgel put the money in his pocket and called for further business.

Mollie looked more closely at the egg. It was resting on a bed of straw. Her eyes could see the spell Merlin had put there, the very magic that made the egg so strong. It was a thin layer of earth and fire elements, so fine she could hardly detect it.

Well I didn't see it the first time, she thought. *Though I was a bit busy to take a proper look.*

The spell was there, yes, but it was being broken with each stroke of the mallet. Mollie guessed she was the only one who could see it. She doubted it would last another night of constant pounding, and when the magic armour broke, the egg would be as fragile as any other egg on Earth.

I have to do something fast. I just don't know what. She scratched her head and jiggled her foot. *I can't just walk up and take it otherwise the whole place would go berserk. I'm still invisible and they'd think a ghost was stealing it. I need a distraction.*

Mollie turned and ran in the direction of Wendy. Maybe the horse could do something—if she could be coaxed.

Chapter 50

Whitestaff was so disappointed with his own time-trial he could barely concentrate on Armay's. He watched her anyway, trying to show her the support she had shown for him.

'Nice and smooth. Ha,' said Graggy as the blue Palal weaved through the light-circles. 'See how she has learned from your flight?'

'My failure, you mean?'

Graggy gave him a pained smile.

'Well, I won't sugarcoat it, friend. You'll come last in this one.'

'Thanks,' said Whitestaff, rolling his eyes.

'Let me finish, O Golden One. You'll come last, BUT, speed isn't your thing. Speed is my specialty.' He put his claws to his chest and raised his head proudly. 'Leave those rings to *me*. You just worry about strength events. You'll win those paws down.'

Whitestaff looked back to see Armay soaring through the sky. She was nearly finished, and he could see by the grains in the timer that she'd easily beaten him.

'But this isn't just speed, Graggy, this is brains too.'

'Huh?'

Whitestaff couldn't be heard over the other dragons. Armay had just finished and they were calling out and whistling.

'Good job,' Graggy said as she flew back to the centre.

'Better than my time, right enough,' said Whitestaff, unable to keep the bitterness out of his voice.

'Don't be like that,' Armay replied, a little out of breath. 'We won't know who does best until they weigh the grains. Besides, I'd be happy for you if you won.'

'Sorry,' Whitestaff said softly. 'You're right. I just wanted to do better.'

'Last is good for you,' Nap butted in. 'Get used to it.'

The other dragons ignored him.

Susset reset the rings with a dramatic wave of her arm and Cracone counted Nap in for his flight.

The Re'dahl shot off like a rocket, going straight up for the top ring like Whitestaff and Armay had done. Cracone struck his rod in excitement, urging his son forward, his still amplified voice echoing in everyone's head.

'GO SON! SHOW THEM HOW WE FLY!' Cracone laughed and blasted and bellowed and howled. He was loud, loud, LOUD!

Whitestaff folded his ears down, trying to block it out a bit. The two next to him were doing the same.

'He's certainly worked on his speed,' shouted Graggy to Whitestaff.

'What?'

'He's gotten faster. Look!' Graggy pointed.

Whitestaff could see at once it was true. Nap must have trained hard to reach the speed at which he was travelling. The rings popped so fast around them it sounded like a chain of fireworks going off.

'He's gotten quicker,' agreed Whitestaff, 'but not smarter.'

'What do you mean?' asked the Gra'dahl, raising his voice above the din.

Whitestaff gave a wink. 'Think about it. We all went for the ring that was furthest away.'

'Hmmm, and?'

'Well, you're the smart one,' Whitestaff shouted back. 'You tell me if that's a good move or not.'

Graggy chewed his claws in thought, repeating the question to himself.

Slowly his eyes widened.

'If you save the furthest ring until last, then you don't have to double back!' He did a small jump and clapped his paws.

'What do you mean?' asked Armay.

'Well,' said Graggy excitedly, 'if you fly all the way to the top first, then you have to fly all the way back down to get the other rings. If you leave the top one for last, it's a one way trip. It should shave seconds off my time!'

'What?'

But Graggy didn't hear her either. He didn't even bother to watch Nap as he came back to the podium, grinning as the whole Stadium called his name.

'Guess they know flying when they see it,' he said to the others with a smirk. 'Beat that, *Gra'dahl.*'

Graggy didn't respond. His eyes were glowing, his muscles twitching. He was crouched low and looking from ring to ring, planning his route, doing some quick maths in his head.

Whitestaff looked over and saw Graggy muttering to himself. He caught snippets, something about 'velocity' and 'virtual acceleration'. Whitestaff didn't understand a word.

'Next contender, Graggy for the Gra'dahl,' Susset announced as she floated in front of him.

She tried to make eye contact with Graggy, but his head was moving wildly. She wasn't even sure he heard her or the audience cheering.

'On my mark,' barked Cracone.

Graggy was still down low, eyes flitting from ring to ring, mouth moving as he thought aloud.

He's not even listening! Whitestaff thought.

'Graggy?' said Armay, for she too was worried he was going to miss his start.

'If I take the… then come back avoiding the major currents of the west…' Graggy mumbled.

Cracone lifted the Royal Rod.

Graggy still gave no sign he was ready.

Nap blew from his nose and shook his head in disgust. 'Typical Gra'dahl.'

Cracone smacked the rod down hard.

'GO!'

Chapter 51

Mollie made her way to where she thought Wendy should be. She was running hard and still invisible, when suddenly she stopped with a skid.

Was that who I thought it was?

She retraced her steps a little way, looked down a poorly lit alley, and saw a heavyset figure with a big black beard.

Bob!

Bob, or Blackbeard, was surrounded by a knot of people. Some were his crew (Mollie recognised a few faces from the Barren Arms) and some were obviously not. The clothes they wore were too fine for a start, and they kept looking around suspiciously, as though they were mice about to steal a cat's dinner.

They were huddled around Bob and were talking in low voices. Mollie crept closer to them to eavesdrop.

'What I'm saying,' said one of the nervous men, 'is that we are totally outnumbered.'

Bob pursed his lips and shook his head. 'What I'm saying, *mate*, is that the rest of these fair folk, these show people,' he gestured around him, 'don't even know what's going on. My bet is it's only a couple of them.'

'What makes you so sure?'

Bob was about to answer when he looked up and straight at Mollie. He stared at her hard, sniffing as he did so.

Mollie froze instantly.

He can't see you, you're invisible, she told herself. *Plus he seemed nice last time you met him.*

But she stood absolutely still nevertheless. Barely daring to breathe.

Blackbeard made a funny little shape with his hands. His crew nodded and he continued.

'What makes me sure is that carnival folk are mostly decent. If they got a reputation as being untrustworthy, no town would have them, would they?'

One of his crew said something, but too softly for Mollie to hear.

Blackbeard responded. Mollie could see his lips move, but now all of the conversation was held in whispers.

So she crept closer and waited. Nobody looked up—they were too intent on their discussion. She took a few more baby steps in. Suddenly the group started to break away, moving off in all directions and not looking back.

What's going on? Mollie wondered as she tried to watch everyone at once.

Where are they all going?

The worried men blended in to the fair so quickly Mollie had lost sight of them within ten paces.

Now Blackbeard and his crew were all that was left.

And they moved so fast! As quickly as she could draw a breath to yell, they had bounded over to where she stood and surrounded her, knives out and pointed at her neck.

Blackbeard seized her wrists with his tattooed hands, his grip like iron chains.

The shock of it all made Mollie Adkins lose her spell. The air and moisture dropped off her like a shed skin, leaving the young woman perfectly visible and scared.

If Blackbeard recognised her at all he didn't show it. His face was twisted with outrage and his voice dangerously soft.

'What have we here then, boys? A stowaway listening to our private dialogue? How long have you been here you little devil?'

Mollie gave a whimper.

'That's the witch from Gibbon, Captain. The one Jake warned us about.'

'I can see that, you fool.' But he did not relax his grip. 'I don't like sneaks, *girl*. I don't like them one bit.' He leant in close to her face.

She tried to conjure a magic missile, but her mind wouldn't relax enough. She was far too panicked.

'P-p-please,' stammered Mollie. 'You're hurting me.'

But Bob didn't move his eyes boring into hers.

'Hmmm,' he said. 'I don't know what to make of this. I doubt you're the one we're after, but you *were* being sneaky. I have a lot to lose here.'

'She was being sneaky, Captain,' said a crew member. 'An' you don't like sneaks!'

'I know that, you fool,' Blackbeard said out the side of his mouth. He stared intently into Mollie's eyes and saw she was scared and in shock. He eased his grip, and when she didn't try to run, he let go of her completely.

Tears gushed down Mollie's cheeks as she began to cry uncontrollably.

This was bad news because they were attracting looks from people passing by.

The crew looked to their captain, who gestured for them to put their knives away quickly.

'There, there,' he said, returning his attention to Mollie. He patted her gingerly on the shoulder. 'Don't cry. We didn't mean to upset you. I do think you owe us an explanation though.' He turned to his mates for support. They shrugged their shoulders and looked at their shoes, suddenly ashamed of themselves.

'See here,' Blackbeard persisted as Mollie's crying got louder. 'We didn't know it was you. I could see your shadow. I could smell your perfume and I heard your footsteps and I thought the thief was on to us. I'm really sorry, but you shouldn't be sneaky.'

'Captain don't like sneaks, you see?' someone offered apologetically.

Blackbeard shuffled closer and put his arms around the sorceress. She let him. She cried into his thick coat until her shivers had subsided.

'I'm sorry, Bob,' she blubbered. 'I only went invisible because I don't like all these people. I haven't seen this many people in the one place, and I need to get the egg, and Audrey and Cudgel are breaking it—and—and…'

'There, there,' said Blackbeard again, not following a word she was saying. 'Come with us and well get you a nice cup of tea and a biscuit.'

'But Captain, all our biscuits got weevils in 'em.'

'I know that, you fool. You bunch really aren't helping me much tonight, you know.'

The big man sighed, put his hand on Mollie's elbow, and guided her back to his camp.

Chapter 52

'GO, GO, GO!' shouted Whitestaff and Armay in unison. They needn't have bothered, for Graggy had taken off like an arrow from a bow as soon as Cracone had banged the sceptre.

He aimed at the ring nearest to the King, popped through it then made a sharp arc to another ring between two pillars. The atmosphere buzzed as his wings cut through the air. Graggy had become a green spear, thrusting through each circle of light so fast most of the dragons had trouble just keeping their eyes on him. They were all gobsmacked, especially Nap.

'Latos!' he breathed. 'And I thought I was fast.'

Round the outside of the Stadium he tore, whipping up a gale as he did so. He flew so quickly past Olfar that the old dragon's eyebrows blew into his eyes, making him blind for moment.

All of the Palal were on their feet, but the loudest acclamation came from the Gra'dahl. Nobody had ever seen flying like this!

Pop-a-pop-a-pop went the rings. Plunk … plunk … plunk, went the timer.

Soon the only ring left was the highest one. Graggy heaved his body toward it like a boulder out of a catapult. Up he went, faster and faster.

Pop. He exploded through it and gave a whoop of glee.

He opened his wings wide to slow down and lose momentum. When at last he stopped, he turned around and headed for his podium, amid a standing ovation.

'Well, we know who came first,' said Whitestaff loud enough for Nap to hear.

'Yes, and it wasn't a Re'dahl,' agreed Armay with a grin.

'Latos,' said Nap again.

Whitestaff and Armay rubbed Graggy on the head with their tails and told him how great he was to watch.

Graggy gave a wheezy laugh as he tried to catch his breath. 'Thanks, you two,' he said, 'Told you to… *puff*… leave those… *puff*… rings to me.' He then collapsed onto the platform and rolled on his back, chest heaving as he panted heavily.

'Well,' said Susset to the Stadium, 'that was some amazing flying from our Contenders. But who was the quickest? We will now weigh the grains and find out.'

She summoned a monstrous set of scales with four dishes on it. On each plate she placed a pyramid of grains. 'These are what had fallen into the bottom of the timer in each race,' she explained.

'How do we know whose is whose? They're all clear?' asked Whitestaff.

'Just watch,' said Graggy, still short of breath.

The plate on the left sank down the furthest and glowed bright yellow.

'In last place,' Susset said, 'is Whitestaff for the Kai'dahl.'

'I knew it,' said Whitestaff angrily.

'So did I,' taunted Nap.

The next plate of grain radiated a blue tinge.

'In third place, Armay for the Bo'dahl.'

Armay nodded, as though she expected the result.

'In second place,' continued the sorceress, 'is…'

All eyes watch the plate carefully. It glowed … red!

A big cheer from the Gra'dahl came forth, for they had figured if Nap had come second, then Graggy had to be first as he was the only dragon left. There were some groans from the reds.

No one bothered to listen as Susset announced Graggy as the winner, as they were too busy celebrating or sulking.

'Well done, my friend,' said Whitestaff, hugging Graggy's neck with his tail.

'Quite a brilliant flight.'

The three partners turned to face Nap, surprised to hear him give a compliment.

They saw Luzahmin had already dashed from her seat to hang off Nap's shoulder.

'Don't speak to them, darling,' she cooed in his ear. 'We don't know if Susset fixed the timer against you.'

'How dare you suggest that!' said Armay in disgust.

Luzahmin turned her nose up and whispered something into Nap's ear. Whatever it was made him smile evilly.

'As I said,' he continued, 'that was great flying Graggy. Pity for you the speed challenge is over. And to you, *Kai'dahl*, you may have had the crowd on your side at the start, but I knew when they saw how pathetic you really are, they'd change their minds about your colour.'

He said no more because other dragons had left their cushions and were flying over to pass on their congratulations.

Soon the four were drowning in well-wishers.

Cracone broke it up with his bellowing voice.

'All right,' he boomed. 'So ends our first trial. Back to your places, you lot, hurry up, that's the way. The sooner you sit back down, the sooner we can get this over with and have our Council Meeting. Oh, hurry up, Clarence. You too, who is that? Ugos, move it would you. Great, that's the way. All ready? Yes? Oh, Latos! Would you sit back down!'

He cleared his voice and waited for quiet, though with his voice made so loud he didn't really need a captive audience.

'Congratulations to those in the top *three*,' here he looked at Whitestaff and flashed his teeth.

Blood rushed to Whitestaff's face and fire burned in his chest.

'My son put in a terrific effort that I'm sure impressed you. It was Graggy, however, who we will hear about tonight over dinner and probably for many dinners to come. The boy had extra wings on his *feet*, I'm sure of it.'

Everybody laughed at his joke.

'So without further ado, can Susset please show us the Points Board.'

Susset nodded her head and spread her arms wide. The sky shimmered above her and the Points Board was displayed. It was simply a huge tally box, the letters and numbers were taller than trees so all could see it easily. It read:

Contender	Event 1	Total
Graggy 1st	3	3
Nap 2nd	2	2
Armay 3rd	1	1
Whitestaff 4th	0	0

Whitestaff stared at the big zero next to his name, crushed to see he was coming last.

Not for long, he thought, gritting his teeth in determination. *Not for long.*

Chapter 53

Mollie sat on the edge of a campfire, trying to ward off the chill in the night air.

She was composed again, wide awake, and more like her normal self. She had become used to the people around her and was over her initial fright at being seized at knifepoint by Blackbeard and his crew.

Blackbeard was more relaxed too. He was reclining against a hay bale, listening intently to Mollie's chatter as were his shipmates. She had been telling them everything she had found out about Audrey and Cudgel.

'And so,' she said matter-of-factly, 'it must be those two you are looking for.'

'She has a point, Captain. We are looking for sneaky thieves, and this here lass has found sneaky thieves, aye.'

The crewmember who spoke was named Rio. He had sandy blond hair that covered his ears and most of his face. Rio had long ago given up brushing his locks out of his eyes, so he kind of looked like a sheep dog.

'True, mate, true,' agreed Blackbeard, closing his lids and thinking. 'Tell me, Mollie, do you think these two have done this sort of thing before? The thief I'm looking for must be a bit of an expert. Made off with most of my booty, he did. In fact, he made off with lots of people's things.'

'Aye,' Rio added. 'This thief is like a ghost. The only thing that sort of gives him away is he always strikes wherever the fair is. It was Captain here who put it together, weren't it boys.'

The rest of the crew hoyed in agreement.

''Tweren't nothing,' said Blackbeard with a self-satisfied smile and a shrug. 'I just asked around a bit and I found other folk what had been ripped off. Put it together like a puzzle. That's who you saw us talking to. I convinced a lot of them to come here and help me track the dirty burglar down.'

Mollie could tell he was very pleased with himself.

'I think you are absolutely right, Bob. Audrey and Cudgel have enough in their van to feed an army. Plus I heard her boasting about it. She said when most of the town is at the fair, she goes and robs them. They still work to mask what they are really doing.'

Blackbeard gave a wicked chuckle.

'Well, my lads. Looks like we've finally found them.' He rubbed his hands together and the fire reflected and danced in his eyes. 'Let's get our loot back.'

His crew gave a hoy and laughed too. But it wasn't the kind of laugh people make when they are happy. It was the kind of laugh that put a chill back into Mollie's bones and made her a little bit sorry for Cudgel and Audrey.

Chapter 54

Much of the Palal's exuberance had faded by the time they took their seats in the King's Court. The greens, however, were more talkative than usual, and the reds more resigned.

When Cracone demanded silence in his booming threatening bellow, the mood became almost solemn.

The King's previous good humour had left him and he opened the meeting with thick sarcasm. 'We are here because our esteemed Kai'dahl couldn't make up his mind last time. So in the interest of saving daylight, I'll cut the usual ceremony.'

There were nods from the other dragons, and Whitestaff couldn't help but feel embarrassed.

'Whitestaff, on the question of "Do we move closer to the Dire?" what have you decided?'

Whitestaff stood up higher on his legs and tried to look his fellow dragons in the eyes as he spoke.

'I thank you for permitting me the time to make an informed decision, Your Majesty. I have flown out to the area in question and have found it is all that you say.'

Cracone nodded. 'So then you are in favour of the move? Great, let's begin—'

'Actually, Cracone,' Whitestaff interrupted. 'I am not in favour of the move at all. To start a war with the Nazoor would cost many lives and—'

This time the King broke in. 'You impertinent, insolent dragon.' He jumped to his feet in anger. 'You said you would vote with us if the land was good. How dare you get us all back here for this nonsense!'

Other dragons murmured in agreement.

Don't lose your head here, Whitestaff told himself. *You knew this would happen. Just stick to the plan.*

'If you'll allow me to, my King, I have a reason and an alternative.' He tried to make his voice strong. 'You see, my fellow Council, the blue dragons complained of dwindling food supplies. But why not harvest the fruit from the Dire spires? Surely taking food from the area isn't banned, is it?'

Some of the talking stopped. His question gave them pause for thought.

'Well, err, no,' said Cracone. 'But that is only half of the solution. We need the extra space.'

'Yes, we do,' shouted someone from the Bo'dahl section.

'I have thought of that too. There are more spires further to the south, and some other spires here that could handle another dugout or two.'

Cracone remained silent, his jaw set hard. Whitestaff could see he was fuming.

Finally he said, 'You're just looking for excuses not to go to war. You are a coward.'

Everyone in the Court drew a collective breath. That was the second time the King had insulted him so publicly. Now all eyes watched Whitestaff to see how he would react.

In fact, the name-calling didn't affect Whitestaff in the slightest. He had been called far worse things before on Earth, and in this case, it worked to his advantage.

'Well, Majesty, you are right and wrong. Right about me not wanting to go to war. You see, I am new to this planet, new to my fellow dragons. Already I have come to appreciate what a brave, noble, proud race I belong to. Would I want to see them all wiped out? No. I would not want to see one life lost unnecessarily.'

Some of the Palal smiled, touched by his speech. He saw he was winning them over, so he pressed on.

'I would much rather leave killing as a last resort. Why not try other methods first and save the bloodshed? You say we need more space! That's because there are more of us now. We owe that to peace. I say preserve the peace for as long as possible. Harvest the food from the Dire and use more of the land we already own. Problems solved. No one dies.'

A few of the Gra'dahl clapped. Some blues nodded.

Whitestaff took a chance and continued speaking. 'On the second point though, Cracone, you are dead wrong. If war were pushed upon us then I would fight tooth and claw for you, for my friends and for the Palal. I never have been a coward, *King*, and I never will be.'

'Good boy!' shouted Olfar from his side. His voice rang out in the hollow chamber. Now everyone looked at *him!* Olfar's cheeks coloured and he dropped his eyes to the ground.

'Well then,' said Cracone curtly. 'I see no further use for us all being here and listening to this waffle. I hereby close the meeting.' He rapped his staff three times quickly and took off, followed by Nap and some other Re'dahl.

Most Palal stayed back a little while and talked.

The speaker for the Bo'dahl Council stood and flew over to him. 'The blues have considered your vote, Whitestaff. Your insight is impressive. It was a good decision.'

Armay joined him, as did Olfar and Graggy.

'Nice speech,' Armay said with a smile.

'Yes, my boy. Well put,' agreed Olfar. 'Thou have shown the Council the leadership it deserves. By my calculations, if thou challenged Cracone for the throne, he would be heavily outvoted.'

'Not that stuff again, Uncle.'

'I'm just saying. The way thou turned the tide in your favour, only a born leader could do that.'

Whitestaff ignored him and turned to Graggy.

'Come on,' said the younger Green. 'Let's forget all this stuff and celebrate my victory through the rings. Balebeer at my dugout!'

'Finally,' said Whitestaff with a broad grin. 'Someone is speaking sense.'

Chapter 55

Wendy stood with some other horses and munched on long grass.

'Oh, I do hope they skip the fireworks this year,' one lanky beast said. 'They give me such a fright. What about you?'

Wendy didn't answer. She chewed a mouthful of grass and looked thoughtfully at the stars above.

'What should I do now?' Wendy wondered aloud.

'Do about what?' asked the other horse. 'The fireworks? Well, I just close my eyes and neigh a lot, but that doesn't seem to help much.'

'Hmmm?' said Wendy, looking over to him. 'Ooh, sorry. I didn't know I was actually saying that. I just meant to think it.'

'Oh,' said the other horse. 'Something on your mind?'

Wendy gave a deep groan. 'Well, yes actually. I have a friend in there who wants me to do something that would distress me greatly. I'm supposed to be her horse, but I carried her all the way here, you think that would be enough, right?'

'Of course,' he agreed. 'Some humans can be terrible masters. They never think of us noble beasts. My master for instance hasn't fed me properly in over a year. Look, you can see my ribs!'

Wendy looked him up and down. He *was* in poor condition.

'Don't get me wrong. Mollie feeds me well enough.'

'Ahhh, but she rides you till exhaustion?'

'No. She's never done that,' Wendy admitted.

'Right,' said the skinny stallion. 'Then she neglects you? Doesn't give you any attention? Bought you at a low price and wants you just for profit?'

Wendy blew through her nostrils.

'No, nothing like that. She actually rescued me from this horrible man who kept me in a cage.'

The other horse neighed savagely. 'What! You mean to tell me you have a perfectly good owner who cares for you and *saved you*, and you're out here when she needs your help? Is that right?'

'W-w-well, yes… I suppose… it is true,' Wendy stammered.

'What sort of horse are you? Our kind would never think to desert a friend like that. There's plenty that would trade places in a second.'

Wendy looked taken aback.

'I mean, here I am with barely a morsel of food all week! I'll go in and help her! Maybe she'll take me in. What's she look like?'

But the words of the strange horse had hit home and Wendy trotted off in the other direction, scarcely holding back tears of shame.

He's right, she thought. *I am very lucky to have her for a friend. Twice she's saved me and I turn my back on her the second she wants real help. Sorry Mollie.* She picked up her pace and headed into the showground. *I'm coming! I'm coming!*

Chapter 56

Whitestaff, Armay and Graggy were about to get the fun started when they heard a dragon land heavily behind them. They turned to see a troubled looking Olfar.

'Sorry to interrupt thy merriment, but if thou could save the drinks for later and sit down in front of me, that would be good. I have something vitally important to tell thee about tomorrow's Tournament events.'

Graggy was about to protest, but Olfar looked so sombre that he just shrugged instead and put down his frothy glass of balebeer.

'I apologise again. I know thou three just want to relax. Perhaps thou can. Later.'

'What is it, Uncle?' asked Whitestaff in concern. 'You don't look so good. You look so serious and for you, well, that's saying something!'

Olfar lowered his head and beckoned them to sit in front of him.

'I'm not entirely sure how to put this, but I think it's fair thou should know about one event in particular that's coming up tomorrow.'

Graggy clicked his tongue with disapproval. 'We're not supposed to know, Olfar.'

The older dragon motioned for him to be quiet.

'I know, I know. I'm on the rules committee, remember? But Nap knows. In fact, it was probably Nap's idea. So it's reasonable to share this secret.'

Now that he had the attention of the younger dragons, Olfar tugged his beard and went on. 'The first challenge tomorrow is a game of chicken, and it's one

Whitestaff will win. First place is awarded for the dragon who gets closest to the ground.'

Whitestaff screwed up his face. 'I don't get it. Explain, Uncle.'

Olfar drew a breath. 'The Contenders will all dive below the cloud cover, straight at the dirt. Whoever pulls up last wins.'

Whitestaff smiled. 'But that's easy, Uncle. I've got that one in the bag. I'm not afraid of touching the ground at all. Pretty stupid to come up with a challenge like that. Right guys?'

Armay and Graggy looked at each other.

'Err, it's quite clever actually, in a sadistic sort of way.'

'What do you mean, Graggy?' the golden dragon asked.

'What he means,' answered Olfar, 'is Nap designed this challenge to put a cloud over thy win. See, if thou do go closer to the ground, thou would gain the points in a way that would make thee very unpopular.'

Whitestaff threw his front legs in the air. 'Again with this nonsense. It's just the ground for the love of...' He shook his head in disbelief.

'If you do get the closest to the ground,' Armay added, 'and you do win the Tournament, all anyone will remember is that you won it in a tainted way.'

'Not you too,' Whitestaff glared at her. 'I thought we were past all that rubbish.'

'Let me explain,' the Bo'dahl pleaded.

'Explain what? That you are just as stubborn as the rest of them? That you think I'm unclean?'

'No, it's not that.'

Whitestaff ignored her.

'I thought you were different, Armay. I really did.'

'Please, listen! Nap just wants to lower you in the eyes of all the other Palal. It must be what he was so happy about today. Winning this challenge will net you points but no one will want to talk to you. If you win you'll play right into his plans. Don't do it!'

'Armay, if you're asking me not to go through with this, then you just don't understand me at all.'

He gave her one final look of contempt and flew back to Olfar's place in a huff.

When he got into the dugout, his head swam and his vision blurred as though he'd drunk a whole barrel of balebeer. The queasiness in his stomach had returned and he was shaken and a little weak.

He flopped on his soft cushion to sleep. *Maybe you've just had a big day,* he thought.

But he was wrong, very wrong.

Chapter 57

'Wendy!' cried Mollie as her horse cantered over. The young Adkins threw her arms around Wendy's honey coloured neck and kissed her warmly.

'I'm sorry,' said the mare, her voice choked. 'I shouldn't have deserted you. I'm a bad, bad horse.'

Mollie tried to calm her by patting her head and stroking her nose. 'No, don't say such things. I totally understand. I don't want to see Cudgel either.'

'But you're here anyway,' Wendy stated. 'You're facing your fear to help a friend. I will do the same.' She stamped a hoof in determination. 'By the way, it took me so long to find you. What are you doing standing around in the dark? You can't expect to find anything here.'

'I know. I've found the egg already. I've met up with Bob from the Barren Arms and we've got a plan to get the egg back. We have to keep out of sight for a bit, that's all.'

They were standing behind a massive pavilion. There was little light and no side shows or stalls, so it was the perfect place to hide.

'What's all this, sorceress?' Blackbeard asked as he shuffled over. His face was hard to make out in the gloom.

'Oh,' said Mollie, not knowing how to answer. She figured she'd shown him too much of her power tonight. *Maybe I'll just keep a few secrets. I wouldn't want him to know everything!* 'Ummm, my horse just found me, that's all. Must have smelled me out. She'll be good for a quick get away.'

Blackbeard's eyes darted around. 'Bit obvious though, a horse! We're meant to be, you know, inconspicuous.'

'She can help,' said Mollie quickly. 'She can... ummmm... I've trained her really well. Just give her an order and she'll follow.'

'Right,' said Blackbeard rolling his eyes. 'Let's just stick to the plan, shall we?'

Mollie gave him a grin and a false salute. 'Aye, Captain.'

Bob chuckled good-naturedly and saluted back. 'Cheeky.'

Presently a figure crept up to them from the shadows, his face obscured by long hair. 'All in place, Blackbeard.'

'Thanks, mate. Mollie, let's move.'

Mollie turned to Wendy. 'Come on. This is it.'

'How exciting,' said Wendy, her skin prickling all over. Her voice came as whisper in Mollie's head. 'By the way, who is that blond one?'

'His name is Rio,' she whispered back.

'Oh,' Wendy said. 'Tell him he needs to trim his mane.'

Mollie tried not to giggle as they made their way into the light and over to Cudgel's van.

'Ooo,' said Mollie suddenly. 'I've just had a great idea.'

And she shared it with the others. They all agreed it was a very good idea.

Chapter 58

Whitestaff absolutely did not want a repeat of yesterday's performance. He was the first one at the Stadium and waited patiently on his podium for the others to arrive.

He felt bad today, as though he hadn't slept in a decade. He flapped his wings weakly.

I wonder what they do if a dragon is sick? he wondered.

Susset was the first to appear. She came with the rising of the sun, looking resplendent as usual.

'It's happening,' she said to him, looking him up and down.

'What is happening?'

'Look at your body,' she said, pointing to his chest. 'You're fading.'

Whitestaff looked down. The gold glowing scales looked pale and washed out.

He gave a gasp. 'You mean—'

'Yes, your essence is fading. It's time for you to go home,' the sorceress told him bluntly.

Whitestaff eyes grew wide. 'I can't, not today,' he protested.

Susset shrugged. 'You might have enough energy to get through today, but I did warn you this would happen.'

Whitestaff rolled onto his back and closed his eyes.

The woman floated over and stroked his belly.

'I'm sorry, Whitestaff. But have hope. The first event is an easy one. I'm sure Olfar told you.'

The dragon didn't reply.

'I can give you a little bit of magic, if you wish. It wouldn't be entirely wrong,' she whispered.

Whitestaff shook his head from side to side. 'It's okay. I just hope Graggy wins. I'll be happy if Graggy wins.' Then he sat bolt upright. 'But everyone will see me weak.'

'I think it's time I explained everything to the rest anyway. Leave it to me.'

Whitestaff hummed and lay back down. He watched the plain sky above; they were too high for clouds. 'When I go, Cudgel will be there.' His voice was soft and scared.

Susset continued to stroke his underside. 'Hmmm, I don't think so. I've got a good feeling all of this will work out. Your mother would have told you the same.'

Whitestaff liked the sound of that. Since landing in Sorteya, he'd heard mainly about Frendrek. Olfar mentioned his mother a few times—her name was Leeza—but the old Gra'dahl was closer to Frendrek, and so talked about him more often.

'I have to go,' said Susset after a long time of gentle patting. 'Others are starting to get here, and I need to take my place.'

Whitestaff roused himself and looked around. The Stadium was slowly filling up. Time for him rocked back and forth; his vision would blur and then clear as his very spirit ebbed away.

Before he knew it, the place was tightly packed, and Graggy, Nap and Armay were next to him. His friends were quiet, still unsure of what to say about yesterday.

Armay was the first to break the tension.

'Are you ill, Whitestaff? You don't look yourself.'

He nodded in reply, too tired to speak. Besides, Armay was not someone he wanted to talk to.

Cracone opened the day with the usual ceremony and staff banging, then it was Susset's turn.

'Today, a special event. One that will be sure to get your jaws jabbering.' She gave Whitestaff a knowing look. 'But first, let it be known that I have assessed the health of one of our Palal Contenders. Our Kai'dahl, as you know, came to us from his portal.'

All the Palal now locked onto Whitestaff.

'And his time with us is nearly done. He will need to revisit Earth once more to rebuild the dragon spirit he is now losing. As you know, one cannot survive without one's spirit. Whitestaff is wilting like a flower, and for him, the Earth is his sun.'

There were sympathetic groans from the audience. Whitestaff hid his face. With all the looks of pity he was getting, he began to feel like he did back on Earth in Cudgel's cage.

Armay slid over to him.

'You poor dragon. Is it true?' She sounded on the verge of tears. 'I'm so sorry about yesterday, I didn't mean to hurt your feelings. Please, please talk to me. This is terrible.'

The big gold dragon looked in her eyes and saw genuine concern.

'I know,' he said at last. 'Apology accepted. If you'll accept my apology for overreacting.'

Armay nodded eagerly, her eyes moist.

'The second trial will require this,' Susset continued to address the spectators. Above her the sky shimmered. A massive rectangle of wavy water appeared. 'And these,' she said, producing four thick bands of silver.

'These shackles go around each dragon's neck. They are connected by magic to this screen of water above me. Watch.' She floated over to Nap and put the band around his neck, doing up a clasp at the front. Instantly Nap's face appeared on the screen of water above. He looked up and saw himself magnified by a thousand. He grinned from ear to ear and winked.

'Merlin taught me this trick,' she said to Whitestaff and Armay. 'He said one can't have an event without it. He called it a "Big Screen" and said they're very popular in the future.'

Whitestaff looked dumbly at the wall of water. His face popped up as soon as the band was fastened.

With each dragon's image now clearly visible, Susset explained the rules of the trial. It was as Olfar had explained; a game of chicken with the ground—closest to the dirt wins.

The dragons flew to the edge of the spire. Cracone counted them in.

When he said 'GO!' each Palal dived straight down, like meteors headed for the dreaded ground.

Chapter 59

The air howled in Whitestaff's ears and burned his eyes as he plummeted downward.

He came through the cloud cover with beads of moisture on his scales. His wings were tucked in and his neck stretched forward as far as it could go.

Through squinted eyes he could see Graggy's green tail thrashing from side to side in front, his long legs pulled under his stomach.

He guessed Armay and Nap must have been just behind him; he could almost feel them.

He didn't dare turn around.

I'll get those points, he told himself. *I can still win this thing!*

The ground was like a big, brown, never-ending plain. Shapes and colours were revealed as he fell towards it. First he picked out some large boulders, then some pointy tops of small spires. He could see a river here and there, then some yellow blobs that he knew were clusters of yellow balefruit.

Down, down, down he went, falling like a stone, his ears flailing at the sides of his head.

Suddenly, Graggy's wings ballooned out before him, and the green dragon pulled himself out of his free-fall.

Whitestaff risked a look behind him. Nap had already spread his wings, but hot on his tail was Armay, her jaw clenched, her forehead crinkled.

Back to the ground, Whitestaff could see smaller rocks, crevices and pockmarks on the surface. He chanced a few more seconds, and then flung his wings out as far as they could go.

The audience at the Stadium watched all of this on the screen. They ooohhhed and ahhed with each second of the drama.

But Whitestaff hadn't counted on his loss of strength. The force of the air friction pushed his wings up and over his head, the same way the wind can turn an umbrella inside out. He kept falling and falling.

Panicking now, he clawed at the air in vain.

Oh no, he thought. *This is the end.*

He shut his eyes tight and focused on pulling his wings down. He grunted with effort and strain as he slowly brought each massive wing level. As he slowed his descent it became easier to hold his wings out. He opened one eye to find himself only a dragon length from the cold and unyielding dirt.

The spectators above let out a collective sigh of relief.

And there he hovered, looking at the brownness below, knowing the other dragons had pulled out long ago and that he had won.

But he was dead wrong.

For Armay glided next to him, not speaking, just flapping her wings gracefully. She came around to meet him face to face. They were frozen like that for a moment, then she dipped a few feet closer to the ground.

Whitestaff's eyebrows shot up in surprise, but not to be outdone, he lost some altitude to match her.

The crowd watched the screen aghast. No living dragon had ever come *that* close to touching *it*.

Again the two dragons looked into each other's eyes.

'Don't do it, Armay,' said Whitestaff. 'Don't get any closer. You'll dishonour yourself.'

She looked at him and smiled patiently.

'If you think all that nonsense bothers me, Whitestaff, then you don't understand me at all.'

Her gaze was warm and caring. She gave him a joyous smile as she slowly drifted down.

All Whitestaff could do was watch her sink. She went slowly, like a baby bird's feather falling from a tree. She put down a sky-coloured claw.

And touched the ground.

The bare earth crunched. But Armay didn't hear it.

She placed a paw on the ground, then two legs, then all four. She stopped flapping her wings and sat down; all the while she looked up at him peacefully.

Those in the Stadium were too shocked to talk. Their mouths hung open. Even the King was lost for words.

But Armay wouldn't have cared even if she saw the looks on their faces. Her mind and hearts were with the gold dragon who was watching her from above.

'I think it's a stupid rule too,' she said softly.

Both of Whitestaff's hearts swelled with love.

Chapter 60

Mollie's nerves jangled. Her heart beat heavily, pumping too much blood to her head. She could hear the *thump, thump, thump* of it pounding in her ears. Her stomach was doing acrobatics, her brain felt like it was filled with gas.

But there was no backing out now; the stage was set.

She inhaled deeply then marched up to Cudgel.

'I'll give it a go,' she said, remembering to look him directly in the eye.

Cudgel had been calling to the fair-goers who mobbed his little van, but none of them stepped forth. They just stared at him. At first he thought they were making up their minds about whether they should give his egg a smash or not. But no one before him spoke or made any move that suggested they would part with a gold coin.

At first he found it all frustrating. He wanted to yell at them *Pay up or go away! You're jamming up the queue for my business. Move on, would yer.* He wanted to shout that at them, but he didn't dare. For he knew word of mouth was the best form of advertisement, and if he offended too many people, the spenders would avoid his attraction.

The other reason he didn't yell at them was because their expectant, cold, accusing expressions made him nervous.

What are they doing? He wondered. *Why are they all watching me? They don't know, do they?*

When Mollie came to him and presented a gold coin, Cudgel was glad for the distraction.

'Ho, my dear lady,' he said at the top of his voice. 'I doubt whether you'd be able to lift the mallet.' He began to chuckle but then suddenly stopped dead.

His eyes opened all the way. He went white. Sweat broke out across his brow. He recognised her.

'You're-you...' he pointed at the girl and backed away. 'You're the mullytill what took me 'orse and lost me dragon! Audrey! Come out here.' Cudgel licked his lips, his voice barely a squeak.

'Give her a go,' yelled someone from the knot of people.

'Yeah,' demanded another. 'Let the girl try. She paid good money.'

'Err... umm...' Cudgel began to realise he was being somehow set up. 'Ahhh, due to unfortunate circumstances, we will have to cancel the Egg O' Wonder for this evenin', we wish you a good night.'

Cudgel ducked his head and made a grab for Whitestaff's precious egg.

A man from the group quickly got himself in Cudgel's way. It was Rio.

'Give her a bash at the egg, mate, or I'll declare shenanigans and call someone of authority over here to deal with you.'

Cudgel stopped in his tracks. The last thing he wanted was unnecessary attention, especially from the law.

Think of all that money sittin' in the van.

'Oh, all right then,' he said holding up his hands. 'Jus' one bash at it and then I'll 'ave to retire. Past closing time, yer see? Very tired.' He yawned for effect.

More onlookers had turned up by now to see what all the fuss was about. Even a passing family of nobles pressed their way through to get a better look.

Mollie heaved the mallet above her with great effort. Before she could bring it down a mad horse rushed at them.

'Wendy, right on cue,' Mollie said as the mare rushed past.

Wendy gave a whinny, making sure she had everyone's attention. She pranced and danced in front of Cudgel's house on wheels. Then, when she was certain she had everybody's interest, she bucked and kicked a gaping hole in the side of the van.

But that was not all, for as soon as the wood splintered and broke, all of the hoarded treasure Cudgel and Audrey had stolen spewed forth like twinkling lava out of a volcano.

The people looked on in stunned silence.

Blackbeard was the first to break it with a piercing bellow. 'Hey, that's my mother's silver vase!'

'He's got my platinum goblet,' yelled Rio.

The people who Mollie had seen Blackbeard talking to when she was eavesdropping also stepped in.

'That there is my wife's necklace.'

'And *my* wife's ornate bracelet collection. These two have been robbing us blind.'

Cudgel backed away slowly, hoping to escape notice. Mollie caught him creeping from the corner of her eye.

'There,' she said, fixing him with a finger. 'He's trying to run.'

Half of the crowd bolted for the treasure, the other half chased after Cudgel, who had never moved so fast in his life.

As for Mollie, she picked up Whitestaff's egg in the confusion and mounted her horse.

'Giddy up, Wendy. And a job well done.'

'That was exhilarating,' said the horse, her voice jittery.

Mollie steered Wendy though the bedlam, the egg tucked safely under her heavy coat.

She was about to make a getaway when someone grabbed her leg.

I knew that was too easy. She looked down, half expecting to see Audrey.

Instead it was Blackbeard.

'Good work, young sorceress. Good work. Now I'm not always an honest man, but what I steal I take on the high seas, looking my enemy dead in the face. I hate these sneaks, and I don't think I could have got all my booty back without you. You're a good girl; don't let any one tell you different. I hope we'll meet again.'

He turned back to the loot so quickly Mollie didn't even get to say anything in return.

'Let's get out of here while we can,' urged Wendy.

Mollie didn't reply. She kept her head down and rode Wendy with deliberate slowness out of the showground and into the star-filled night. When Wendy thought they were far enough away, she galloped like a thunderstorm and the two headed for Gibbon en route to home—smiling and cheering as they went.

Chapter 61

The four dragons returned to their podiums and were received with mixed reactions.

Some of the dragons in the Stadium gave unenthusiastic shouts of hooray, some spoke to those around them in exasperated whispers; some began to clap but stopped when nobody else joined in.

'She actually touched it!' some were saying.

'Like she meant to do it. Why?' asked others.

'Well, she disqualified herself for some reason. Maybe she's sick too?'

But all of this was lost on Armay. She was distant. Every now and then she would look over at Whitestaff and give him a smile, which he returned. But she didn't say anything. Her mind was somewhere else.

Graggy didn't know what to say. Part of him wanted to hug them both, another part of him wanted to slap them silly with his tail.

Nap didn't even look in their direction. His jaw was locked so tight it looked as though he might crush his own teeth.

Susset flew over and squeezed Armay's shoulder. The two looked at each other with hidden understanding. The sorceress turned to the dragons in the Stadium.

'As you could see, Armay touched the ground...' There came more gasps from the audience here. 'Therefore she will receive no points for this trial. The winner is Whitestaff, second Graggy, third Nap.' She waved an arm and the updated tally box appeared.

Contender	Event 1	Event 2	Total
Graggy 1st	3	2	5
Whitestaff 2nd	0	3	3
Nap 2nd	2	1	3
Armay 4th	1	0	1

"I'm a tie for second,' Whitestaff said to himself. 'But still a long way off first place.'

He did some calculations in his head.

'I'm still in this race. I can't give Nap the victory.'

The gold Palal, however, was fading fast. He was shrinking too. He was only just bigger than Nap now and his body ached all over.

Most of all though, he told himself, *I have to win this for Armay, especially after what she did.*

He turned to her.

'I will come back, Armay. I will leave tonight, but I will come back. I have to fight Audgar. I have to be the Champion. I have to!'

Armay met his eyes. 'I know,' she said. 'We all have a destiny.'

She turned back and wouldn't say anymore.

'Finally,' announced Susset, 'the last Trial. To see who is the overall Champion, to find who will challenge the deadly Nazoor in claw-to-claw combat in six months time. I give you: The Rocks.'

BOOM!!

Ten massive boulders levitated in the middle of the Stadium. A glass tube as deep as a well appeared too. It was filled with purple liquid.

'Each Contender will break as many Rocks as he or she can,' Susset explained. 'You have until the balejuice runs out of this tube. The dragon who breaks the most rocks is the winner. First will be Graggy for the Gra'dahl.'

Cracone winked at his son and counted Graggy in.

The green dragon blurred into flight on the King's mark, as he did so the purple juice in the tube began to drain away. He surged towards the first gigantic stone and lowered his shoulder for the charge.

There came a sickening crack as Graggy hit the Rock and bounced off it. He screamed in agony and fell to the Stadium floor. He hit with a dull thud that reverberated through the grandstand. The rock he had collided with split in two.

Many dragons flew over to Graggy and helped him to his feet. Whitestaff and Armay leapt off their podiums and raced to their friend.

'Are you all right?' Whitestaff asked his voice thick with worry.

'No,' said Graggy. 'Not at all.' He winced in pain as he touched his shoulder. 'It's broken,' he said. 'I can't even feel my claws.'

The dragons parted to make way for Olfar, who examined the leg and shoulder with an expert eye, prodding and poking and asking lots of silly sounding questions.

'Well,' he said after a time. 'It's appears to be broken.'

Graggy shook his head, clearly vexed. 'That's what I said.'

Olfar ignored him. 'I'll have to get Nitegale of the Bo'dahl to set it right for you. I think you'll be off it for at least a season.' He turned and found another dragon. 'Get this boy to the infirmary, broken shoulder bone. You there,' he pointed to a tough looking Re'dahl. 'Help carry him, grab someone to assist.'

'Latos,' said Graggy hotly, not caring to mind his language. 'I was winning too. Well it's up to you now Whitestaff. Don't let me down.' He gave Whitestaff a salute with his tail as he let the others lift him.

'I won't,' Whitestaff called as the dragons carried him off.

'All right,' yelled Cracone, his voice drilling into everyone's head. 'Back to your places. Let's get this over with so my boy can win this thing.'

A few cheers came from the Re'dahl. Boos came from the green dragons.

All the dragons went back to their seats and everybody clapped as Graggy was taken from the field.

'Next up, Armay for the Bo'dahl,' Susset called when everyone had settled.

Armay didn't look too keen to ram a rock after Graggy's effort, but she readied herself anyway.

The balejuice ran out of the bottom of the tube as soon as Cracone yelled, "GO!", and Armay flew towards her first ball of stone.

Instead of shoulder barging it, she hit it with the thick part of her tail, making the rock crack in a few places. She turned around, got some more momentum and then hit the rock again, splitting it in two.

POW!

She gathered herself and chose another target. She repeated her tail smashing until the second rock crumbled. Panting heavily and looking sore, she started on a third, belting it over and over. But time had run out, the last drop of juice plopped out of the pipe before the rock broke. She flew back to her pedestal and landed gingerly.

'Are you hurt?' Whitestaff asked.

Armay nodded, her nostrils flaring in and out. 'It hurts and I'll be bruised tomorrow. When it's your turn, give it all you've got.'

'Sure,' he agreed. Then to himself thought: *Not that I've got much left to give.*

Susset reset the rocks once more.

'Next will be Nap for the Re'dahl.'

Chapter 62

Mollie and Wendy made it all the way back to the Barren
Arms in Gibbon before dawn. The nervous energy of their
daring rescue had worn off hours ago, and now they were
both exhausted. Mollie's eyes were sandy and Wendy's legs
were giving way. Both of them nearly nodded off more than
once.

They were relieved to finally see the inn. Wendy
stood shakily as Mollie undid the saddle and the other
attachments. As soon as she was unburdened, the horse
slumped to the ground and dozed immediately.

Mollie did the same when she got to her room. She
didn't care about the cockroaches or the smell. The bed was
hard but she was so tired she would've slept in a briar patch.

The sun was nearly at its peak when she awoke the
next day.

She gave Jake a wave as she let herself out. The
stout man just glared after her. As soon as she was gone, he
ran up to her room to look for damage. He was almost
disappointed to see the room was unchanged. Well, actually
it looked a bit cleaner.

Mollie found Wendy just waking.

'Get up lazy bones,' she teased. 'I've been up for
hours.'

'You have not,' said Wendy groggily. 'Have you?'

'No. But it sounded good.' They both laughed a
little.

Mollie saddled up the horse and they made their
way to the little cottage where they hoped Esmae and Terry
and Bramble would be waiting.

They weren't disappointed either, for the three of them came dashing up the road when they heard Wendy's hoofs on the dirt.

Mollie saw them coming and held the egg aloft like a trophy.

'Good girl,' said Esmae, beaming proudly.

'Good woman, you mean,' Terry corrected. 'Why look at her, she's shot up a couple inches since she left not even two days ago.'

Mollie smiled back at them, dismounted, and ran into their embrace.

Bramble nuzzled Wendy's neck and talked into her ear. Wendy looked pleased with herself and nuzzled back.

'So tell me,' said Terry Gritbole, 'did you smash him up with a ball o' magic? Did you wash him away with a torrent of water? Blow him to next week with a hurricane?' What did you do?'

'Well,' said Mollie with a grin. 'I didn't use magic at all. I used my brains.' She turned to Wendy. 'And my friends. With those two things, I didn't need any extra powers at all.'

Wendy neighed in agreement.

'Well, darling,' said Esmae. 'I have taught you something. And you have the egg. Let me go to the kitchen and see what I can do with that pheasant Terry caught. We'll all celebrate.'

The older Adkins and Terry went off into the house. Mollie took her egg over to the barn and laid it on a bed of straw. She crouched down next to it and spoke.

'Wherever you are, Whitestaff, I hope you know I've got your egg. And if you ever come back, I'll be here to take care of you. You're safe now, my very first friend.'

Chapter 63

Back in the Stadium, Nap was punishing the rocks that lay before him.

He bashed them with his barbed tail and his shoulder. He even headbutted one.

Cracone was louder than ever, urging his son on with both curse words and encouragement.

He'd destroyed *six* large boulders altogether when the time had run out.

The other Palal cheered him loudly and applauded his efforts. With Graggy out of the race, Nap was now favourite to win.

'Beat that, Whiteworm,' Nap taunted as he flapped back to his place.

Whitestaff had to admit, Nap's rock breaking was impressive. Six rocks and he didn't even look drained.

'I can give you a little boost,' Susset said in his ear.

'I won't need it,' said Whitestaff back, hoping his voice sounded more sure than he actually was.

'Now for the Kai'dahl. Can he break more than six?'

Cracone counted him in and he took off for his first boulder. He tail-smashed it with all his might and yelped in pain as he did so. The boulder was harder than rock; it felt like steel.

Whitestaff was losing strength with every second, but he was still tough enough to break the rock with his first hit.

He flew to the next one and smashed it too, his tail already tender.

The next rock took a tail whip and a shoulder barge to crack it. Three down.

He glanced at the timer, the juice was below half.

At this rate I'll never make it.

He threw all his remaining strength into the next two rocks, splitting them both with shoulder barges.

Weaker now, he attacked the sixth rock. But he didn't have much left to give. He slapped at it with his tail, barely chipping the surface.

His body was battered and worn and the juice was running out.

Some of the Re'dahl had already begun to celebrate because they could see Whitestaff couldn't crack a sixth.

Thoughts of Nap winning and rubbing his face in it gave him enough anger to give the rock one last smash. He used all his might, shattering it into pebbles.

Now it's a tie, he thought. *But if this goes to a tie-breaking event, I'll lose for sure. I need one more to win!*

He looked again at the tube and saw he had barely any time left. It was over; it had to be a tie.

Whitestaff thought of Armay and her sacrifice for him, he thought of Graggy and his broken bone. He thought of his father who he'd never get the chance to meet, and his mother who he'd never get to embrace. And lastly, he thought of Nap, whose jeering voice echoed in his brain. It all made him very mad.

So mad, in fact, he burned with anger. His chest boiled with it—churning hot fumes in his throat.

He approached the seventh rock just as the last drop of balejuice was about to fall.

He opened his mouth.

Nap started to dance.

He breathed deeply and hotly.

Cracone raised his staff.

Whitestaff belched a ball of molten fire. It hit the centre of the ball of stone and exploded it into dust and rubble.

The last drop of Balejuice dripped out and splashed on the floor.

It took the crowd of dragons a second or two to work out what they had just seen. But when they realised they had just witnessed the greatest Tournement victory ever, they were ecstatic. And for the second time in his life, Whitestaff heard the entire Palal race cheering just for him.

It was a glorious sound.

Contender	Event 1	Event 2	Event 3	Total
Whitestaff 1st	0	3	3	6
Nap 2nd	2	1	2	5
Graggy 3rd	3	2	0	5
Armay 4th	1	0	1	2

Chapter 64

Whitestaff was in Susset's dugout reflecting on his win. He had been named the Dragon Champion in front of all the Palal. He accepted the medal Cracone presented him, waving feebly to the crowd at the Stadium as the sorceress conjured fireworks and confetti.

Nap ignored him, but Whitestaff was too weak to care.

Then when the speeches were given and the proper ceremonies over, everybody swept him off his podium. They took turns in carrying their new fire-breathing hero back to the spires.

Armay was with him for the whole journey, as were Olfar and Susset. Graggy was still in the infirmary being tended to by Nitegale, the Bo'dahl healer.

They had a little party at Susset's, but her place was so cozy and comfortable that everybody got sleepy, wished him farewell and good luck, then went to their homes for rest.

Whitestaff wondered again if the dugout was enchanted in some way.

In front of him was the shimmering portal that would take him home.

On one side of his wasting white body stood Susset and Olfar. Armay sat huddled next to him on the other.

'Nephew, thou did thy father proud this day, of that I'm sure. Thou made me proud too. Thou really showed us something, breathing fire like that. I'll have to rewrite some textbooks now!' He hugged his nephew fondly, cleared his throat then straightened.

'I'll bid thee goodbye for now, Whitestaff. Till six month's time. I'd better fly before I make a fool of myself and cry.' It was too late for that, however, because the old dragon had tears trailing from his eyes down to his pointed grey beard. He gave his nephew one last squeeze, then turned away to go home.

Susset was about to say something when three dragons appeared at the entrance.

'Just came to see you off,' said Cracone. 'And to let you know if you're not here in time for the battle with Audgar, Nap here will take your place.' He rested a heavy paw on his son's shoulder.

'I just came to say goodbye too,' said Luzahmin. 'Now you'll be all that Father will talk about. Maybe I should move in with the Nazoor for some peace.'

Whitestaff couldn't tell if she was making a joke or not, so he just thanked her and said goodbye. Luzahmin and Cracone turned to go but Nap stepped closer to Whitestaff.

The red dragon leaned in close to his ear and said something only Whitestaff was meant to hear.

'Next time.'

With that he turned and joined his father and Luzahmin. The three took off as suddenly as they had appeared.

'Are we ready?' asked Susset.

'No,' said Whitestaff. 'Give him a minute, he'll be here.'

No sooner had he spoken those words than Graggy appeared at the entrance. He was being assisted by a blunt-snouted Bo'dahl. He was also bandaged heavily and was very short of breath.

'Sorry, I'm late. Is he still here? Oh, there you are.'

'Didn't want to go without saying goodbye, my friend.'

The two shook tails, then hugged warmly. Whitestaff was careful not to crush Graggy's shoulder.

'What about you, eh? I heard you breathed a fireball, by Latos! Fire! What next? And you beat old Nappy boy.'

Whitestaff chuckled. 'Beat him good.'

'Well, I guess this is it,' said Graggy. 'The sooner you get through there the sooner you can come back.'

'That's right,' Whitestaff smiled. Then his face fell. 'Cudgel,' he said with bitterness. 'Will I have enough strength left to take my egg back?' he asked Susset.

'Probably,' she replied. 'But don't you worry about that. I have a feeling everything will work out all right. Trust me.'

'Me too,' said Armay. 'Could we have a minute alone?' Graggy and Susset looked a little embarrassed, but agreed and gave Whitestaff one last hug each.

When they were gone, Armay touched Whitestaff's head with her tail.

'You were great today,' she said.

'So were you. Especially when you landed on the ground.'

Armay smiled. 'I've wanted to tell you for a long time that you were right. But every time I tried to, it came out wrong. I thought I'd show you instead. Actions speak louder, and clearer, than words.'

'They sure do.'

'Anyway,' she continued, 'you taught me that. You showed me silly superstitions don't matter. It doesn't make a jot of difference if you touch the ground, live on the ground, or were born on the ground. What matters is friendship. What matters are your actions.'

'Well said,' Whitestaff remarked.

'Plus, I think it's my destiny to break a few rules. Just like it's yours to go through that portal. Go now,' she said, giving his tail one last squeeze with hers. 'Go back to Earth and come back in six months. It's your destiny. I'll be waiting right here when you get back.'

Whitestaff nodded and picked himself up off the floor.

'Seeing as you are a no-good ground-dweller now,' he joked, 'there is something you must do.'

'What is it?'

'Closer to the ground, at the bottom of the spires, are yellow balefruit. They'll help Graggy's shoulder. Get some and make him eat it.'

'I will,' Armay promised.

Whitestaff stood shakily and wobbled over to the portal. He looked back, gave Armay a bow then entered through the shimmering curtain.

Chapter 65

For a while Armay's voice lingered on. Or *was* it her?

'It will all be good. It will work out in the end. Don't be scared.'

He couldn't be sure if it was her voice or just a memory. He had a strange sensation that his mother's voice would sound exactly the same—warm and soothing—then it faded away.

It was all black around him. He blinked his eyes but couldn't see.

He could feel though. And his hearts sank when the pads of his paws felt the soft crinkle of straw beneath them. He could smell Wendy close by. Her musky scent was all around him.

'Back in the cage,' he said to the blackness. 'I don't want to go back.'

'You could stay here,' suggested a voice from the void around him.

'Who was that? Where are you?'

'I am here, with you. In limbo.' The voice sounded like an old man to Whitestaff.

'Why can't I see you?'

'Because there is no light.'

'Who are you?'

'A friend. I know you don't want to go back to your prison. So I thought I'd let you know you can stay here.'

'Where is this place? Am I dreaming?'

'This place has no light and no time. You can stay here forever and ever. You'll need no food or drink. Forget the hardships of Earth. Just let it all go. And stay.'

Whitestaff didn't answer, but he didn't move either.

'Tempting, isn't it' said the voice. 'Just float here for as long as you like. Time just flies by.'

'I shouldn't stay,' Whitestaff said.

'Why not? We all know what is waiting for you back on Earth. Do you really want that again?'

'No,' Whitestaff admitted. 'But someone once told me a leader presses on no matter how tough it gets.'

Laughter greeted Whitestaff's ears.

'Is that what you are, dragon? A leader? Do you have the courage to walk headlong into a hopeless situation all alone?'

'A good leader is never alone. Let me show you.' Whitestaff put his head down and marched forward again. With each step the straw grew more real, Wendy's scent filled his nose, but there was something else too.

Strawberries and sugar?

'Good for you,' said the voice as it faded away. 'Good for you.'

The blackness around Whitestaff was fading. He blinked more and more.

There was light. There was a person in front of him.

Then he heard a voice.

'Whitestaff? Is that you? Have you really come back?'

Then he saw her clearly. Her ink-black hair, her pixie-like face.

'Mollie? Mollie!'

Whitestaff gave a sigh of relief that sent his shoulders slack.

'Mollie,' he said in a raspy voice. 'I am so happy to see you.'

The two wrapped each other up and held on tight.

'I got your egg back.'

'You did! Where are we?'

'In my barn at home. Whitestaff, where have you been? Did you get home? Did you find other dragons? Did you find the ones who were calling you?'

Whitestaff tried to nod his head but it was too weak.

'Yes to all of the above, Mollie, and that's not all. In about half a year's time I'm going to go back to them. I'm going to go back to be their Champion. When I return to that planet of the dragons, I know what I have to do.'

'What is it? What are you going to do?'

'Mollie, I am going to defeat an enemy in a Tournament. Then I, Whitestaff the Kai'dahl am going to make myself King of the Palal and—' He broke off into a fit of coughs.

Of course, Mollie didn't understand a word he said.

But she didn't doubt any of it either.

'I bet you will,' she soothed as she stroked his pale back. 'I bet you will. And until then, I'll take good care of you.'

'Mollie?'

'Yes, dragon?'

'Thank you. One day I will repay you for your kindness. One day, Mollie, I will save *your* life.'

Mollie looked down at the dragon, his head cradled in her lap and his small body tucked into a ball. His green eyes were already closing as exhaustion overtook him. She regarded his fragile white body and nodded to herself.

'I believe you,' she whispered. 'I really think that one day you will.'

As Whitestaff slept in Mollie's arms, he dreamed of things to come. In the future he saw himself fight the Nazoor for the glory, and peace, of his race. He saw himself as the King of the Palal, sitting on the royal throne with his friends by his side. He saw Nap and Cracone and all of the Palal and the Nazoor bowing before him. He saw it all and he knew it would all come true. All he had to do was rest and wait.

And be ready!

We hoped you enjoyed reading The Last Dragon Home.

If you have any feedback for this novel, we'd love to hear from you. We also pass along fanmail to our authors. Drop us a line at arinhousepublications@gmail.com

'Like' our 'Last Dragon Home' Facebook page for competitions and updates on the next book in the Dragon Wars series!